WWII SOLDIER FLIER PRISONER PARTISAN

MISSING IN ACTION AND PRESUMED DEAD

RICHARD J. NOYES

Copyright © 2013 by Richard J. Noyes
All rights reserved.
ISBN-10: 1481139991
ISBN-13: 9781481139991

WWII Soldier Flier Prisoner Partisan is a work of fiction. With the exception of incidents participated in and related to me by Lt. L.C. "Chet" Lake, any resemblance to events, or actual persons living or dead, is purely coincidental.

A Sampling of Praise for
Soldier Flier Prisoner Partisan
from Readers Nationwide

"In the global struggle for freedom that marked WWII, the theaters of combat raged across land, sea and air and in pockets of underground resistance. Of the many heroic individuals portrayed in *Soldier Flier Prisoner Partisan,* two young Americans, one an infantryman the other a pilot, see action in all four arenas across North Africa and Europe; and it is through their eyes that this epic novel unfolds. This outstanding book is an unflinching look at WWII from the underground up. Its lean, compelling style vividly puts you at the center of nonstop action. You will feel the tension, you will share the agony, you will relive the terrifying moments and face the life-or-death decisions that these extraordinary people had to make every day. One word rightfully could be added to the title: "Patriot." At heart, this is not just another war novel but a gripping account prompted in part by real-life recollections that dramatize the diverse ways in which WWII was won."

-Richard A. DeLia, Screenwriter and
Webmaster, Berkeley Heights, NJ

"I favor novels with narrative drive. *Soldier Flier Prisoner Partisan* is pretty much nonstop action that kept me turning pages. I liked that the author didn't go in for a lot of filler or extraneous descriptions. The book moves forward with terrific pace. Discovering the WWII feats of the two Americans is a ride well worth taking."

-Forbes Robertson, Financial and Business Consultant, Niles, IL

"I love a good action story, and *Soldier Flyer Prisoner Partisan* fits the bill. I was taken in at the first page, getting to know the two American soldiers. But it was the second half of the book, when the heroes fight the Nazis with the partisans, that entranced me. The bravery and camaraderie of the group was highlighted in one exciting episode after another. This story is a perfect balance of the courageous soldiers and the fearless combat nurses they fall in love with."

-P.A. O'Halloran, Director, Art Production, The Designory, Inc., Long Beach, CA

"Richard Noyes' latest book, *WWII Soldier Flier Prisoner Partisan: Missing in Action and Presumed Dead*, helps to capture a time that is too quickly receding into a dim memory with the passing of WWII veterans. It captures the emotions of those often too young to be placed into such extreme situations. Their guts and heroism unfolded in an exciting and enthralling way. I found myself reminiscing about stories told by my father who was also in the European Theatre. As a nurse, I can relate to the medical scenarios and wonder if I had been born earlier if I would have chosen to serve. My four years of high school German were put to the test! I look forward to the next book by this talented author."

-Connie A. Michell, BSN/RN; Warren, PA

"I don't often read war books, but a friend recommended *Soldier, Flier* and I am glad she did. I was swept up in the continuous action, the love affairs and the main character's lives. The scenes of rescues from the Nazis had me speed-reading. The plot has it all—the passages at the end of the book choked me up!"

-Celia Nelson, Realtor, At Properties, Winnetka, IL

ABOUT THE AUTHOR

After long stints with IBM and Westinghouse, Richard J. Noyes was Associate Director of the Center for Advanced Engineering Study at the Massachusetts Institute of Technology. Noyes is now a business consultant for public and private sector organizations.

Also by Richard Noyes and co-author Pamela J. Robertson: *Larceny of Love*, a contemporary novel of action, love, danger and emotion. Trace the interwoven careers of three men in jeopardy and the accomplished women in their lives, plus compelling inside looks at cutthroat technology, big-time sports and Machiavellian Hollywood deals, 280 pages, Amazon.

Also by Noyes and Robertson: *Guts in the Clutch: 77 Legendary Triumphs, Heartbreaks and Wild Finishes in 12 Sports*, Illustrated, 329 pages, Amazon, with a Foreword by Drew Olson of ESPN and Past President of the Baseball Writers Association of America.

Order e-Books of *Soldier Flier* and the two books above from amazon.com, barnesandnoble.com, googlebooks.com and other e-Book distributors. Also use the Kindle app on your mobile devices. Order paperback copies from amazon.com

DEDICATION

WWII Soldier Flyer Prisoner Partisan is dedicated to Lt. L.C. "Chet" Lake, (1924-2008), B-17 co-pilot, American hero, 15th Air Force, Second World War in Europe.

ACKNOWLEDGMENTS

Chet Lake, to whom this book is dedicated, was my brother-in-law. He was a self-effacing man who never extolled his successes, and they were many. Following his discharge from the U. S. Army Air Corps in 1945, Chet finished college, married my sister Carolyn, and they raised three fine children. Subsequently, Chet embarked on a highly successful career as owner of industrial equipment businesses. He was a good friend and relative to me and my wife, best man at our wedding and a terrific guy who was great fun to be with.

Chet rarely talked about his Second World War experiences. Occasionally, however, he would relate anecdotes while sparing most of the details. The stories, abbreviated as they were, fascinated me to the extent that I asked Chet if he would mind if someday I used the incidents in a novel on World War II. He said, "Write anything you want. It's okay with me."

Chet's wife, Carolyn D. Lake, also gave her approval: "I loved the book. It perfectly captures the sacrifices and victories of World War II. A wonderful and exciting read told from two different viewpoints, with a thrilling climax. Chet would have been very proud."

Some of the incidents Chet Lake described are in *WWII Soldier Flier Prisoner Partisan*, and since I know very few particulars, most of the writing related to these incidents was imagined by me. But the five anecdotes mentioned by Chet inspired the fiction directly related to them. The occurrences include, and are limited to, Chet's assignment as a flight instructor; the trip to Foggia, Italy; the damage to and crash of his B-17; the capture, jailing and escape from the Germans (the means of escape from prison used by Chet Lake closely correlates to the techniques used by the fictional characters in the book); and his months fighting the Nazis with the Polish partisans of which almost no details are known. Unlike corresponding circumstances in the book, from the time Chet was first captured and during his affiliation with the Polish underground he was, so far as is known, unaccompanied by other Americans.

Sincere thanks to Lt. William Nopar, B-17 navigator, for his technical assistance. Bill flew thirty-five combat missions over Europe while serving in the 8th Air Force out of England.

1

"Sir, permission to go ashore."

"Now hear this, now hear this, Radioman Steven Millen report to Chief Petty Officer Dwyer at the infirmary." Steve looked at his mates, shrugged his shoulders, took his headset off, straightened his cap, threaded passageways and climbed up and down ladders.

"Now hear this, now hear this, the smoking lamp is now lit." Steve didn't smoke but felt the need for a cigarette. He entered the antiseptic infirmary to see Chief Petty Officer Dwyer, the medical officer and the executive officer talking without smiling.

As Steve saluted, he thought: *What the hell is this all about?* "Radioman Third Millen reporting, sir," and removed his cap.

The exec said, "Millen, the medical officer here told me that your physical last week showed your arches have collapsed. The slight heart murmur they found last year's no worse and not considered risky, and that alone wouldn't have mustered you out. But now, along with the flat feet, you know we can't have flat feet in the Navy. Your medical discharge is effective today. Sorry, but those are the rules."

Steve's insides dropped. "But, sir, I love the Navy, the Lexington. What'll I do?"

"I wish there were exceptions, but none are permitted. Good luck, Godspeed and all the best."

The medical officer looked pained as he left with the exec. "Sorry, Millen."

"It's tough luck, Millen, but you know the Navy, there ain't no in-between," Chief Dwyer said. "You're a good sailor and a helluva radioman. I was going to recommend you for second class. Come on, we'll get your gear. At least we're in port. We'll draw your pay and small stores. I already have your medical discharge papers. They don't fool around in this man's Navy. I'll get you train fare home, Chicago, right?"

Even though Steve was now wearing civvies, he stopped at the top of the gangplank and saluted the officer of the deck. "Sir, permission to go ashore." Then he saluted the flag, and finally he turned toward his gathered buddies and saluted them. He walked down, duffel on his shoulder, eyes glinting into a new life. It was spring 1941, and he'd just turned twenty-one.

Steve Millen grew up in a northern suburb, and his parents' house was just over the Chicago line. The people in the neighborhood liked Steve and welcomed him home after two-and-a-half years. Although he was his usual smiling, good-natured self, the friends and neighbors knew he was sad about the discharge and didn't bring it up. Then everybody felt good again when Steve had a sudden turn of good fortune. The local stationmaster retired, and Steve applied for the job. The company liked his telegraphy skills, service experience and maturity. He got the job, and it was just a half-mile from home.

Steve took the local girls out for ice cream in his Dad's convertible, radio playing hits of the time like 'Frenesi' and 'In the Mood.' One girl he liked was spoken for. He didn't have any other favorites, but they all were fond of him, not least because of his Nordic features. Steve was no innocent. He'd been to foreign ports, but he wasn't about to cat around in the neighborhood.

He let the kids on the block hang around the station. The girls and boys were all given tasks under his rigorous, but kind, training and supervision. When the commuter trains were due in the evening, they lit the lanterns, hung them on the gates and took turns raising and lowering the gates with the big ratchet handle. On winter nights, Steve liked watching their happy, expectant faces in the glow of the approaching locomotives' headlights.

He taught them rudimentary Morse code, and under careful watching let them throw the switches when a freight needed to go off on a spur to make way for a passenger train. They also helped him keep the station and grounds shipshape. Steve also liked to work out doing one-arm pushups, endless sit-ups and one-legged squats. The kids, of course, imitated him, and using two hands and legs he taught them proper techniques.

The family doctor told Steve that picking up one-hundred marbles a day with his toes would strengthen his arches, and it did. The kids watched him pick them up and drop them in a can. Soon they all wanted to try it. So Steve had them bring their own marbles and cans. Then they had contests: who could do the most or the fastest without dropping any. The floor of the old train station was now scrubbed clean as the Lexington's deck. But it sagged with age; and the aggies ran all over as the kids scrambled after them, laughing and tumbling over each other.

Joe Millen, Steve's father, a First World War combat infantry veteran, was a lieutenant in the town fire department and amateur magician. Occasionally, on his days off, he came over to the train station and performed card, coin and other tricks for the local kids. Steve had his dad's knack of making everything seem like fun. Joe had two daughters, and when they married and left, he and his wife had only Steve at home. And they were thrilled to have him back.

Steve had been an all-scholastic wrestler, a football guard in high school, co-captain of the team and a leader by example. Several college football coaches recruited him because he was often in the other team's backfield looking for the ball carrier. It looked like he could have gotten a full ride to the University of Illinois. Steve's mother and father were not happy when he decided to join the Navy.

"Sorry, I know how you feel but I want to see some things, get around, maybe grow up a little and, who knows, go to college later."

"Look at it this way, Steve," Joe Millen said. "You've got the marks, and you won't get that scholarship money later. There'll be some new guy they want."

"You're probably right, and I know what you're saying, Dad, but I want to do this."

Helen Millen said, "We want you to be happy, Steven, just be sure to write and come home on leave."

"I will," and he did, and now he was back at home, they hoped for good.

One of Steve's neighborhood friends was a Coca-Cola truck driver. On one of Steve's days off from the train station the friend asked him to ride along. Downtown deliveries included two of Chicago's popular burlesque houses. Steve and his buddy ran up the fire escapes carrying a case of Coke in each hand. The strippers walked around backstage in various stages of undress, unmindful of who was around. Steve liked that a lot.

Chicago's Navy Pier on Lake Michigan was also on the route, and Steve got a kick out of talking to some of the sailors who were there to build a new naval training facility. That night, he was full of stories for the gang outside the corner store about the burlesque houses and his talks with the American sailors.

No one in the neighborhood took the Pearl Harbor attack harder than Steve. He wanted to be out there on his ship. When the Lexington was sunk in May 1942 in the Battle of the Coral Sea, Steve didn't smile much for a while. The neighbors knew he was thinking about his dead shipmates and left him to his thoughts. His main thought soon became: *I'll try to join the Army*.

Joe Millen had been a firefighter for over twenty years, had a substantial pension built up and was about ready to stop chasing fires. When he learned that Steve was going to join the Army, Joe applied for the stationmaster's job. Steve gave him a crash course in telegraphy and found that his dad had a gift for it. Joe got the job and kept it for the rest of his life.

2

"You're just too good an instructor to let go."

When he was fourteen, a dreadful tragedy struck Rick Heydon's family: His mother, who was a legal secretary in a downtown law firm, was killed in a Loop crosswalk by a drunk speeding around a corner the wrong way on a one-way street. Rick's father was in the Merchant Marine and away for weeks at a time. Rick and his twelve-year-old sister, Shirley, were latchkey kids from an early age. With their mother often coming home late from work, they had learned to clean and shop and cook and were pretty much self-sufficient. But now, with their mother dead and their father home only occasionally, the leadership role shifted to Rick and the responsibility for a sibling who was devastated by her mother's death.

Rick and Shirley were bright and good students, and their mother had instilled in them a strong work ethic. Rick was identified as academically gifted at an early age. Moreover, he was intellectually curious and a voracious reader.

A few months after the accident, two men from foster care, probably tipped off by a prying neighbor, came to the house. Rick's father, Arthur Heydon, who was a bruiser, happened to be home on leave. The men spoke of the need for more guidance for the children in a facility. Arthur took them by their collars and heaved them out of the house with the warning, "Over my dead body." They never came back.

With the help of a widowed aunt who came by twice a week to bring food she had prepared and look after Shirley's clothes and well-being, Rick took care of his kid sister. In addition to studying at every opportunity, he worked most days after school, many nights and always on weekends leaving no time for sports which he was good at. Rick was six-two, two-hundred pounds, and the coaches drooled when they saw his speed and finesse playing basketball and touch football in high school gym class. Late in Rick's senior year, Arthur Butler retired from the Merchant Marine and found a job as a foreman in a factory six blocks from their home.

Rick read the valedictory at his north-side Chicago high school graduation ceremonies. With the top honors and college entrance scores in his class, he entered Northwestern University on an academic scholarship. To save money, he commuted to and from college. Before and after his father came home for good, Rick was known in the neighborhood as 'Running Rick' because he ran everywhere: to high school, to the store, to his part-time jobs, to Shirley's school to check on her, and now to the el or the bus for the trip to Northwestern and his sprints to class through the tree-lined campus. Occasionally, when he got a ride from a neighbor who worked in the area, Rick ran to school through Evanston's leafy streets. He admired the grand old houses and hoped some day to live in one of them.

During the first semester of his sophomore year, Rick took an anatomy class and found it fascinating but challenging, especially the dissections. One day, he forgot to bring his textbook from home, and he needed it for an upcoming quiz. He asked the girl sitting next to him if he could borrow her textbook, and she handed it to him with a little grin. Rick got the information he needed and passed it back.

When the class ended, Rick walked out with his classmate, introduced himself and thanked her for helping him. She was lean and tall. He thought at least five-ten, wore glasses, was shy and had attractive features, flawless skin and luxuriant hair. Her name was Beverly, and she was a freshman. Rick asked her to have lunch with him. She said in a soft, gentle voice, "I'm sorry I have to go to volleyball practice. We have a game tomorrow at three in the gym if you care to come." He went and saw that Beverly was a capable blocker, spiker and leader. Rick waited for her to change, but she came out with a gang of teammates, gave him a small wave and quick smile and left with her group.

Rick's further attempts to engage Beverly were unsuccessful. She was always polite, but his efforts to know her better never went anywhere. Then one day she wasn't at class, nor was she in the following class. Rick wandered over to the gym and asked some girls in a pickup volleyball game if they knew a player named Beverly. He raised his hand to eyebrow height. "Oh, she transferred out last week. I didn't hear where she went." Every few weeks over the next couple of years, Beverly crossed Rick's mind. Although he didn't know it, she didn't forget him either.

After completing two years of college, Rick decided to enlist in the army and apply for officer candidate school with the intention of becoming a pilot. He ran to catch the train downtown and lined up inside the recruiting station. He got talking with the guy in front of him, "Hi, I'm Steve Millen." Rick and Steve immediately hit it off, discovered they were both baseball fans, went through the enlistment drill, and on the way home stopped for a burger and a beer. Both men said they were in the phone book and agreed to meet after the war and take in a Cubs or White Sox game.

Rick got into OCS and flight school and wanted to be a fighter pilot, but at the time the Army Air Corps needed multiengine pilots, and he entered training in Sioux City, Iowa. Rick had never flown, but he'd diligently read up on it, talked to pilots when he got the opportunity, sat on the sly in the cockpit of a Stearman trainer to familiarize himself with the controls and was ready for his first flight.

While waiting for the instructor, Rick checked the wind sock and the gauges on the control panel. He thought through the takeoff and watched to see if his mental checklist matched the pilot's actual procedure. It did. The instructor took off, climbed to four-thousand feet and demonstrated a few maneuvers. He told Rick to take over and immediately liked his handling of the plane. He asked him to do some more difficult turns and later asked Rick if he wanted to land the plane.

Like the takeoff, Rick had rehearsed the landing many times in his mind. He knew what he needed to do, and now was his chance to put muscle memory to work. The instructor watched as Rick banked smoothly into the downwind leg at eighty-five knots. As expected, Rick glanced over at the landing point midway through the leg. He soon turned base leg while again lowering the flaps and throttling down. He headed upwind at sixty-five knots, lined up on the runway, adjusted the flaps another notch on final approach while compensating for a slight yaw, made a perfect three-point landing and taxied into position. The instructor hadn't seen that level of innate flying ability in a trainee before, especially in a balky tail-dragger like the Stearman. "Are you sure you haven't flown before?" And he let his superior officers know Rick Heydon's name.

Rick was twenty-one when he got his wings. Flying thrilled him. The soaring freedom provided pleasure and fulfillment he had never experienced before. His skills were so advanced that they asked him to stay stateside and train new pilots. Rick begged for an overseas assignment, and they told him that if he gave them six months he would get a plane and his wish.

As a 2nd Lt., Rick was transferred to Blytheville, Arkansas as a flight instructor. He loved teaching prospective pilots who got the same kick out of flying that he did. He didn't enjoy, but was good at, preparing the men who lacked sufficient flying aptitude for their eventual washout. Rick's continuing push for a combat assignment was endlessly stalled, and the six months turned into eighteen. "You're just too good an instructor to let go, and we're making you a first lieutenant."

Finally, a new commanding officer capitulated, and Rick was sent to Alexandria, Louisiana, for multiengine training. Following that, the B-17 crew, with Rick as pilot, assembled in Kearney, Nebraska. They flew to Presque Isle, Maine; Gander, Newfoundland; the Azores; Morocco; Tunisia; and finally to their base in Foggia, near the spur above the heel of the Italian boot.

3

"Old Yellow-Belly's come to save us."

Steve Millen told his parents, friends and neighbors, "The army will take anyone who can breathe and walk, has flat feet, whatever." Actually, his diligent exercise with the marbles had vastly improved arch lift and strength. He said goodbye to family and friends and took the commuter train into Union Station Chicago. He didn't need to buy a ticket.

After sorting through scenes of mass confusion, Steve and some newfound buddies boarded a train headed for infantry basic training at Fort Wheeler, Georgia. Steve had already been through boot camp at the Great Lakes Naval Training Center. So he clued the group on what they might expect based on his own experiences.

Steve had told the recruiting officer about his radio operator grounding in the navy and later in civilian life, but the information fell through the bureaucracy like rain down a storm sewer. After a month of basic training, Fort Wheeler administration got around to learning more about the recruits' backgrounds.

The Signal Corps was desperate for talent, and soon Steve was on a train headed north to Fort Monmouth, New Jersey. His telegraphy and other communication skills were tested; and he was headed south again to Ft. Benning, Georgia, to join the 142nd Armored Signal Company in the 2nd Armored Division commanded by Major General George S. Patton. Personnel logistics was not the army's long suit in early 1942, as weeks of valuable time were wasted shifting G.I.s around in classic screw-ups. At least Steve stayed on the east coast; some men needlessly criss-crossed the country.

Steve liked the feel and rhythm of the trains and the chance to watch the East Coast scenery flash by. He especially enjoyed the shoreline views and the brief stops in Washington and Philadelphia; but it was wartime, and the trains were crowded and the food bad. He met Betty Ann Prather, a pretty southern girl, on the Georgia-north-to-D.C. leg. After discovering mutual interests and sharing a few laughs, they moved closer on the dimly-lit seat and became affectionate toward one another. Under different conditions they might have gotten together. Late in the trip she fell asleep on Steve's shoulder. Betty Ann said when she woke, "You're nice and a good kisser. I'll be working at the Agriculture Department. If you're ever in town with a little time be sure to look me up."

Several days later, after traveling hundreds of wearying miles, Steve landed at the right place where he was needed just in time to train for Operation Torch, the Allied invasion of North Africa. Crossing the Atlantic a few months later, most of his shipmates in the convoy were seasick. Steve, who had retained his sea legs from the navy and knew enough to keep his eyes on the horizon, was one of the few Army personnel with enough stomach to stay on deck and look for U-boats.

The pitch and roll of the deck, the hum and vibration of the engines, the dip of the bow and the crash of the waves against it, the 'shoosh' 'shoosh' of the wake and the feel of the scattering spray on his face filled Steve with much joy and some longing. When he wasn't on deck, asleep, working out or undergoing training, he hung out in the radio room sharing scuttlebutt with the Merchant Marine sailors, enjoying the slang and idioms he knew so well.

Steve watched the convoy's long arc of ships stretching to the horizon, with escort destroyers darting in and out searching for German U-boats hiding in the darkened sea. Thanks to luck and diversionary tactics, the troopships, loaded to the gunnels with soldiers and all the paraphernalia of war, made it through without incident, and Steve's battalion prepared to invade the beaches near Casablanca.

U.S. and British intelligence cajoled, threatened, bribed, planted misinformation, used false promises and tried every other trick they knew to get the Vichy French leaders to split with the Nazis and not resist the invasion. Eisenhower and Patton weren't sure what to expect when they invaded. They quickly learned that the reception was unwelcoming, with heavy Allied casualties.

The Vichy French Navy put up strong, initial resistance. The Allied Air Force and Navy promptly sunk most of their ships and damaged the rest. The invasion was postponed due to foul weather, but the next day Steve's landing craft bobbed and churned through heavy swells on its way toward the Moroccan shore. He briefly watched dogfights overhead and wondered whether his buddies on the Lexington had time to say the sailor's prayers running through his mind.

He went down the ramp in the first wave and headed toward the beach with roiling water up to his collarbone and bullets spattering the surface like raindrops in a downpour. He held his M-1 and radio overhead. The soldier next to him was small and choking from swallowing seawater. Steve, who was a half-inch under six feet and built like a linebacker, put his M-1 and radio in his right hand and thrust them aloft. He took the near-drowning soldier under the armpit with his left hand, lifted him enough to keep water out of his mouth and nose, and they made it to the blood-stained shallows.

French Vichy soldiers fought aggressively. Rifle, machine gun and artillery fire were intense, and the American troops who reached the shore hit the sand. Accurate snipers were a vexing problem, and one took down an American officer who was out in front trying to mount an advance while most of the troops were hunkered down or inching up the beach on all fours with bullets whining overhead. Steve shed his M-1, radio equipment and pack, ran out through a swarm of bullets, knelt, put the wounded man over his shoulder and raced back yelling, "Medic!"

After Steve found a medic, deposited his comrade and got back to his gear, Master Sergeant Deets chewed Steve out in a loud, angry voice from a few yards away, "Goddam it all, Millen, don't leave your fucking radio again, asshole." Deets didn't like Steve who was a natural leader men gravitated toward. After Steve's daring rescue, his fellow soldiers looked to him even more and continued to hate the martinet Deets.

A minute later, Lt. Fosburg, the platoon leader, elbowed over to Steve's position. "Get on the horn, Millen, and tell gunfire support to breach that high seawall and level the buildings beyond *now*." After Steve called it in, Fosburg said, "Good job getting that guy, it was Lieutenant Rabe a friend of mine. The medic said he'll probably live. I'm getting you another stripe."

Fosburg then yelled to his men, "Saddle up. As soon as the Navy starts shooting we're up and running. Eat sand when I do." Then to Steve, "Stick with me, I need radio contact."

The barrage opened up with a deafening roar. Lt. Fosburg was on his feet and started up the beach. A machine gun bullet entered his mouth killing him instantly. Steve looked around, and although the men who were not casualties were up, they were frozen in their boots. Steve looked at Sgt. Deets who was face down with his hands covering his helmet. Steve yelled, "Follow me," and with a long swing of his arm motioned the troops forward. Then he got on the radio while on the run and told gunfire support to hold fire.

Steve heard bullets buzzing like wasps and the flat thudding impacts striking those around him, as they fell silently dead or wounded screaming in pain. He threw a grenade over the seawall and raced through an opening, with over one-hundred men following him through that and other gaps. When troops on the flanks of Steve's platoon saw the charge, they got up and advanced on the run. The Vichy troops who retreated were shot down. Those who held and fought were shot, bayoneted, or smashed with rifle butts in hand-to-hand fighting. The Americans bivouacked under a low ridge to duck machine gun fire from buildings one-hundred-fifty yards ahead. The beachhead at Casablanca was established.

Steve called in the coordinates requesting fire support on the buildings. He heard, "You've got—" and the rest was garbled, as Navy fighter-bombers flying in low-level echelon formations thundered over dropping bombs and destroying the buildings.

Good we stopped here. Sounds like the deck of the Lexington when a squadron warmed up and took off. He then checked around lugging his radio and M-1 making sure the wounded got water and attention from medics.

Captain Carson, company commander, along with Sgt. Deets, came up with more troops and took command. Deets bellowed, "Good job, men, I knew we'd get them."

One of the soldiers whispered to those around him, "Old Yellow-Belly's come to save us." And a nickname that stuck was born. Word filtered back to Captain Carson that Steve led the charge, and he was made Corporal Millen. His buddies thought it should have been sergeant.

4

"We took a few rounds in the chin turret, but they missed me and the bombsight."

Rick Butler flew his B-17 into Tunis, the next-to-last leg of the long journey to Foggia, Italy. As they descended over the never-ending stretches of sand under a pitiless sun, Rick felt contented that he was a flier and not a ground soldier. Now that southern Italy had been secured by the Allies, the 15th Air Force moved its main base of operations from Tunisia to Foggia. After refueling and stretching their legs, they took off and headed north under an azure sky with the sun-speckled Mediterranean reflecting brilliantly below. They landed in Foggia with a light touch and taxied into line among an array of B-17 and B-24 bombers.

The crew disembarked on a sultry day and reported in. They soon learned they weren't there for rest and recreation. Their job was to bomb targets in southern and eastern Germany. Plus Nazi objectives in eastern European countries like Poland, Czechoslovakia and Romania that were difficult to reach from England.

Ploesti in southern Romania was the first target. They were told that the Ploesti oil fields supplied up to one-third of the oil needed by the Nazi war machine. And they quickly found through hellish experience that German fighter protection and anti-aircraft batteries around Ploesti were probably the most concentrated of the war. The run would include 98 B-17's and 127 B-24's, and the bombing approach would be made at seven-hundred feet.

Rick and his co-pilot sought out the ground crew, talked about the plane and thanked them for their support. At the mess hall that night, one of the veteran pilots said to Rick, "Better say your prayers before you go beddy-by, rookie, because a lot of us aren't coming back from tomorrow's show. And if you do come back, you'll probably be shot up. The flak's as thick as snow in the Rockies, and the Kraut fighters bite like crazed rats." Rick thought: *That wins first prize in the metaphor and simile contest.*

They took off into the sun at dawn, leveled at 18,000 feet over the Adriatic, rendezvoused with their P-51 and P-38 fighter escort, crossed Yugoslavia and Bulgaria, entered southern Romania and descended for the low run over Ploesti. Rick told the crew, "Here we go, squeeze those cheeks." No enemy fighters or ack-ack were seen. Suddenly, the sky ahead exploded in harmless-looking puffs, as though five-thousand smokestacks all started belching at once. The puffs contained a curtain of steel shrapnel, and they were flying right into it. The ball turret gunner could see the anti-aircraft guns on the ground.

A B-17 to starboard lost its tail and plunged. Another blew up on the far port side of a lower squadron, and Rick's plane shuddered from the shock wave. Rick spotted a

German fighter flying upside down coming up at them, and before he could yell, "Bandit twelve o'clock low," it zoomed over them, machine guns spitting death.

Rex, the bombardier, shouted, "We took a few rounds in the chin turret, but they missed me and the bombsight. Rick, vector three-five-eight, hold it, ready to pull up . . . bombs away. Let's get this big-assed bird out of here." The plane, along with others in the formation, jerked upward as the bombs released and lightened the load. The pilots used that momentum to climb out of danger, circle and head southwest for home base, as their bombs showered paths of destruction.

Sevy, the top turret gunner, said, "The Kraut who just missed us has a P-38 on his tail. Wait . . . all right, he blew him up in a fireball. Must've been a cannon shot up the ass."

Smitty, the co-pilot, looked over at Rick. "Let's hope it doesn't get worse than this. I need a butt and a few stiff snorts."

5

"Old Blood and Guts will come with his big tank and pull us out."

Once the Navy's aerial bombardment leveled the buildings beyond the beach, LSTs unloaded American tanks, and they rumbled forward with more troops advancing behind them. Despite a few minor skirmishes with diehard Vichy soldiers and sporadic sniper fire, the serious fighting for Casablanca was over. Steve heard on his radio that the landing in Rabat was in mopping-up stages, and they were still battling around Safi.

A runner handed Capt. Carson a package. A minute later, Carson walked over to Steve. "Patton's headquarters wants radio operators with cryptography know-how. You know cryptography, Millen and can tap it?" Steve said he did. "Well, get over there on the double. Take these orders with you. Wait, I'll sign them and add a message about your leadership, your promotion and a medal."

Steve saw one guy from his squad and asked him to say goodbye to the rest. He needed to find the location of Patton's headquarters, and he did with the help of an MP with an Irish mug. "It ain't fah, g'down that street, turn the connah. Oh, shit fahgeddit, folla me."

Steve saw a column of shuffling Vichy French prisoners, escorted by MP's, weapons at the ready. *Poor bastards, I bet they wish they hadn't hooked up with the Germans.*

Steve asked the MP who was guiding him, "Where you from in Boston?"

"Southie."

"Did you know Joe McNamara, went in the navy?"

"Lived up on B Street, was killed on the Lexington. You knew Joe Mac?"

"I did, good man."

"You on the ship?"

"Before the war."

The MP pointed. "The buildin' you want's over theah. Good luck, pally."

Steve thanked him and hustled across the street to a large white house with a big MP standing on each side of the double front door. He showed his orders to one of them who thumbed him inside. "See Lieutenant Wilson."

Wilson sat Steve down at a small desk with a telegraph key. "OK, soldier, use this sheet for the code and tap out, all Krauts are pussies. . . . Good, you're fast, but there's two s's not three in pussies. You'll do. Go see Sergeant Ridgely, first door down that hall."

With his helmet for a pillow, Steve got a lousy half-night's sleep on the floor in the house next door. He never got comfortable and couldn't stop thinking about Joe Mac and other buddies who went down with the Lexington.

The convoy left at 0300. Steve hadn't ridden in a half-track before and soon learned that with two tires up front and a tank-like track propelling from the rear it didn't ride like a Cadillac. He had no idea where they were going and neither did the M-2 half-track's driver and two gunners. Lou, the chunky driver, said, "I just follow the vehicle in front of me. Where he goes, I go. I just the hope the stupid son of a bitch doesn't go over a cliff or into the drink."

Brownie, one of the gunners, said, "Relax, Lou. We're heading east into the sun, only sand dunes ahead."

Lou's canteen was always half empty. "We'll probably get into quicksand."

Pete, the other gunner, was pipe-cleaner thin and nicknamed "Fat." He said, "Old Blood and Guts will come with his big tank and pull us out."

"Sure, Fat, maybe if he's behind us; if he's leading, Patton wouldn't go back for his mother."

Steve read a coded message: *Designated units will head Oran, condition unstable.* He knew that Oran was several hundred miles northeast of them in Algeria. The convoy headed north, then vectored eastward, south of Fez and beyond. Steve kept his take on the intelligence to himself.

The half-track was near the end of the convoy, and even though the canvas roof was on and their mouths and noses were covered with cloth they ate dust all day and broiled. When they stopped for refueling from one of the tankers, Brownie uncovered the .50-caliber machine gun, oiled and then tested it once the tanker moved away. Steve watched him work, asked a few questions which Brownie answered while stroking his beard, and stored the information. Then he watched Pete maintain his .30 caliber.

The men could see how the monotony of the desert drove people crazy: now gravel, now sand, now more sand, and always the unpitying sun, a blinding white disk fixed in the sky. They lived on rations and restricted water intake. Throats parched stomachs angry, butts sore from the bumping on unyielding seats, constipated, nerves raw, they rolled on into the endless unknown. As Steve studied the dramatic cloud formations over the Atlas Mountains to the north, he smiled to himself when Pete said, "We should've joined the Navy."

6

"Jump, you bastards, jump."

In late 1943, not long before Rick Heydon arrived, American and British bombing raids on German-held airfields and nearby targets killed thousands of citizens in and around Foggia. Then the British Eighth Army liberated the area allowing the rebuilding of the airfields for use by the Allies.

Rick learned from fellow officers that going into Foggia to look for girls was a waste of time. The bitterness from the bombings remained. He went anyway and found that that some young women had returned to the city, but they were more interested in his money than they were in his good looks and he passed.

Other than the short delay to repair the chin turret, Rick's B-17 was in constant use on bombing raids. Mercifully, they were never sent back to Ploesti, but were always thinking it could come and they might not be so lucky next time. Crew members rotated back to England, especially radio operators and gunners. Rumors had it that they were needed for a cross-channel invasion.

German anti-aircraft fire and fighter attacks were not as intense northwest of Romania, but bad enough to destroy many planes. Rick saw a B-17 plummeting in a sickening cartwheel with its port wing gone. Another took fighter cannon fire in the bomb bay, blew up, and a single parachute burst from the fireball, opened and floated down with no one suspended from it. The B-17 directly above it was blown upside down and pancaked in with no sign of recovery. Rick and Smitty thought the pilots were either dead or unconscious.

Still another, with much of the tail shot away, spiraled down trailing smoke. Except for the sad and eerie empty chute, there was not a sign of anyone bailing out of any stricken plane. Rick knew some men from the doomed crews and watched in horror with damp eyes and constricted throat as he croaked, "Jump, you bastards, jump."

Rick also saw planes so badly shot up they had to ditch in the Adriatic. One hit a wave and broke up. Some floated long enough for the men to evacuate and get into rafts. Other B-17's that looked intact sank like stones with all hands.

Then the harrowing approaches to the Foggia runways where the mechanicals needed to control landings were so badly damaged that runways were missed never reached or overshot because the flaps wouldn't go down, the brakes were out, or the plane couldn't go around to land into the wind.

Some of the men got to home base dead or critically wounded by machine gun bullets, shrapnel or fire. But the B-17 was an amazingly durable aircraft, one that could withstand brutal punishment and died hard. It got many crews down safely when you wouldn't have bet a dime on their chances.

They never knew whether it was phosphorous or some other kind of white-hot projectile, but one found its way inside the fuselage of a B-17 and rattled around near the waist gunners. One of them raced over; and in a display of matchless heroism, picked up the deadly missile, dashed screaming in agony to the open gun door, and pitched it out. The instrument of destruction fell through the formation and exploded out of range. Despite the thick flying gloves, six fingers were burned off and the base surgeons were barely able to save the rest of his hands. The fearless airman won the Distinguished Flying Cross and the enduring gratitude of his squadron's crew members.

7

"Sandstorm coming, cover the machine guns and get your asses under a tarpaulin."

The convoy stopped for fueling, and the four men sat in the back of the M-2 in their sweat-stained desert camouflage. Lou griped, "Why the fuck would they send us, what, four hundred miles? What's wrong with the First Armored? I heard they're already over at Oran."

Brownie wore a bad Van Dyke Beard and assumed the role of the group's resident philosopher. He believed it was his responsibility to put things in perspective. "Look at it this way, Lou, you might see some new beaches and find some broads. And it's only about a hundred more miles, right, Steve?" Steve nodded.

Pete said, "You're both full of shit, we're going to beat up Rommel."

"Bullshit, Fat, Rommel's over in Egypt," Lou said. "I heard the Brits already fucked him over."

A grinning Brownie said, "Why don't you two quit yapping, and I'll give you both a geography lesson." The suggestion was met with an acid bath of derision.

Steve smiled at the scuttlebutt. *All I know is from coded messages I'm supposed to keep to myself, and these guys already know more through the grapevine.* There was one fresh thing he could tell them. Unhappy with the military failure of Vichy French forces in North Africa, German and Italian troops invaded Vichy France. The Nazi-sympathizing French Marshal Petain had made a Faustian bargain and lost.

The sun's huge, red, slightly-flattened disc slid from sight, and as it does at that latitude the temperature dropped and night came on like a cloak. The convoy, shadowy in the half-covered headlights, kept moving, but it would soon stop for the night. Pete and Brownie, the two gunners, and Steve stayed topside. Lou went to the cab and drove on while muttering to himself. Steve worked the radio. He tinkered, tuned and listened to verbal and telegraphic chatter. Then he heard, "Attention all units, batten down for sandstorm 090 degrees."

The wind picked up from the south. Steve looked out and saw in a searchlight glow from one of the trucks up front what looked like a high, solid tan wall accelerating toward them. He covered the radio and shouted to Brownie and Pete, "Sandstorm coming, cover the machine guns and get your asses under a tarpaulin." By now, Steve was the accepted leader of the crew.

Lou shouted, "Fucking beach is coming to us." The gunners got the .50 and .30-calibers and themselves covered. Three minutes later the sandstorm hit with gale force. The convoy kept moving in an apparent attempt to drive out of the storm. Lou yelled over his shoulder to Steve, "I can't see shit, and the compass's gone screwy. I think we're off the road, whatever you call this sandbar."

The storm raged, rocking the half-track. The pitting of the windshield sounded like pebbles rattling in a can. Steve hollered, "Cover your ears and face below your goggles and keep driving, Lou. It may keep the engine and track from clogging. Go slow, if we hit something it'll be soft."

"Hope Brownie's right about no cliffs around."

They crept along blind seeing no other vehicles. Hearing them above the racket from the storm was impossible. Suddenly, after about thirty minutes, the storm passed as abruptly as it arrived. They stopped under a full moon and starry sky. And they were alone, very alone. Pete and Brownie slid out from under the tarpaulin, uncovered the machine guns and fired a few rounds into the sand. Steve never liked the sound of the angry burps, but this time they sounded reassuring.

He tried the radio again without success. "OK, guys get into your pajamas and I'll read you a story."

Pete said, "Make sure it has broads with big tits in it."

The other three were soon snoring. Steve lay on his back, hands behind his head, looking up at the blanket of stars. A shooting star darted evanescently across the northern edge of the Milky Way. *Hope that's a good sign.* He thought back to a Pacific night when he stood watch on the Lexington and how the sky seemed to stretch forever. It felt like a long time ago.

Steve woke at the edge of a refulgent dawn to see that they were in a gully surrounded by dunes ten or fifteen feet high. *This sand saddle is a bad place for an ambush.* He looked to the rear of the truck. A Vichy soldier stood on a dune one-hundred feet away staring at him. The soldier saw Steve looking at him, turned tail and disappeared over the edge.

Steve shook the rest of the crew awake. "Enemy around, man the guns and point them north." He thought of helmets, but it was too late and sat at the radio cranking for power while prodding and cursing.

"Lou, get this crate rolling straight ahead pronto." Lou hopped down, jumped into the cab, the motor turned over, and they rolled down a slight grade. It was a good thing they got going because a Vichy French Panhard armored vehicle with its telltale brown and black markings appeared over the rise, and its cannon shell just cleared the cab roof and thudded into a dune ninety feet ahead.

Brownie swung and armed the .50 caliber and Pete the .30 caliber. Before they could fire, a machine gun from the Panhard cut them down splashing blood on Steve and the radio. Steve dove for the truck bed, a move that saved his life as the machine gun continued to spray along with small-weapons fire. Lou swerved the M-2 left, saving it as another cannon round whistled by on the right.

Lou scrambled out of the cab and ran for a far dune hollering, "Run, Steve, before they blow us up."

Steve yelled, "Come back and we'll outrun them," and was drowned out when bullets chased Lou across the sand and ran up his back flinging him face down and dead.

The M-2 coasted over the lip of a low dune and stalled with its tail in the air. Steve hoped that the tail section hid him from view and the Panhard crew hadn't seen him diving for cover. He also knew they might launch another cannon shot and blow him to pieces. After seeing Lou killed, Steve knew a run for it was hopeless and stayed put. He thought of waving something white, but even if he had they might think it was a ruse and still kill him. So there he sat wondering what the Panhard crew would do.

They did the stupid thing. Steve saw through a space in the tail that three crew members skidded down the slope of a sand dune toward his M-2. One of them wore a holstered sidearm. Another's rifle slung from his shoulder. The third carried a submachine gun in position for firing. Steve knew he had to kill him first. He crept across the truck bed, slippery from Brownie's and Pete's blood, thinking of how he was glad he'd watched his buddies prep their guns.

The .50-caliber was closest. Steve pulled himself over Brownie's legs and looked up at the gun. It appeared that Brownie got it primed just before he was hit. From the way the three approaching Vichy soldiers were amiably chatting, it sounded like they believed that all threats were dead. *Why didn't they just blow up the M-2 or at least lob a grenade into the bed? That's what I'd do. Why didn't I get a grenade out of the ammo box?*

Hot with revenge, Steve jumped to his feet, pivoted the .50 caliber and raked back and forth across the three men. He wasn't a killer by nature, but he liked seeing this death dance. Then he was a target. A figure shooting a rifle appeared out of the Panhard's hatch. Steve instinctively ducked and popped up firing just as the Panhard was enveloped in a bloom of red fire. The intense blast, which must have ignited ammunition carried in the Panhard, knocked Steve onto his back banging his head onto the truck bed.

He was dazed and suddenly overcome with fatigue and sadness, as he tried to blink away the blurry images and thudding pain. He crawled to Pete's body, straightened his limbs and closed his mouth and eyes. Because of the loud ringing in his ears, Steve never heard the American tank come over the ridge as he fixed Brownie's body. Then he vaulted over the side of the M-2 and went to Lou. *These were good guys. I'm glad I got the chance to kill those fuckers.*

With tear-filled eyes, clenched throat and bursting skull, he turned over Lou's body. As he wiped the sand from his face, a hand touched Steve's shoulder. He whirled into a defensive crouch, fists balled ready to fight. An American tank captain said, "It's okay, soldier. We'll take good care of your buddies." A big sergeant came over, reached down for Steve's hand and pulled him up. The sergeant and the captain looked at Steve's blood-smeared face, hands and uniform. He was almost senseless, as his eyes rolled back in his head. Sinking to his knees, two red streams coursed down the back of his neck from blood-soaked hair.

8

"Die you Nazi maggot scum."

Rick's flight commander believed in occasionally rotating crews, and in this mission Rick didn't fly with his regular men. The pilot of the B-17 he was assigned to was disabled with shrapnel wounds. The target was deep into Germany near the northern Polish border. Anti-aircraft fire was light, and no enemy fighters were seen. They dropped their bombs at twenty-five-thousand feet and turned toward home.

Rick's plane was in the middle of the high squadron and his regular plane, *Rascal*, named as a variation of Nebraska where the crew first met, was on the outside. A Focke-Wulf fighter came out of the sun, and its lucky and devastating cannon round blew off the starboard horizontal stabilizer and the starboard wing beyond the outside engine. *Rascal* rolled over nose down and never recovered. Seven of the crew members who flew from the States to Foggia with Rick died in the crash.

Smitty, his co-pilot; Laddie, the navigator; and Rex, the bombardier, all good friends were in the plane. Rick tried to scream, "Jump!" But nothing came out. He watched in anguish as the plane disappeared below.

The lone Focke-Wulf damaged two more B-17s before it turned on Number 7, Tail-End Charlie, the most vulnerable aircraft at the rear of the squadron. The tail gunner murmured, "Die you Nazi maggot scum," and paid back for dead gunners he'd known by delivering a twin .50-caliber blast into the Focke-Wulf's cockpit sending it into a death spin.

Following debriefing, Rick walked around the base alone for an hour watching vainly for *Rascal* to return, even though he knew from low squadron reports that it wouldn't. He became physically ill, recovered, went back to his bunk and wrote letters for later mailing to *Rascal* crew members' wives and parents.

9

"Watch it, soldier, we can't fraternize."

"He's in the Hundred-Forty-Second Armored Signal Company, part of Patton's group. What? . . . Oh, they were sent over to help out. Got in a firefight with some Vichy between here and Fez, they told me."

Steve tried to open his eyes, but they were glued shut. He tried to talk and nothing came out. He heard another voice approach, "Is this Millen, the guy they brought in from the desert last night?"

"Yes, Doctor, the back of his skull is swollen. The wound is stitched. He's trying to wake up. Here's his chart."

Steve swiped at his eyes, looked around and tried to sit up. He groaned, put his head back down and groaned again. "Where am I? What's going on?" His mouth was gummy, and after the blur cleared he saw two nurses and a doctor, all wearing stethoscopes. He also saw that he was in a large tent, and other G.I.'s lay on nearby cots.

The doctor said, "You must have been knocked backwards and banged the back of your head. There's no facture; it's a good thing you have thick hair, but you had a concussion and were unconscious for over twenty hours."

A G.I. in the next cot said, "He told us all about it in his dreams, quite a story."

Major Lucas walked over. "Corporal Millen, you're now Sergeant Millen. Good job out there. Do you feel like talking about it?"

The doctor said, "Maybe he should wait until . . ."

"No, I'm okay . . . the last thing I remember was my buddies getting hit. I shot three Vichy, then it's a blank."

"A tank came looking for you guys and blew up the Panhard killing a man in the turret," Major Lucas said. "I guess the Vichy were lost like you were. They found you tending to your crew and brought you in."

"Did they bury my guys?"

"In a cemetery outside Oran, you can go there when you're better. Captain Carson wrote in your Casablanca orders that you led a charge at Brushwood Beach, and now this. You're up for a medal, maybe two." Steve's eyes kept closing, and everyone except one of the nurses left. The last thing he remembered was the nurse touching his cheek and squeezing his shoulder reassuringly.

She was there the next morning when he woke hungry, head feeling better. Her name was Suzanne Cousineau, and she was lovely, smart and sassy. She said in undertone, "I washed you while you were asleep, and you got an erection. I knew then you'd be okay." Steve grinned and pulled the sheet over his face in mock modesty, while a smiling Suzanne tucked a strand of butterscotch hair behind her ear.

After Steve could stand without his head pounding, he walked in the yard. Suzanne often joined him when she got a break. They made each other laugh. "You married, engaged, does your girl know what happened? You should tell her." Because of his face and body, Suzanne assumed he was attached.

"No, I don't have anybody back home. I'm just a lonely virgin."

"I'll bet."

"How about you?"

"My husband was shot down, about a year-and-a-half ago, in the Battle of Midway, Navy torpedo bomber pilot. They never had a chance, I heard. I think the whole squadron went in. I hope he got his torpedo launched and sunk something and knew he did it, before . . ."

"I'm sorry," and took her hand.

She pulled her hand away. "Watch it, soldier, we can't fraternize. Lieutenant and sergeant, we'd be in the stockade and not in the same cell. . . . You've got a nice hand. I like you."

"Where you from and how'd you get here?"

"Baltimore. I just got my nursing degree so I joined up. After I got my commission, they put me through six months of school for anesthesia and psychiatric training and sent me here."

"You don't look old enough."

"I finished high school at sixteen, and nursing school was two years."

"Why not the Navy?"

"I get seasick."

Steve smiled. "I want to go out to my buddies' graves, but they won't let me drive yet with my head. Would you drive me on official business?"

"Probably okay, I'll check with the head nurse."

A week later, the corporal at Graves Registration told Suzanne to follow his jeep, and they drove to the plots where

Lou, Pete and Brownie were buried. The corporal left; and Steve, accompanied by Suzanne, went to each grave, said a silent prayer, touched the crosses and thanked them for their sacrifices. Later, he got their home addresses, made sure next of kin were notified and sent letters to Lou's and Pete's parents and Brownie's wife.

They resumed their walks and talks. Steve told Suzanne that getting away from the hospital earlier in the jeep made him feel much better. She said, "You need the break, I can get it again. I found a date palm grove a few miles south of here. I like to walk there. I'm off tomorrow, want to see it?"

"Sure, I like dates."

It was a pleasant patch of green oasis with stately palms, dates for the picking and a freshwater well. And best of all, it was deserted, at least for now. Suzanne and Steve were now good friends and immensely enjoyed each other's company. But it was more than that, a current ran between them. It was all they could do not to hold hands or each other.

Suzanne stopped, reached up and picked a date, bit off the ends, squeezed out the pit and fed the rest to Steve. He chewed and swallowed as Suzanne walked away. He quickly stepped to her side, took her upper arm, swung her around and kissed her parted lips, liquid with date juice.

They devoured each other: kissing feverishly, nipping and inhaling skin, opening clothes, touching with abandon, while sinking moist, turgid and combustible to the matted surface. When they were finished fifteen minutes later and the breathing quieted down, Suzanne said, "That was worth going to the stockade for. I would have faced a firing squad. I love you."

"I've been in love with you for . . . I want to marry you, and I could eat up your beautiful body. I need a commission."

Steve was transferred to Oran to work with a team of cryptographers developing code for the invasion of Sicily. Suzanne and Steve took risks and met every chance they got: at the oasis, behind buildings, at the beach, in remote cafes in the town, always looking over their shoulders, unable to keep their hands off each other, always hoping to make love.

They had their orders and met for the last time. They'd found a tiny bar down an alley. The owner had rooms. Through experience and womanly intuition she read their predicament and let them use an upstairs room for their passion. They tasted each other's tears when it was time to part.

"If you get home first, don't sit under the apple tree. You have my parents' address and I have yours. I know I'll find you."

Although her eyes overflowed and her voice choked, Suzanne tried to smile. "I'll find you, my love."

10

"They also serve who only stand and wait." —John Milton

In July 1943, the 2nd Armored waited in transport ships off the beaches during the invasion of Sicily. Steve's unit wasn't ordered into action for two weeks. Everybody else on board was going bananas, but Steve had experienced the waiting game during his time at sea, and he practiced his telegraphic cryptography and wrote letters to Suzanne he couldn't send. He endlessly exercised, walking and running on the deck and doing hundreds of pushups, squats, sit-ups and pull-ups on the bottom rung of a ladder. Ironically, Suzanne was on a hospital ship close by tending to the wounded. And although each knew the other was in the invasion force, they didn't know where. They ached for each other.

Steve's unit finally landed in Sicily, remained far behind the lines and for two months never got close to the action. Suzanne continued serving on the hospital ship. Both were in the invasion of Italy at Salerno, Steve as a squad leader in the second wave and Suzanne again nursing wounded troops offshore.

11

"They want to kill us, Luis."

Colonel Johnson, the flight commander, called Rick into his office. "Heydon, two generals with stars up the keister need to get to England by Wednesday. You'll fly them in tomorrow to a base," he looked at a paper, "Bury St. Edmunds, north of London. Good name for a cemetery.

"The bigs don't get in here until 0400 hours. You'll leave immediately. Too bad it's not at night, but that's the way it is. It's a little over nine-hundred miles. You'll be okay on fuel at twenty-nine thousand because you'll have no bombs and a light crew. Maybe you can go higher. We'll give you a couple of ferry tanks in the bomb bay. Just take a co-pilot, navigator, radio operator, tail gunner and one more gunner who can move around as needed. The radio operator can handle the top fifty or waist guns, if need be. I'm giving you a good co-pilot, Jeff Granville, who knows the flight engineer routines, and he also knows how to use the radio on the way back, because you're leaving the radio operator in England. They need them there for the next round. I don't have to tell you what that's going to be, any questions?" The colonel puffed on his cigar and blew a smoke ring that hung like a halo over his somewhat irreverent head.

"Fighter escort, sir?"

The colonel took the cigar out of his mouth. "You'll have two P-51s as far as they can go. You may get more fighter support over France and you may not. Depends how busy they are over Germany. We've arranged for one coming back from England, but don't count on it. They said they'd try. With the light load, you'll be flying higher than usual. Maybe their radar will miss you. Get these guys there, Heydon, or you might as well not come back. I know I'll be out on my ass if you don't deliver them. Savvy?"

"Yes, sir."

Despite Rick's mention of its vulnerability, the three-star general took the bombardier's seat because he wanted it. The two-star took a look at the navigator's position in the nose and quickly opted for the less-exposed flight engineer's seat behind the cockpit. The P-51s joined them sixty miles north at 20,000 feet. They climbed together to 29,000 and continued the mission under clear skies. The navigator asked the crew and passengers if they were all getting oxygen, and the replies were affirmative. No enemy fighters or anti-aircraft bursts were sighted. The P-51s peeled away over southern France, and no new fighter escort appeared. The radio operator tapped a coded message asking for backup. No reply was received. Later, when they were two-hundred miles from England another message obtained clearance from British Air Defense.

Everyone, including the brass, was on visual alert the entire trip and they proceeded uninterrupted. Shortly after clearing the French coast, the radio operator, on Rick's orders, contacted the tower at Bury St. Edmunds and got permission to come right in. The weather over the English Channel was dismal, and they bobbed like a buoy in a gale.

With radar guidance down to three-hundred feet, Rick brought the lurching B-17 down in gusting wind, drenching rain, and pea-soup fog. He broke through the low ceiling a little short, gunned the engines, pulled the nose up a bit, throttled back and made a polished landing 1,000 feet down the runway.

The generals disembarked white-faced and rubber-legged. Rick got a mumbled, "Thanks, Lieutenant" from the two-star. While the plane was refueled and maintenance-checked, the crew was debriefed by a stout British officer with carmine-veined cheeks and a plummy accent. They could barely understand what he said. After stretching their legs, the crew was fed a greasy mutton meal by the British cooks. They said goodbye to the radio operator, the weather cleared, and they took a nap on the grass in the sun.

Later, an American intelligence officer briefed Rick, Jeff Granville and the navigator, Bob Cincotta. "I can't believe you guys came up here without enemy contact. They must have been celebrating Hitler's birthday or something. Anyway, there's no good way back there. I'd go a fairly straight line: Paris, Lyon, Marseille, right down the middle. That's no Mexican hayride, but probably slightly better than east and west of that route; angle east between Corsica and Sardinia, split Naples and Rome and on into Foggia. Your biggest problem may be Luftwaffe out of northern Italy. They've got Focke-Wulf fighters with great range, and they can fly higher than you. If you see them you'll have a high pucker factor. What's your ceiling again?"

Cincotta said, "Twenty-nine thousand and change."

"I'd keep the change and push the ceiling, and I'd bust it as much as you can when there's any hint of bandits or ack-ack. Oh, sorry, no fighter escort they're all busy over the Fatherland. Good luck. Oh, one more thing, your plane's got a magneto problem. The mechanics say it's fixable. We might get you out of here before midnight so you can fly most of the way in darkness."

The tower at Bury St. Edmunds cleared Rick for takeoff at 0300 which gave them a little over an hour before daylight. Like the flight up, they saw no threats on the way down, until they were just north of Corsica at 29,500 feet. The tail gunner called out over the intercom, "Bandit diving on me." That was the last they heard as machine gun fire from a Focke-Wulf killed him, and a cannon round tore up the vertical stabilizer.

Another Focke-Wulf came out of the portside sun. Its cannon shot wasn't flush, but was close enough to gash through the back part of the nose and mortally wound Bob Cincotta. The shell exploded just beyond the plane shredding the starboard wingtip. Rick said to Jeff Granville, the co-pilot, "Check what happened down there."

Another cannon blast entered the left rear quadrant blowing out mechanicals aft of the bomb bay. It was fortune calling that the radio operator was not in his seat. But just as Granville stepped out, the same shell ripped through to the right of the cockpit opening killing him. Rick now had minimal control of the rapidly descending plane with the far right corner of the windshield out and the rest dotted with blood. The wind tore at Rick's flight suit, the right side of which was smeared with scraps of Granville's flesh.

Rick lunged toward the windshield to wipe the blood away, but the blasting, frigid air drove him back into his seat. He tried, through a sliver of vision, to keep the rocking plane steady. Miraculously, it didn't go into a spin but continued to rapidly lose altitude. Mercifully, the Focke-Wulf pilots must have thought that they finished off their prey or were low on fuel and broke off.

Just before Sergeant Luis Alvarez, the all-purpose gunner, tapped his shoulder, Rick thought: *Am I the only one alive on this aircraft?* They were now at 10,000 feet, so Rick pushed his oxygen mask aside and hollered, "Anyone alive back there, Alvarez?" He shook his head. "Check below and see if Lieutenant Cincotta's dead. If he is, get his dog tags."

Alvarez quickly came back shaking his head again and holding Cincotta's dog tags. Rick shouted against the din, "I guess it's you and me, Luis. I'm going to try to put this baby down in the drink."

Luis spoke loudly next to Rick's ear, "I saw land to starboard, an island I think, why not land there?"

"It's Corsica, we just liberated it, but I can't steer the plane, the vertical stabilizer must be gone, and the autopilot's not working. I don't know the winds and what's wrong with the controls. I'm not going to rely on banking it in. So we can't get over there and line up on a runway. I'm going to ditch between Corsica and Sardinia, closer to Corsica and hope we can get help from one of them. You know how to use the radio?"

"It's blown up, and there's a hole in the fuselage."

"Oh, good . . . you know how to get the life raft out and ready?" Alavarez said he did. "Get it out of the compartment, but don't inflate it yet. Then come back up here."

Rick had the engines at max, but they continued to lose altitude and were now at 7,000 feet and losing 1,000 feet per minute. The edge of the south Corsican coast appeared ahead, and Rick could see the mountains of Sardinia in the distance.

Alvarez came up to the cockpit door. "The hatch by the radio compartment fused from the shell heat, but I think I can get the aft starboard hatch open and deploy."

"I'll give you your choice, Luis, you can bail out and take your chances with the Mae West or ride it in with me. I'm not sure how cold the water is, or if anyone would ever find us. Me, I'm sticking with the plane."

"So am I."

"How did you avoid getting hit when the shell came through?"

"I was going back to the tail to check on Red. It was bad. He was a buddy . . . I took his dog tags." Luis patted his pocket.

"I'm sorry . . . I want you to go back now, shed your parachute, check on the Mae West, take your boots off, buckle yourself in good and pray the water's calm. You know the escape hatches? Check all of them."

"Probably nothing on the port side aft of here, it looks like the shell came up and in from a low angle below. Can I ride up here, sir? I'd like to watch."

"You've got balls, but they'll do you no good dead. The cockpit's the worst place to be when we ditch, might cave in, and the bubble under us is open and will fill up. If I get killed or trapped, don't hang around, because the plane will go down with you in it. Get the hell out fast, and swim away from the plane or it will suck you under when it sinks. Try to make the Corsican shore."

"We're both going to make it."

"You're a good man, Luis. I think we're going to make it, too. Now scoot. Oh, wait, hold this wheel steady while I get the boots off . . . okay, thanks. Now get back there quick and pray our luck holds. Only one out of three cannon shots exploded inside the plane."

They were now at three-thousand feet and about two miles off the Corsican shoreline. Rick began the prop-feathering procedure: *Two-thousand feet, feather outside starboard engine; feather outside port engine; inside starboard, descending too fast, one-thousand; feather inside port, nose up, five-hundred; water looks fairly calm, no big waves, no spray, tail too low, you're gonna tear it off, nose too low, you'll flip, nose up, here it comes, like a bucking steer, we're down.* The B-17 was in its death throes groaning, creaking and taking on seawater fast all over the plane.

Rick unbelted and looked for Granville's dog tags. He couldn't find them and began to retch from the stress of searching the mangled body. He headed back toward Luis who was in water up to his knees working on the hatch. It opened, they peeked out and saw that a dinghy had divinely deployed, inflated and floated a couple of swim strokes away between the starboard wing and the hatch. Rick said, "Go out and secure it. I'm going back for the Norden Bombsight and throw it overboard. No, shit, I forgot, we didn't bring one, and the plane sinks anyway."

Luis asked, "What's that?"

Rick looked out. A surfaced German U-boat was three hundred yards to starboard and heading their way. Crew on the deck swung a machine gun and cannon toward them. The B-17 was settling fast, as the water rose and gurgled around their chests. They swam out and bellied into the raft. "Unbuckle it, Luis. If the Krauts want to kill us, we can't do anything about it."

Luis unbuckled, and they pushed the raft toward the tail. The sub's cannon boomed, and the shell took out the top turret. "They want to kill us, Luis." Heavy machine gun fire stitched high on the plane's fuselage just clearing their heads. Rick and Luis tried to paddle around and away from the plane to avoid more gunfire from the sub which was less than two-hundred yards away.

Suddenly, the sub crew swung the deck cannon and machine gun up and away from the raft. Rick and Luis heard a plane and looked up to see a PBY Flying Boat. It dropped several depth charges all of which splashed close but not close enough to damage the sub. The crew was unsuccessful in hitting the PBY with cannon and machine gun fire. Their guns lowered, pivoted again and commenced firing in the opposite direction, while the Americans got wash from the depth-charge explosions.

Between the cannon blasts from the sub, they heard a high-pitched, whining roar. Rick stood for a better look. "Can you believe it, Luis, a PT Boat and they're launching torpedoes?"

The twin wakes appeared ready to bracket the sub, while the PT Boat's machine guns raked the sub's deck as the crew ran for their lives. One torpedo just missed the sub's nose, and continued on passing within ten yards of the barely visible B-17s tail. The other torpedo must have hit the munitions hold because the U-boat exploded in a gigantic ball of flame, quickly sank and exploded again under water.

Rick and Luis rocked violently and were nearly swamped from the waves caused by the explosions. Then the PT Boat came roaring past, seeing the plane for the first time just before it sank out of sight. Meanwhile, Rick and Luis, wallowing in the PT Boat's wakes, furiously paddled away from their plane sinking nose-first. The PT crew saw them, slowed, circled in a wide arc and pulled within thirty yards. "Hey, you flyboys want a lift?" Luis and Rick looked back at the bubbles rising from the now underwater B-17. Both saluted and Luis crossed himself.

The crew took Luis to their quarters for a change of clothes and some hot coffee. The three officers outfitted Rick, and after he gulped a coffee they talked on the bridge. Rick asked, "Where did you guys come from, and how did you and the PBY know we were here?"

The PT Boat captain, Will Evers, said, "We *didn't* know until the PBY reported you down. We were both out looking for the sub. He's been nosing around for a few days, and we haven't been able to get him. The PBY tracked him this morning, then they spotted him surfaced and going after you and called us over. I guess the Kraut commander got sick of being chased and wanted a little target practice on a downed plane. The prick got too hungry for his own good. Lucky we were only a mile-and-a-half away. What happened to you guys?"

"It looks like we all got lucky. The sub focused on us and didn't spot the PBY. When they started shooting at him they picked you up too late. Anyway, we're on the way back on a roundtrip from Foggia, Italy to England dropping off some brass. We got hit by several Focke-Wulf's north of Corsica. They shot up the plane, and we had to ditch down here. The rest of the crew was killed in the attack, only Sergeant Alvarez and I made it thanks to you guys."

"We're based in Sardinia, and we'll head back there direct, unless we spot some juicy targets. We'll let them know at the base you're on board. Maybe they can fly you, or there's a boat to Italy." Evers signaled the helmsman, and the Packard Marine Engines revved with a thunderclap boom. Rick held fast with both hands, as the PT Boat's nose lifted and sliced the water into high-plumed wakes.

12

"That's your squad. The squad leader got it this morning."

Following the initial landings, German counterattacks jeopardized the beachhead at Salerno and Allied casualties were high in a ten-day pitched battle. Action was light on the section of the beach where Steve's battalion deployed, and before the heavy fighting began he and other radio operators were moved offshore to work on coding and messaging. He remained onboard for three months, as his ship cruised slowly north providing supplies and communication along the Tyrrhenian Coast in support of Allied troops engaged in dirty and costly battles to break a succession of German defensive lines between Naples and Rome.

As we have learned, Steve was a self-contained person. He was grateful to have escaped death on the Salerno beaches. But the long confinement on the ship was almost beyond his capacity to endure. Transfer requests were ignored. He'd experienced many snafus in his service career, but this was his first fubar, fucked up beyond all reason.

He had no way to inquire about Suzanne's current posting and didn't feel comfortable writing to her parents. He decided to keep himself in peak physical condition, while becoming more proficient with the tools of his trade, particularly the latest coding protocols. Having access to coded messages allowed him to keep track of the battle for Naples and the savage fighting to crack sturdy German defenses along the Volturno and Barbara lines.

Suddenly, in a rush and for reasons unknown to him, he was taken by launch to the shore and assigned to an infantry battalion designated to attack the Gustav Line which ran across the Italian Peninsula near Cassino. Due to the intense demand for cryptographic telegraphers, he quit trying to keep track of which unit he was assigned to. Brass kept trumping lesser brass, and he was constantly being requisitioned and on the move. Movement, however, came in fits and starts, and often they sat for days in the same spot waiting for new orders.

Steve knew the expression, 'See Naples and die' but never got to see the city fabled for its beauty. He caught a faraway glimpse of Mt. Vesuvius with the summit wreathed in purple haze and was grateful for the view. He spent most of the time in an armored vehicle bouncing on bad roads, hunched over a radio sending and receiving coded messages. The messages told him where he was, where the unit was going and where they thought the Germans were.

The unit got into some fierce firefights as they neared Cassino. Once, when they were beaten back, he got up to get his M-1 and go out and help. A brigadier general riding in the compartment said, "Sit down and keep tapping, Sergeant. We've got enough people out there. I need a radio operator, not a hero."

Every time he saw a truckload of nurses at a stopping point and could leave the vehicle for a break, he ran over, saluted, and asked, "Do any of you happen to know a

Lieutenant Suzanne Cousineau?" No one did. A few times one of the nurses looked at Steve's stripes and then looked at him funny.

"She's my sister," Steve poker-faced.

Upon hearing this answer, one nurse asked him, "What's your name, Sergeant?"

"Millen, ma'am."

"How come she's Cousineau and you're Millen?"

He was ready for that one, "Same mother different father, ma'am."

The armored vehicle shuddered and vibrated from a German artillery onslaught as they neared the base of the mountain with the monastery, Monte Cassino, on top. The Germans were dug in up the mountain and on the top hiding among the bombed-out ruins, with thick walls and piled-up rubble giving them cover from American air strikes and artillery batteries.

Company Commander Captain Knowles called Steve over, "Third battalion wants you as a forward artillery observer. I don't want to give you up, but he outranks me. Grab your M-1, put a few grenades on your belt, get a hand-held radio and report to the battalion commander. He's the lieutenant colonel scrunched down behind the sandbags over there about fifty yards. Run low and fast, there's a shit-load of snipers behind those high rocks up there."

"Millen, I'm sending up two platoons. You'll lead the first squad in the left platoon starting over there by the big white rock. See that ridge halfway up the mountain? We can't see over it. Get up there and give me coordinates. See the platoon leader, Lieutenant Melo, the tall guy by the field piece."

Steve squatted beside Lt. Melo. "You've been in combat before, Sergeant?" Steve said that he had. "This may be your worst one." Melo pointed to a squad of about ten men. "That's your squad. The squad leader got it this morning."

Steve thought: *I hope it's not worse than the desert.*

Lt. Melo gathered his squad leaders. Steve thought: *We're too tightly bunched, one mortar round wipes us all out.*

Melo said, "We can't get a spotter plane in here, ack-ack and machine guns too heavy. There may be some mines, but most have probably been stepped on. This platoon and Lieutenant O'Reilly's on the right need to get over the ridge and give artillery coordinates. Millen, you're first up."

Steve ran crouched over to his squad, told them to spread out, saddle up and listen up. A corporal stood, walked over to Steve and got in his face. "Who the fuck are you to come in and big-man us? They should have promoted . . ." Steve sat him on the ground with a short right hand, hunkered down and resumed:

"We're going over that ridge up there, and we'll shoot some Germans on the way. We *will* get over that ridge so I can call in coordinates and fire support can start blasting the Krauts off the mountain along with their heavy stuff that's carving us up." Steve pointed to the man he just knocked down. "If I get it, you, corporal, what's your name?"

"Roche."

"Okay, Roche, you're assistant squad leader. Here's how you use the radio."

A moose of a Pfc. looked over Steve's shoulder as he explained the radio to Roche. "What's your name?"

"Carlson."

"I like your attitude." And to rest of the squad, most looking young and scared, "Check your M-1s and have extra clips ready. Where's the BAR ammo bearer?" A hand went up. "Make sure you all have grenades. Drink some water now. Stick together and watch each other's backs. This mission is *going* to succeed."

Steve pointed. "See Lieutenant Melo over there, taller than the rest? I follow him, and *you* follow me." A mortar shell burst over two-hundred feet in front of them, and they all flattened. Another sprayed steel on their far left, and they stayed down coughing, covered in dust and dirt.

Lt. Melo and Lt. O'Reilly got on their feet and signaled everyone up. The two platoons climbed the rugged, rocky mountainside spread out and making themselves as small as possible. Steve liked it when a few of his men slipped and other squad members helped them up and along. They took no fire on either flank.

About halfway to the ridge, a previously unseen German machine gun nest opened up. Steve slipped on a smooth rock and went to one knee. A bullet skimmed his helmet. Lt. Melo was cut down along with four other squad members, including Corporal Roche. Steve still had Carlson and hoped he understood the radio instructions down below. Steve was now leading the platoon.

Carlson came up out of breath beside Steve, "Jeez, Sarge, you climb like a fucking billy goat. I've got an arm. Want me to throw a pineapple into that gun?"

"Yes." He called up the remainder of the squad and the one behind. "Not too close. Stay separated. You can hear me. Carlson's going up to lob one. When I say 'fire' let's lay down some heavy shit on the nest. Brooks, put the BAR on the tripod . . . Carlson, when I say go, you go. Get your pieces up, ready, fire . . . hold fire. Go, Carlson!"

Meanwhile, Carlson laid down his M-1 and pack and put a grenade in his right hand. When Steve yelled, "Go" he climbed one-hundred feet bent forward like a sapling in a hurricane. He pulled the pin and dropped to one knee as he launched the grenade in a motion that resembled Joe DiMaggio throwing out a runner from deep center field. While the grenade was in the air, the machine gun opened up. Everyone, including Carlson, sprawled, the grenade landed true, and the firing stopped. Carlson waved them up.

A German soldier with a rifle popped up from behind a rock near the machine gun nest. An alert squad member shot him through the nose, and his face disappeared in a gush of blood.

Steve looked over to see the rest of Lt. O'Reilly's platoon bogged down. *They need a Carlson.*

A man handed Carlson his M-1 and pack. Steve said, "You climb with me, Carlson," and they made headway up the steep, boulder and bush-strewn incline under withering small-arms fire. Then the Germans up on the ridge, now two-hundred yards away, began rolling armed grenades over the edge. It was hard to see them among the rocks and the few stumps and bushes that survived the bombardments from above and below. Most of the grenades detonated before they reached the Americans. A few brave G.I.'s picked them up and threw them to the platoon's left. Others, not so lucky, lost limbs or were blown apart.

Steve could now see why O'Reilly's platoon was behind them and not moving. They were taking mortar fire from behind the ridge, and now Steve's flank began to get it: the barely audible chuff, followed by silence and then the blast with shrapnel spraying 360 degrees. While thinking about that and climbing hard with sweat stinging his eyes, a bullet grazed Steve's left forearm, tearing his sleeve and darkening it with blood. Another bullet shattered Carlson's right tibia, knocking him flat howling in pain.

Brooks, one of the five remaining squad members, had lost his two support men. He moved up, put down his BAR, produced a cloth from who knows where and tied it around Carlson's leg. He gave him a sip from his canteen, picked up his own weapon, and crawled up beside Steve as if to say, "I'm with you." Steve was glad that Brooks was built like a shot putter and could handle the BAR and ammo alone.

Steve looked back down the mountain. The trailing squads were disintegrating under the mortar barrage. The explosions and body damage were horrific, and a full retreat was underway. Steve called down on the radio, "Millen, forward observer lead squad, we're moving up."

"Go and go hard."

They moved around and past dead Americans who had not reached the ridge on earlier attempts and couldn't be retrieved. Steve thought: *The Germans are battle-hardened and very good.*

Steve and his remaining men, joined by six others from the squad behind them, got to the edge of the ridge and bivouacked under a slight overhang. The other squad's sergeant wasn't there, and when one of his men saw Steve looking, he quietly said, "He's dead."

A German soldier, suspecting that Americans were below him, leaned over trying to see them. The private who just spoke to Steve shot the German through the throat. He tumbled over the edge coughing blood on the Americans and rolled down the steep grade until pinned by a boulder where he lay writhing in death spasms.

Steve soft-voiced, "Spread out, six feet apart, leave room to toss grenades. Throw them back over your head like this." He demonstrated empty-handed. "And throw them as far as you can. As soon as they go off, boost me up for a look-see. Now get them out, and we pull the pins on the count of three and toss them quick."

This isn't exactly military procedure. One could go off and kill us all. But I'll take the chance it works so we get off this fucking mountain.

"Okay, on three: one, two, three, pull, throw!" Ten went over and exploded like a firecracker chain. One hit the underside of the lip and dropped four feet below them. They looked at it wide-eyed hoping it would roll and dove for the ground. It did roll and exploded harmlessly eighty-feet below. Steve looked down through the acrid smoke to see that the rest of his platoon, plus O'Reilly's platoon, was in full retreat with some pausing to rescue wounded and bring back the dead. The eleven of them were the only Americans high on the mountain.

"I need to look over, lift me." Steve scanned the perimeter as a few rounds zipped past his head. One kicked up dirt and blinded one eye. Through his good eye, he saw a narrow plain backed by another steep slope. The place was littered with dead German soldiers and live ones scurrying about under sharp-voiced orders. Several mortar and machine gun emplacements, plus howitzers, were manned and sat waiting for use.

Steve tapped arms signaling he wanted down. He tipped his canteen into the blocked eye, then got on the radio and called in the coordinates. The answer came back, "Get out of there and down the mountain. We're letting go in two minutes."

"We're staying under the rim until you start blasting, otherwise the Germans will run out and shoot us in the backs."

"Okay, it's your call, but you guys better haul ass once we start."

The first shell landed too close to the edge shearing it off and showering dirt on the Americans. Fortunately, the heavy earth fell beyond them, and except for a cascade of muck down the backs of their necks and a few mouthfuls of Italian soil none were hurt. Steve hollered, "Move out, spread out more, pick up wounded and dead. Wounded first, we'll take the dead if we can." He gave the orders none too soon, as the explosions above made hearing impossible. The ten men would have followed Steve anywhere.

They rescued as many wounded as they could. Two men carried Carlson. Lt. Melo wasn't dead, but he'd taken a bullet through the chest and was comatose. Steve got Melo's long frame over his shoulder, and the squad slowly picked bloody paths down the mountain.

Two medics ran up the lower slope with a stretcher and took Melo off Steve's shoulder. One of them opened his shirt and examined the wound. "No artery, it's flesh, needs plasma, he'll probably live."

Near the bottom, a private ran up to Steve. "Sarge, report to the company commander."

"You're now Staff Sergeant Millen. I just saw in your record you're up for a Bronze Star for North Africa action. I'll second that motion with a recommendation that includes valor. Now get that arm bandaged and grab your gear. We have orders, we're moving out, only God knows why, and you're staying with this company."

"Thank you, sir. I recommend Pfc. Carlson for a promotion and decoration. He took out a German machine gun nest. Without him, we wouldn't have gotten to the ridge."

13

"Oh, Reeky, my name is Alisea."

"I don't know how we're going to get you out of here, Heydon. They're bogged down south of Rome fighting the Germans over some monastery on a mountain. The rest of the boats are north supporting another invasion. I'll bet it's Anzio, nice beach. We'll try and notify Foggia about you and Sergeant Alvarez, but these days a lot doesn't get through. You might as well have yourself a little vacation, nice local girls."

Luis Alvarez found a girl and never wanted to leave Sardinia. Despite being a possible stand-in for Gregory Peck; well, at least in a wide shot, Rick had his usual bad luck with women. He frequented a local club that featured a Corsican singer of smoky looks and voice: "Underneath the lantern/By the barrack gate . . ."

Rick turned around to see who she was singing to and realized it was him. She came over on her break for drinks and cigarettes. "What is your name?"

"Rick."

"Oh, Reeky, my name is Alisea."

During the second visit, she put her hand on his thigh under the bar. Rick had the buoyant look and confident feeling of a man who was certain he was going to get laid. A few minutes later, when Alisea returned to the bandstand

and things had cooled a bit, he thought: *I hope this freakin' movie doesn't have a bad ending.*

On her next trip to the bar she asked "Reeky" to walk her home. On the way, Alisea's yielding body pressed against his, and her kisses were moist and probing. When they reached the door of her darkened little house, she said, "Wait here while I check."

After Alisea went inside, Rick heard in low-toned, heavily accented but clear English, "You, soldier boy." He pivoted to see mister-quick-with-the-knife, a muscular, mustachioed Corsican bandit from central casting lacking only a bandana and wide leather wrist band. "You like your balls you don't touch my woman, *comprenez-vous?*"

Rick nodded and walked away thinking: *He looks like Gilbert Roland.* He wasn't cupping himself but did look back a few times. *I guess he came back earlier than expected from the latest string of robberies and was tipped off by a friend from the club.* Before being out of earshot he heard the thug yelling and slapping and his wandering-eyed girlfriend screeching in pain. Rick never returned to the bar and felt lucky he wasn't knifed instead of getting a warning.

He busied himself hiking and sightseeing in the hilly, sylvan countryside and writing letters to the families of his dead crew members. He hadn't flown before with Bob Cincotta, the navigator, but had gotten to know him around the base. Bob, a prolific writer of fiction and poetry, asked Rick to read some of his work. He thought it showed overflowing talent. *War robs the world of so much potential.*

In writing some of the letters and thinking of the young wives, like Bob's, who would read them, Rick realized that he'd never had a loving relationship with a woman and thought about what it might mean. Sex was always the first priority. He'd had a couple of brief affairs with lonesome women back when he was a flight instructor in Blytheville, Arkansas. And with the near-death experiences and the newfound comprehensions he was now aware that he wanted someone who loved him and cared deeply, a life partner and lover.

After a month on the island, Rick was tanned, rested and fit. After endless badgering, he finally got himself and Luis on a boat to mainland Italy. ". . . No, Luis, you aren't staying here. The MPs will find you and shoot you for a deserter . . . no, I'm not putting you in for a transfer. I have no authority, and we need gunners back in Foggia. They're sending half of them to England. Say goodbye to your girlfriend, tell her you'll see her after the war, pack your stuff and be at the dock tomorrow at 0500 hours, and don't be late."

14

"BY SOME CHANCE HAVE YOU SEEN A NURSE NAMED SUZANNE COUSINEAU?"

Steve's restructured squad, blank-eyed, rain-soaked, filthy, pestered by flies and mosquitoes and played out huddled in a truck in a seemingly endless convoy. They tossed and pitched for hours on shell-pocked roads from Cassino up the Italian coast with sporadic glimpses of the Tyrrhenian Sea: Cervaro, Formia, Gaeta and in between tiny villages ravaged by war. And always the war-weary Italians peering out hoping the Germans wouldn't come back once the Americans passed through.

They finally got out of the truck near a port in a coastal town and lined up for creamed beef on toast, also known in the Army as shit on a shingle. A corporal walked around calling, "Sergeant Millen! Sergeant Millen!"

"Here."

"The company commander wants to see you now, Sergeant."

"I figured I'd lose you, Millen, can't hide much these days. They want people to write code. It's in your records from Oran and Sicily." He pointed. "Report to that ship over at the end of the dock; see Captain Adcock, adjutant to

Brigadier Lessor. I wrote up your medal recommendation. Good job."

Steve walked over to where the men in his squad were chowing down. He thanked them, wished them luck and headed for the ship. On the way he saw a group of nurses talking. "Excuse me have any of you by chance know or know of a nurse Suzanne Cousineau?" One of the nurses looked at him quizzically. "She's my cousin."

Most in the group shook their heads no. The nurse who gave Steve the look knew from his voice and expression that this was no casual inquiry. She brushed one forefinger across the other while clucking tsk, tsk, tsk. Then with a mischievous smile, she said in a stagy French accent, *"Ah, Cousine, Cousineau, oo la la."* The nurses all laughed. Steve couldn't suppress a smile despite his disappointment.

Like the invasion of Sicily, Steve wrote code and sent and received messages from a ship in the harbor off Anzio and managed to work out regularly. The chow was better, the billet was more like the Navy, and he didn't miss being constantly on the move chasing Nazis and sleeping on the ground in rain and mud.

He knew from the lack of gunfire and the messages going back and forth that the Anzio invasion was a cakewalk. The generals figured that the Germans had given up on holding Rome, and some forward reconnaissance units got within thirty miles of the city without serious opposition. Then everyone wondered what happened. Why didn't we push our advantage, break out on a broad front, put the Germans on the run and liberate Rome in a sure-fire military and propaganda victory? But we didn't.

While the allies were napping, the opportunistic German commander Field Marshall Kesserling brought up massive reinforcements. He embedded howitzers and mortars on the hills circling the beach and rained death on the Americans. Ships in the harbor were sunk and badly damaged with a huge loss of life. Steve's ship pulled out of range early and avoided harm.

Tanks deployed by Kesserling pointed their devastating 88 mm guns at the Americans on the beach killing and wounding thousands. Anzio was one of the worst American military debacles of the war in Europe, and it could have been avoided had aggressive forward action been taken early in the invasion.

After weeks of havoc, the reinforced Americans broke out of the now-widened beachhead, the Germans retreated to a stronger northern position and Rome was taken. Steve got off the ship, was given new orders to a place he thought was on the Adriatic coast. *Why there and why me, and who figures this shit out?* Because all roads supposedly lead to Rome, Steve's unit rode through. He caught glimpses of some landmarks: the Tiber River, Vatican City, the Coliseum and lots of fountains.

The Italians cheered, and he saw pretty, smiling girls in summer dresses and was reminded, as if he needed it, of Suzanne. The driver was going around in circles and needed directions. They were allowed to get out of the truck near the Spanish Steps. Nearby, a comely American captain stood next to a grinning major. His body language displayed all the appearances of courting. Steve approached them and saluted. "Excuse me, Captain; are you with the Nurse Corps?"

"Yes, I am. What do you want to know?"

"By some chance have you seen a nurse named Suzanne Cousineau?"

"As a matter of fact I have. We were on a ship off Anzio together."

"Do you know where she is now?"

"No, I don't. She was among a detachment of nurses that was sent ashore."

"Was that after the breakout?"

"No, they were sent during the worst part of the fighting." She saw Steve's face darken. "I probably shouldn't have told you that. I don't know where that group is now. I'm sorry."

The guys on the truck knew that Steve had gotten bad news, and when he stared into the middle distance they left him alone. It was June 6, 1944.

15

"You'd better take your pistol, a submachine gun and a few grenades."

The convoy rode east just south of the German lines. Steve was again put in an armored personnel carrier to transmit coded messages. It seemed that Italy had become the forgotten war. All anyone wanted to talk about was the invasion of Normandy. Through the clutter, he picked up that the Germans established a new defensive line that stretched eastward through the central portion of the Apennine Mountain chain and on to the Adriatic coast. And he understood that soon he would be out of the relative safety of the armored truck and moving north to help shatter that line.

Despite that prospect, Steve's spirits quickly reconstituted. Although he couldn't bear to bring her photo out, he willed himself to believe that Suzanne survived Anzio, was the radiant woman of his memories and would be his lover and friend once more.

As in the battle of Monte Cassino, Steve was an artillery observer leading a squad in a forward platoon. He knew that most artillery observers were officers and had gone to school for special training. He also knew that, like his assignment at Monte Cassino, most of them were dead or wounded, and he was a necessary replacement.

Also like Monte Cassino, the Germans were entrenched and experienced. Unlike Cassino, the hills were heavily wooded, and the enemy was potentially behind every tree. Some of the veterans had been in brutal fighting on the German Winter Line, and their attitude was fatalistic. One, who had been in the Battle of San Pietro, said, "If you're going to get it, and you eventually will, it might as well be here."

Before the climb toward entrenched German positions began, two advance scouts were dispatched to separate quadrants. No messages were received and neither returned. Since no shots were heard it was assumed that they escaped along a flank and were working their way back, or been captured, or killed silently. After a heated debate, the artillery laid down a heavy barrage above the topmost perimeter of the scout's agreed-upon range. The fire control officers didn't know what they were aiming at and what effect the shells might have.

Steve gathered his squad. "We're going into an unknown situation. The best way to avoid being killed is kill them first. Keep separated, but keep me in sight and watch my hand signals. Speak only when absolutely necessary. Help each other, and we'll get through it and out the other side. Check your weapons."

Allied units fought with the Americans in the battle of Monte Cassino. Steve's squad had not been in close proximity to them, but now they were. Steve especially liked having the Polish and Italian contingents on their flanks. These soldiers were known to be steadfast and brave. Three platoons of different nationalities, Italian, American and Polish, dispersed over a three-hundred-yard-wide front, entered the forest and climbed a steep foothill of the mountain chain.

Since no German small arms were heard, it was uncertain whether the enemy was above them, and if they were, what their strength might be. Suddenly, a quarter-mile into their ascent, the answer came down hard as they were slammed by mortar, rocket and grenade blasts and raked by machine gun fire.

Steve didn't need to wave his men down. Troops across the line flattened reactively, or because they were killed or wounded. When the shooting stopped Steve waved his men up, and they crawled toward him staying wide apart. His squad was intact, unlike other close-by squads where some men didn't move or rise and others raised an arm beckoning for help. Trailing medics moved in to help the wounded and dying, many crying out in their suffering.

Steve's platoon leader sent runners to his Polish and Italian counterparts asking for a meeting. He told Steve to keep moving up and he would rejoin them. Since his was the lead squad, Steve temporarily led the platoon, and the rest of the squads followed. *Why the hell would they meet? There's nothing to plan. Our job is to keep going until the commander calls it off.* The three platoon leaders did meet and it was brief. They didn't follow the rule of spreading out, and all were killed by a random German mortar shell.

Steve didn't know this. He also didn't know that three other platoons, American, British and Australian, were now bringing up the rear. Nor did he know the carnage caused by the German howitzer shells whistling over the three lead platoons and exploding and ripping bodies with shrapnel throughout the rearguard platoons. He did know that the front line was advancing and dying under concentrated and well-placed mortar and machine gun fire. *How do the Germans know where we are?*

He found out when the concussion from a mortar blast knocked him to a sitting position, and he saw a German spotter talking on his radio high in the trees. Steve pointed up to squad members nearby, and they shot the German off his perch. A runner from the Italian platoon on his left, obviously sent because he spoke enough English, told Steve of the platoon leader's deaths. "Who sent you?"

"Sergeant Giaccone."

Steve reached for his radio, brought it to his ear and a sniper's bullet knocked it to the ground. Steve rolled behind a tree pulling the runner with him. He shook his numb hand and tried the dead phone. He sent the Italian courier back to his platoon with the words, "Tell Sergeant Giaccone to follow me and move when I do."

He told two riflemen to find the sniper in the trees and kill him. Close-by a squad member was bleeding through his shirt but ambulatory. No medics were about. They were all busy getting other wounded down to the base of the hill. "Sample, you okay?"

"Got nicked by shrapnel, I think."

"Go down the hill, find the company commander and tell him Sergeant Millen sent you. The platoon leaders are dead, and I'm leading the three front platoons. It's bad but we're climbing. Tell them to get a radio up to me so I can call when we find the German artillery. You got it? Get that wound fixed and get back up here. I need you. And bring medics and ammunition. Now go!"

After Sample was out of sight, Steve thought: *Shit, I forgot to tell him not to get shot by our guys below us*. Luckily, it wasn't necessary, since the rearguard had been largely reduced by shell fire and the survivors had pulled back. Steve thought of a tactic.

"Pass the word. Anybody speak Polish or Italian?" Shortly, two men ran over low to the ground. "Your names?"

"Jaworski."

"Falzone."

"Get over to the platoons on each flank." He pointed. "Go left Falzone and find Sergeant Giaccone. Tell him to keep his troops spread ten meters and staggered in at least two lines. When he hears my shot, advance firing on the count of three. Stop shooting and run forward until the Germans open up and get down. Then we repeat it. You got it? You too, Jaworski?" They both said yes. "I don't know the Polish sergeant's name. Find out and tell him the same thing. Again, they move forward shooting on my shot, thousand-one, thousand-two, thousand-three. Stop shooting, then run forward until the Germans return fire and hit the dirt. If the other two platoons can't hear my shot, tell them to advance firing when we do."

It's probably a bullshit scheme. But we're not going to sit here and wait for German artillery spotters to give our coordinates.

Steve told the men near him what to do and pass the word. In five minutes, Falzone and Jaworski were back and gave Steve thumbs up. The German mortars and small arms were quiet for a few seconds. Steve stood, yelled an elongated "Go!" and fired his M-1. The troops of three nations opened up for, well, it wasn't exactly three seconds, but close enough as they ran uphill through the trees whooping in three languages. For some reason, lost forever in the shroud of war, the Germans didn't answer. By the time they did, the sortie covered two-hundred yards across a three-hundred-yard front with minimal damage.

The men plunked down, caught their breaths, reloaded, shared whatever water was left and waited for orders. Steve could tell from the loudness of the answering fire that the Nazi line was now much closer and could be reached with another charge. It was also clear from the shells thudding below them that the advance came just in time to escape a ferocious artillery barrage on their former positions.

Two corporals had attached themselves to Steve at the hip. "Your names again?"

"Rideout."

"Schmidt."

"Find Falzone and Jaworski. They tell the Polish and Italian sergeants that we repeat the act on my shot in about five minutes. This time when the Germans open up we throw grenades. I don't give a rat's ass how bad the Germans hit us. We keep going until we drop grenades in their laps. Tell them that, and make sure they understand it. Now move it. Wait . . . see if they have mortars. If they do, tell them to fire rounds now set for two-hundred meters for one minute and stop; one minute, and only through openings between the trees."

Steve noticed that two sergeants, one a buck the other a tech from other American squads in the platoon, listened in to his directive. Steve grinned and said to the tech sergeant, "Sorry, I didn't know I was outranked. You want to lead?"

"You seem to be doing okay. We'll be right with you."

"Good, now let's pass the word to get the grenades and BAR's ready and finish this thing off. We need everything we have. Fire mortar rounds now through clearings at two-hundred-twenty-five yards for one minute only, one minute and stop."

After the group separated, Steve noticed a private, who probably hadn't shaved yet, curled under a tree crying and shaking. Steve put an arm around his shoulders. "It's okay, kid, I'm scared, too. You've done a good job and you've done enough. I'm sending you down to tell the colonel that I need a bazooka, a machine gun and a radio and send some big guys to carry them up." The boy stopped shaking and was now just sniffling. "If they want to send you back up tell them Sergeant Millen wants you to stay down there and rest for the next battle, because there will be a next battle and we need experienced guys like you. Now go." The kid went down the hill with the momentum of a snowball gathering size and speed. He had his orders and he was going to carry them out.

A Pfc. ran over to hand Steve a walkie-talkie. "I just found this, Sergeant Millen. Somebody dropped it."

The corporals reported back that the message was on its way to the flanking platoons. Steve said, "We go in soon, pass it down the line to be ready with all weapons."

As the ever-present low clouds released a cold, soaking rain, the mortar fire stopped. Steve thought of a Civil War book he had read with a description of the Wilderness Campaign: *Just like here, rain, fog, smoke, dark, Godforsaken, bloody, not knowing where the enemy is. Maybe war never changes.*

He looked left and right down the line. *We're all the same, scared shitless, wishing we were home, afraid we're going to die.*

He stood and yelled a long "Go!" from the gut and shot off his M-1. This time the Germans didn't hold their fire. Before it ended, at least one-quarter of the troops in the three platoons lay dead or wounded from bullets and shrapnel gashing through them, but the advance never faltered. Perhaps because of their shared hatred for the Nazis, the Italians and Poles got to the German mortar and machine gun emplacements first. They threw grenades into the pits, waited for the explosions and then waded in on a killing rampage, bayoneting and shooting in the backs surviving enemy soldiers trying to escape. No prisoners were taken.

Steve had used all his grenades, and his M-1 was empty. He got on the radio, "Millen, first line in front of enemy position taken and secured, heavy artillery fifty yards above. See flare and shoot over it in five minutes. We're coming out and will recover wounded. Send medics and stretcher bearers up the hill, out."

The flare went off, and Steve ordered the three platoons off their positions. They trudged down the hill listening for the aching cries of the wounded, picking them up and as many dead as they could carry on the grim descent. Steve staggered once while carrying a man with a tormenting belly wound. The two corporals rushed over, relieved him and laid the man down next to an improvised aid station. Then they took Steve by the arms until his head, still foggy from the earlier mortar concussion, cleared and he shrugged them off.

He stopped by some men he knew, saw that they were too far gone, patted and thanked them and moved on to make sure that the less-seriously wounded got care and evacuation. The ground quaked beneath their feet as the American artillery pulverized the German positions. Then Steve shrunk inside as he saw Sample on the ground in a contorted attitude of death, with rending shrapnel wounds to his face and throat. The radio and ammunition he was bringing up lay beside him. *Oh, God, why didn't I tell him to stay down there?*

Just as Steve started to squat and pick him up, Schmidt said, "We'll carry him down," and he and Rideout lifted Sample's body.

When Steve reached the bottom, one of the last off the hill, a runner raced over. "The colonel wants to see you now, Sergeant Millen." He navigated around stretchers loaded with the wounded. Medics gave blood, bandaged wounds and closed the eyes of the dead.

"Millen, all I hear from the troops is 'Millen' this and 'Sergeant Millen' that. Now hold your hand out palm up." He put two gold bars into Steve's hand. "I'm awarding you a battlefield commission. Congratulations, Lieutenant Millen. And don't get too cocky; it's mostly because we need officers, too many killed. The promotion's in your record and here's a copy. I'm also putting you up for the Silver Star."

"Thank you, sir. There were a lot of brave men up there."

"Millen, you look like shit, pardon the expression. Your eyes are two pieces of anthracite sunk back in your head. I'm giving you two weeks off the line." Steve smiled. "Don't get too happy, Millen. I want you back here for the next phase. The Germans are pulling back to a new line higher in the Apennines. The next assault will make this one look like a church picnic; and I want you in charge of the lead platoon. Now, you aren't going to the seashore. You're a stable soldier, and I need you to escort a truckload of men who are basket cases, you know shell-shocked, battle-fatigued, to a hospital south of here so they can get some help. Now get moving, and be back here on the thirtieth or before. Oh, one minute, I don't think any Krauts are left south of here. Anyway, your driver will be armed, and he's been down there before. You'd better take your pistol, a submachine gun and a few grenades. Good luck."

16

"His blood spurted all over my shirt."

Steve was promised a medic and a nurse to help with the mentally damaged men, but both were too busy treating wounded soldiers from the battle on the Apennine hills and didn't make the departure time. They did get a good truck, a two-and-a-half ton, 'deuce and a half,' six-by-six, outfitted with a canvas roof and benches on the side. They also drew an excellent driver and, as it turned out, a first-rate individual in Sergeant "Stash" Losik. And since the roads heading south had more holes than surface, they needed reliable driving skills and equipment.

Steve had a pistol holstered on his hip, a few grenades on his belt and a submachine gun slung over his shoulder. He found the men sitting docilely on the ground near the truck. The scared kid he sent off the hill for a rest was not among the group, and that was good. *Some people get overwhelmed by battle and just need a break, and he was one of them.* As Steve walked over to the men in his charge, he had the gut instinct that it's most effective to talk to intoxicated or mentally unstable people as though they were perfectly normal.

"Hi, men, I'm Lieutenant Millen. We're all going south for a while to get some better chow, play some ball have a shower and a good night's sleep. Look at my eyes. You can see how black and tired they look. That's why they're sending me down with you. The Colonel said, 'Millen, you look like shit.' Was he right?"

Several of the men loved the idea of telling an officer he looked like shit and they nodded enthusiastically. "I saw a couple of you up on the hill, you're Higgins, right?" Higgins didn't answer, just stared at the ground. *There's a project*.

"Just so you know, I'm carrying these weapons in case we meet up with some stray Nazis on our trip south."

"Aren't you Clasby?"

"No, Clasby's dead. I saw him get it through the eye with a bayonet. His blood spurted all over my shirt." The shirt was dirty but not bloody, a*nother project*.

A private stood and walked over for a better look. "You were Sergeant Millen, is he dead?" Steve let that one go.

"Okay, saddle up; take a leak, a dump if you need, fill your canteens and grab some rations." Sgt. Losik helped out with those who couldn't get moving, encouraging, giving a hand up, lifting under the armpits when he had to. *He's a good man*, Steve thought.

Corporal Peters helped others who couldn't perform basic duties. He filled canteens, got rations, always right there. Suddenly, he started wildly punching and screaming, "These are all Nazis! I hate Nazis! They'll kill us!" Fortunately, no one was hit. Steve made sure that he sat between Peters and the rest on the way down. Losik volunteered to take him in the cab, but Steve thought it too risky. As brawny as Losik was, Peters might grab the wheel and put them over a cliff. Also, Losik needed to keep his M-1 on the seat in case any holdout Nazis were on the road.

The men were restive: arguing, muttering and yelling incoherently for no apparent reason. Steve moved around the truck talking quietly and calming the worst offenders. When he sat down again, the ruckus resumed. Just as he was about to read the riot act, Private Norlund, a big Iowa farm boy, hauled out his pride and joy. The men were stunned by its dimensions:

"Looks like an arm at parade rest."

"Be afraid to see it at attention."

Steve was about to tell Norlund to put it away, but thought: *What the hell, at least there isn't a full moon*, and closed his eyes for a few moments of peace.

17

"Exigencies of the service having been such as to prevent the issuance of written orders..."

Rick's and Luis's road didn't lead to Rome. Nor did they see Naples. They were dropped at a small port twenty-five kilometers south of Rome. Right away, MPs, always on the lookout for German spies, gave them a hard time over their orders. Rick knew trouble was likely since administration at the PT base was a shambles. No interest, no accountability, no records, all they cared about was chasing Nazi ships and subs. Rick did get a Lt. Commander to dictate his recollection of transfer orders: "Exigencies of the service having been such as to prevent the issuance of written orders, voco . . . Lt. Richard Heydon and Sgt. Luis Alvarez have permission to return to their base in Foggia, Italy. Please assist them in this endeavor . . ."

The spit-and-polish MP at the first checkpoint relished giving officers a hard time, using a curt "Sir" as a verbal weapon. And the "Sir" sounded suspiciously like "Suck."

"Well, sirk, we've been told to question handwritten orders . . ."

"The typewriter was broken at the Sardinia base."

"You'll have to talk to Lieutenant Freeman, sirk. He's not here right now, should be back soon." Soon is a long time in the army.

Rick tried to get messages to the base in Foggia, but doubted that any got through, assuming they were actually sent. The truck rides were usually short, with the driver often declaring an eastward direction and then heading north or south. One aimless lift from a hapless local headed north too close to the western end of the latest German defensive line, and they found American checkpoint personnel jumpy from talk of Gestapo infiltration.

An over-particular intelligence captain quizzed Rick. He would talk only to an officer, Luis was ignored. "What were army personnel doing at a PT base in Sardinia? How come you only had two crew members in a B-17? Where are you from in the States?" This is where things improved.

"Chicago."

"I went to a place called the University of Chicago. What street is Marshall Field's on?"

A place called the University of Chicago, what a pretentious asshole. "State, sir."

"What street is the Art Institute on?"

"Not a street, sir, Michigan Avenue."

"What town in the area makes watches?"

"Elgin, sir."

When Rick and Luis got back into the truck they glanced at each other and smiled.

They once got a ride in a farmer's horse-drawn wagon and were brought to the farm for a meal and a night in the barn. When this was promised through sign language,

Rick got out the list of familiar Italian terms he'd picked up in Sardinia.

"*Quanto?*"

"*Gratuito.*"

"*Grazie.*"

The Italian people Rick and Luis met along the way didn't know whether all the Germans had left. They did know that if they were caught harboring Americans they would be shot. Despite this threat, everybody treated them with kindness and generosity refusing to accept any money. Several times, the Americans were warned by the Italians that Germans might be near, and they successfully avoided potential danger.

As they bounced along in the farmer's cart, with the horse clopping up a hill, Luis said, "Maybe he's got a daughter."

"I wouldn't expect much serendipity on this ride, Luis."

"What's that?"

"One of my teachers said that serendipity is when you look in a haystack for a needle and find the farmer's daughter."

Luis laughed. "I think I'll look for a needle."

Rick saw a windmill near a stream on the farm: *Me and Luis, Don Quixote and Sancho Panza with Rocinante pulling the wagon.*

They had three weeks of bad roads, worse rides and endless hikes, seeing the small villages and talking to people, many of whom had relatives in the United States. Rick thought of a story he'd read of a nineteenth-century Italian immigrant to America who sent a postcard home: 'Not only are the streets not paved in gold. They are not paved at all, and we are expected to pave them.'

Rick and Luis agreed that rural Italy was beautiful, and they hoped to come back for a vacation some day. They finally traveled far enough to reach the southern foothills of the central Apennines. The Italian workman's truck they were riding in broke down. They tried to help him, but the vehicle was beyond fixing. The unhappy man yelled, *"Questa maledetta macchina non funziona,"* kicked his truck and gave it a farewell salute of no uncertain meaning. He walked east with them for an hour, said *"Arrivederci"* and turned left on a side road. The Americans tramped several hours more, mostly uphill, listening to the quiet sounds of the Italian countryside. At last they reached an American checkpoint at a crossroads and waited for a ride south on their final leg to Foggia.

18

"It was Fiesta down in Mexico."

They heard a truck rumbling in the distance and hoped it was American and heading their way. They saw the familiar star and had rushes of excitement. The truck stopped with a hiss and creak of brakes, and an American lieutenant hopped out of the back with papers in his hand. He looked inquisitively at Rick. "Hey, Chicago, what are you doing out here with that beard?"

"I've been asking myself that same question. Steve, right, at the recruiting? We're trying to get to Foggia."

After Steve showed his orders to the MP at the checkpoint, he took Rick and Luis aside. "Climb aboard, but I got to tell you it won't be easy. I've got a bunch of damaged troops who need R and R. I'm taking them to a hospital in Foggia. I can use your help in keeping them settled them down, okay?"

While Steve was meeting, Stash Losik, the driver, got the men out of the truck and herded them into the brush for bodily functions. On the way back, Corporal Peters spotted Rick and Luis which triggered his Nazi rant. Stash calmed him down, and they all climbed into the truck. It stank of all the bad body odors. Rick and Luis were used to that, but this was worse than anything they had encountered, even sleeping in barns full of animals.

Rick and Luis split up to sit with the most troublesome cases. The already strained and exhausted men were out of patience, and the tension from the rocking, swerving trip and the perpetual swearing, yelling and scuffles was near the explosion point. Steve was drained, and with Rick and Luis on board assisting he quickly dropped off for a few minutes. When he awoke, the men near Rick were laughing at the story of Alisea and her hoodlum boyfriend.

The men on Luis's side of the truck were more rambunctious, elbowing each other, throwing hips to get more room on the bench and inventing profanities nonstop. Pfc. Rhodes, one of the few passive men, could string curses together in all sorts of poetic combinations. He had a deep voice, and his rumbling, rhyming expletives had a kind of dark and soothing beauty. Steve suddenly realized he was enjoying Rhodes's filthy monologue. *Maybe I'm going crackers, too?*

Just when everybody was about to leap out of the truck at high speed, Luis brought out a tiny harmonica that Rick hadn't seen before. Luis played in a low, hypnotic, haunting style. The harmonica almost spoke. Steve imagined a Civil War campfire. Higgins, who hadn't looked up from his down-facing blankness since departure, began to sing in a melodic voice: "Come and sit by my side if you love me . . ." and the men joined in along with Steve and Rick.

Then came, "How dear to this heart are the scenes of my childhood . . ." and more, many more; by the time they pulled into the base Luis had gone south of the border, and they sang, "It was Fiesta down in Mexico . . ." from 'Frenesi,' the hit from a few years back.

The doctors and nurses knew the truckload of needy men was coming, and several came out to greet them. They gathered at the tailgate smiling and shaking their heads in disbelief at the agreeable chorus. When Luis ended 'Frenesi' with a flourish the men stood without further prompting from Steve, jumped off the back of the truck and filed into the hospital.

Steve wanted Stash Losik to come into the hospital and say goodbye to the men. "Thanks, Lieutenant, but they've seen enough of me. I'll grab a bite at the mess hall and be getting this rig back north."

"You're a good man. I hope to see you again. Good luck."

Luis saluted Rick. "I'll go report in, Lieutenant."

"Luis, it was good vacationing with you." They laughed.

He then saluted Steve. "Luis, you saved the day with your harmonica. I don't know who was going to snap first, me or those guys. Thank you."

Rick said, "Steve, come on over to the BOQ when you finish here. It's that long, low building right behind you. I'll get you a bunk, and maybe we go for a beer after, unless they throw me in the stockade for being AWOL."

19

"THE KRAUTS MOVED MOST OF THE ACK-ACK AND FIGHTERS TO THE EASTERN AND WESTERN FRONTS."

Steve went into the hospital and saw that his guys were in good hands. On the way over to the BOQ he saw several nurses hoisting their gear and boarding a truck to ship out. He ran over and asked the Suzanne question, but nobody knew of her. Because of the gold bar he didn't get strange looks. One nurse asked, "Where was she the last time you heard anything?"

"Anzio."

"Oh," she said and looked down. Steve turned feeling sad and helpless. The nurse knew that her negative "Oh" and body language hurt and yelled after him, "You'll find her. We're tough." Steve turned, managed a half-grin and mouthed thank you.

Rick reported to Colonel Johnson. "I heard you got the brass to England, and when I didn't hear more for a while I figured you and the crew went over the hill. Then I got word on the ditch from the Navy. Sorry about the guys, some good men. Write it up. I need the report. Are you ready to fly?"

"Yes, sir."

"It's a lottery finding radio operators and gunners with all those being sent to England for the big show. Ask around, get in line. Take a few days off."

Steve and Rick were natural friends, hanging out drinking beer, shooting the shit. Neither liked talking about their war experiences, and except to each other rarely mentioned it. Both needed to purge and they did, sort of. It wasn't too specific, told mostly in self-deprecating terms, and just enough to let them rationalize it all and re-establish in their own minds that they were, in fact, fairly normal and not cold-blooded killers who dropped bombs and shot people. In their own ways, both admitted survivor guilt:

"I lost the plane and a bunch of men. I'm surprised the CO will let me fly again."

"It wasn't your fault, you had your orders. You couldn't call off the German fighters . . ."

"Still, those guys and other buddies I saw go down . . ."

"Yeah, I'm thinking of a few times when I told guys to do this or that if they wouldn't have been better off, maybe a few more lived, if I kept my mouth shut and let somebody else take over."

"Somebody has to step up. You did what you had to do."

Learning that Steve was a radio operator got Rick thinking. The next day he broached the possibility that maybe Steve might want to fly a mission or two while he was down there. Steve liked the idea and asked to see the inside of a B-17. He immediately understood the radio and the protocol. Rick asked Luis to show Steve how to operate the guns, and he quickly picked that up. Meanwhile, Rick had assembled a full crew, except for a radio operator, and he went to see Colonel Johnson.

"I don't know, Heydon, they're supposed to have wings. Let me think about it. What's this guy like?"

"I brought him along. He's right outside . . ."

"Millen, huh, where'd you go to OCS?"

"I got a battlefield commission, sir."

"They don't give those away. Where'd you do radio and what kind?"

"Mostly cryptography: North Africa, Sicily, Anzio."

"Ever fire a fifty-caliber?"

"North Africa in an M-2."

"Did you hit anything?"

"Three Vichy outside a Panhard, sir."

"Ever fly before?"

"My father had a friend with a small plane at a local airport, went up a few times loved it."

"Is he checked out on the equipment, Heydon?"

"Yes, sir."

"Okay, he can fly."

"Do we need to notify his CO?"

"Screw that, I don't need some chickenshit turndown. Since you left, the Krauts moved most of the ack-ack and fighters to the eastern and western fronts. Our territory's a milk run now. They've been coming back for two weeks without a dent. He'll be okay and be back on his line up north on time. You'll fly within a week."

20

"I'M NOT GOING TO ASK YOU TO GO BACK ON YOUR PROMISE."

Suzanne had some near misses but survived the Anzio beachhead where she showed special aptitude in treating battle fatigue and shell-shock. Recognizing this talent, she was promoted to 1st Lt. along with her closest friend Beverly Deacon, another proficient nurse. Suzanne and Beverly were assigned to work their way east along the Nazi defensive line training combat nurses and medics in the treatment of battle-related mental disorders. After several weeks of hazardous duty their next assignment was to go south to where some of the worst cases had been sent.

Suzanne gathered half the Foggia nurses in one room. Beverly led the other half in a room down the hall for the initial orientation on new remedial techniques. As she was wrapping up the training session, Suanne asked, "Where did this latest group of patients come from?"

"Up north in the Apennines, it must have been nasty. Some of them are pretty bad off."

"Who brought them here? I want to talk to them."

"A Lieutenant Millen."

A thrill of hope mixed with fear shot through Suzanne's body. She tried to keep her voice steady.

"What is his first name?"

"Steven." Suzanne felt like she had to sit down.

"What does he look like?"

"A Viking."

"What a hunk."

"He can park his boots under my bunk anytime."

"He comes here every day to see them. They love him." Looking and pointing out the window, "Here he comes now."

Suzanne looked, dropped her clipboard and ran out the door crying, "Steve! Steve!"

They collided, tipped over and rolled on the grass frantically hugging, kissing each other's faces, laughing and crying.

The nurses watched wide-eyed and slack-jawed. One commented dryly, "I think they met before."

"They're definitely a couple."

"Think they'll do it right there?"

"I hope so."

A major walked by the recumbent clinch. "There is a hotel in town, you know."

The nurses, and now a few of the patients, looked on as Suzanne and Steve walked around holding hands and impulsively clasping each other and kissing. It was conduct unbecoming to officers, and they couldn't have cared less.

Spotting Suzanne's silver bars, Steve said, "First looey. I knew it, outranked again with these butter bars. Can we still get married?"

"Rank's no longer an issue. Where and when?"

"Let's find a chaplain or a local padre and set it up."

"Who'll stand up for us?"

"My friend Rick will."

"I'll get my friend Beverly."

Later, when Rick Heydon and Beverly Deacon, who was tall and raven-haired, met they burst out laughing and walked away holding hands.

Suzanne turned to Steve. "What's that all about? Do they know each other from before?"

"Beats me."

Rick and Beverly walked down an abandoned runway with weeds sprouting between the cracks. "Why wouldn't you give me the time of day at Northwestern?"

"I was a gawky, introverted, at least with boys, string bean in high school . . ."

"You certainly filled out nicely."

"Thank you. I was seventeen and had no experience with boys when I started college. I was terribly attracted to you and didn't know how to handle it."

"Where did you go? I missed you at class and tried to find you at the gym. They said you transferred."

"I always wanted to be a nurse, and the anatomy class got me thinking. So I went to over to the Evanston Hospital School of Nursing. They took me, and here I am."

"May I kiss you?"

"Yes."

". . . Are you still attracted to me?"

"Terribly," and they laughed and kissed again, this time with more fervor.

When Beverly and Rick returned an hour later, they told their friends that they were college acquaintances and hadn't forgotten each other. Now, meeting again a few years later, they instantly knew they'd found what they were looking for, and the mutual attraction was so obvious that it struck them funny. They just had to go off and find out if it was some kind of joke or the real thing. It was the real thing, and they became inseparable.

When Rick noticed Steve's and Suzanne's looks of disbelief, he said, "Exigencies of the service having been such as to prevent the issuance of written orders . . ." Like the wedding three days later, no one, including Rick, knew what the words meant, and they laughed at the absurdity of the Army's bureaucratic lingo.

The priest was independent-minded and was once nearly defrocked for questioning a portion of Church dogma. He disdained any government interference and all types of forms. Father Sapienti used a side chapel for the service, had Suzanne and Steve exchange simple vows and pronounced them man and wife. He didn't ask for rings, and since they didn't have any it was just as well.

After they stepped aside, the priest motioned Rick and Beverly toward him. Although they hadn't yet discussed getting married, it seemed like a good idea at the time, and he married them, too, thinking that's why they were there and recognizing their palpable love. He was a wise priest who was sympathetic to the need for spontaneous, wartime marriages.

The ceremonies were in Italian with occasional Latin phrases. The four caught only a few words, but it all sounded official and romantic, and they felt very married. The captain was right, there was a hotel in town, and the couples had the two happiest days of their lives. Suzanne's and Steve's romance didn't need rekindling. They were like flame and tinder.

Beverly and Rick had hardly even dated as a couple. They'd made out a few times, liked it and wanted more than kisses and caresses but hadn't had an opportunity. Both admitted to love at first sight and agreed they never thought it would happen to them, especially after not seeing each other for several years. Each of them had had sexual relations and enjoyed it, but neither of their experiences was grounded in love and commitment.

The shades in their hotel room were not light-filtering, and the room was brighter than they wanted. Beverly went into the bathroom. Rick lay on his back on the bed, arms behind his head and fully armed. Beverly came out naked and did not flinch from his gaze. He said, "You are beautiful. I love you."

She looked first into his eyes then down below, and said, "Hello." He laughed. She leaned over; the graze of her breasts raised the hair on his thighs, and kissed the tip. Then she stretched out on the bed, head nestled in his arm, jet hair flowing across alabaster shoulders and onto the white pillow.

"Welcome to my boudoir, husband of mine."

"Hello, wife of my dreams." *Beverly still has that warm, low voice.*

"That's sweet . . . I never did that before."

"What's that?"

"Kiss someone there, but now that we're married, I thought . . ."

"Always feel free, and by the way what happened to the shy mouse from Northwestern?"

"I'm still shy, but I was kind of hoping you might turn me into a naughty girl."

Rick said through his laughter, "I think you're halfway there."

Beverly smiled, turned her face toward Rick's, and they kissed softly at first and then with more ardor. His lips descended to her throat, as his fingertips caressed her body. She stroked him with feathery touches he had never felt before, kissed his neck and chest and gave gentle running bites. The sun dipped, and the room took on more romantic tones.

Beverly and Rick derived mutual pleasure from anticipation and extended arousal. And when their rapture achieved unity, the generous, patient lovemaking put them in the tight, tumescent clasp of shared delight. Paraphrasing the title of a Gershwin tune, their love was here to stay.

The time together for both couples was too short; and for the women, the day of the mission arrived like a sharp rap on the door from an unwelcome visitor. Suzanne said to Steve, "I know you promised Rick you'd fly, and I'm not going to ask you to go back on your promise. But I don't feel good about it, I feel awful. I have this sick feeling way down deep that I'll lose you like the last time and never see you again. Finding you here has been such a miracle."

Steve took her hands, looked into her brimming eyes, and said emphatically, "I love you. Don't worry, I'll be seeing you." He hugged and thoroughly kissed her and left.

Suzanne didn't repeat her misgivings to her friend. Beverly knew of the potential danger of a combat mission, but she never doubted that Rick would be back that night and they parted happily and very much in love.

21

"C'est la guerre."

Rick missed flying and felt good sitting in the pilot's seat with the engines revved up. Following takeoff, Luis, his amiable travel companion, would take the port waist gunner's position. Steve would sit at the radio operator's table working closely with the navigator in preparing to establish position fixes during the flight. The rest of the crew was experienced. And an affectionate wife, who had matured into a statuesque beauty, awaited Rick's return.

Steve loved the sound and vibration of the B-17s four powerful engines at takeoff, then the free, soaring sensation as they climbed out of Foggia and headed north over Italy. *Maybe I should have tried to be a pilot . . . no, I'm just a dogface on a joyride.*

Previous raids on the Blechhammer chemical and synthetic oil plants had been tense and often bitter. The trip stretched fuel capacity, and the German anti-aircraft and fighter attacks were concentrated with many B-17s lost. Smitty, Rick's co-pilot, and six more of his crew who flew together on the trip from the States to Foggia went down over Blechhammer.

Today's mission was different. As Colonel Johnson said, much had changed in the last month. The skies were quiet with no telltale puffs or Luftwaffe fighters seen. However,

Rick had the crew on high alert since a pilot on a mission two days earlier said that German air defenses over Blechhammer had tightened up again. The formation flew at 27,000 feet with Rick's B-17 on the far starboard side of the right, rear low squadron.

Rick and his co-pilot, Wes Trowbridge, had taken turns flying the aircraft on the way up, and Wes was at the controls on the bomb run. Rick found that Wes had one glaring fault. He let the plane drift to starboard in the box formation. Rick kept reminding him to tighten it up, and he always responded promptly and with self-deprecating humor. Rick thought of taking over on the final run, but knew that, despite his one shortcoming, Wes was a competent pilot and let it go. By now all the bomb bay doors were open, and Steve activated the camera beneath his feet to take pictures of target damage.

For reasons they never learned, the high squadron lagged and the lower squadrons got under them. The navigator and bombardier were focused on their equipment and unaware of the impending danger. Rick looked up, saw what was happening and yelled in the clear, "Abort! Abort!" But it was too late. All the planes, including Rick's, released on the lead bombardier. Tons of bombs from the low squadrons fell on the German targets. Tons more, released from the high squadron detonated on the B-17s below them.

Eight planes blew up. Seven more, including Rick's, were fatally damaged and many more took severe punishment but could fly. Diverted by the high squadron's slowdown and the lower squadrons flying under them, and his too-late alert, Rick forgot to check on where his own plane was in the formation. As usual, Wes had let the plane drift to starboard, and the dispersion saved their lives. Had they been in the designated position, their B-17 would surely have been blown apart.

As it was, they were in desperate trouble. They'd lost the port inboard and starboard outboard engines and suffered widespread and extreme destruction throughout the aircraft. The racket in the plane at the numerous impact points sounded like shell fire. Rick believed that the lower part of the nose had been blown off. Steve instantly thought he was back in a ground war. Wes Trowbridge was immobile and in deep concussive shock. Rick was stunned but could function since the starboard side of the B-17 took the worst hits, and Wes was between Rick and the hardest shock waves. Burt, the flight engineer, sat dazed.

The plane was first blown over on its port side. Then another series of aerial explosions blew it the other way with the starboard wing down. They were in a deep dive, and Rick doubted he could pull out of it, even though they weren't spiraling. The intercom was out, so Rick couldn't give instructions for bail-out preparations. Even though he knew that the only crew member with a chance to successfully bail out was the tail gunner. Everybody else would probably strike some part of the nosediving plane.

Rick's feet were on the dashboard, with his body extended almost straight, as he pulled back on the wheel with every ounce of strength he had. The wheel and rudder were narrowly reactive, and the wings gradually came to horizontal, but the plane showed no signs of pulling out of the dive. Finally, at 14,000 feet Rick felt some leveling, and at 11,000 he recovered the aircraft avoiding certain death for all.

But the nose was still down a few degrees, the starboard inboard engine shut down, and the B-17 was unresponsive and losing altitude. Steve was at Rick's shoulder. "I took Burt back to the waist. What else can I do?"

"Check below on the navigator and bombardier."

He crawled through the narrow passageway far enough to see and quickly came back up. "Both dead, shards of steel pierced the bubble. The bottom's out. I couldn't get down there. It's a cyclone."

Rick thumbed over his shoulder. "What's happening back there? Can we bail out of the bomb bay?"

"No, explosions jammed the doors shut. The ball turret got blown off, and Black's gone. The rest seem okay, except for the tail gunner. He came up into the waist staggering. Burt's all right now. The radio's out."

"Go back and check on their parachutes. Have them try the escape hatches to see if they can use them to bail out. If they can't, gather them in the waist, get a hatch open and bail them out. Make sure their hands are on the pull ring. Wait, take Wes. Get him ready to bail. Slap his face or something, tell him what to do."

"Can you crash-land it?"

"Not a chance. I can't bring the nose up enough."

Steve got Wes under the arms and half-carried him across the narrow catwalk above the bomb bay. Luis Alvarez was in the best shape, and he helped Steve get the rest of the crew up and ready to jump. Like the ditch off Corsica, Luis got the starboard aft waist hatch open. Steve thought that if men knew they were going to die they'd want to jump. Some did, some didn't. They saved Wes for last hoping he'd wake up.

With three of the men, Steve had to put their hands on the ripcord and bellow over the wind, "Count to seven and pull the fucking cord." They desperately held on to the sides of the door. Steve put his foot in their backs and pushed them out. They were at 6,000 feet, and the plane was dropping faster. Luis and Steve got Wes Trowbridge on his feet. Steve slapped his face not too hard but firmly. They yelled above the wind.

"We can't leave him, Luis. Put his hand on the ripcord, and we drop him out and hope the cold air wakes him. It's his only chance."

"I'm going out with him," Luis said. "Hold him up straight. I'll scissor my legs around his, put an arm around his body and hold his pull ring with the other. Once we're clear I'll drop him and pull his cord. Then I'll pull mine." Luis wrapped himself around Wes like a soft pretzel.

Steve balanced them: *I thought I'd seen guts before, but this.*

"Push us out hard now," Luis said. And they were gone. Luis held on to Wes. They separated. Wes's chute opened, and a few seconds later Luis's chute blossomed.

Steve checked the plane one more time and went forward. "Everyone's out but you and me."

"The explosions blew us in a southeasterly direction," Rick said. "I tried to hold that vector. We're probably well into Czechoslovakia. Walk east when you land, maybe fewer Germans."

"What about you?"

"I'll be right behind you. Now scram, we're below two-thousand and dropping fast. Roll when you hit. It looks flat down there, just a few trees."

Steve went out and Rick six seconds later. They didn't have much time to enjoy the scenery. Swirling winds pushed them closer together, and they came down about three-hundred meters apart. Both of their chutes slowed them just enough before they touched the ground. Unfortunately, a German squad was equidistant between them. The squad split, and each segment headed toward them with rifles pointed. Rick and Steve raised their hands, were disarmed and led to an imposing captain much taller than Rick. He walked between them from behind, put an arm around each of their shoulders, smiled, and said in impeccable French with accompanying shrug, "C'est la guerre."

22

"Missing in action and presumed dead."

Most everyone on the base knew that the raid was a disaster with many planes lost and missing. Some B-17s returned intact, others were damaged to varying degrees, and several had wounded and dead crew members on board. Beverly and Suzanne talked to any returning airman they could reach. Most didn't know much:

"It all happened so fast, everything spinning below us."

"I was watching the planes that blew up and missed some of the damaged ones."

"There was debris all over the sky, it was chaos."

Finally, from another pilot, "I was in the seventh squadron, the back of the formation. I saw Rick's plane rocked back and forth and then with the starboard wing down. It didn't blow up or break apart. They went into a steep dive from twenty-seven thousand. No parachutes, no time for that. They dropped through cloud cover. No radio contact. I want to believe they pulled it out. I'm very sorry, but that's all I know."

Outside base operations, Suzanne and Beverly grieved for hours weeping, trying to reassure themselves, watching, waiting, hoping that somehow Rick's B-17 with Steve and the rest of the men on board would show up. A gray-faced Colonel Johnson came out. "There's no more coming back tonight, I'm sorry. We can only hope that they pulled out of the dive or were able to bail out. If I hear anything, I'll let you know. The best thing you can do now is to go back to your quarters and try to get some rest."

Since Rick's B-17 was reported damaged from proximate aerial explosions, and because it was last seen in a steep dive, the official report listed the crew members as Missing in Action and Presumed Dead. Steve and Rick had named their new wives as insurance beneficiaries and the ones to notify in case of death or missing in action. The women, still in unrelenting torment, wrote letters to their husbands' parents interweaving hope with the dreadful news. Before departing on the fateful mission the men had written notes to their parents and included photographs of their new wives.

Beverly and Suzanne were strong women who decided to continue as though their husbands had made it, were alive and well and in a German prison camp. They watched each day for notices from the Red Cross. The hospital overflowed with physically and mentally injured fliers from the mission. Plus more casualties streamed down from the north, victims of savage fighting on a new, heavily-fortified German defense line. The bereft wives dedicated themselves to nursing without let-up.

Two weeks later, Sgt. Losik drove one of the trucks loaded with new battle casualties. He also carried a query from the colonel who awarded Steve the battlefield commission. Colonel Johnson told the sergeant what happened and responded to the colonel's question in writing: '2nd Lt. Steven

Millen was urgently needed as a radio operator on a critical bombing mission. His B-17 was downed in an explosion over Germany. He is listed as MIA and presumed dead.' No reply came back.

23

"They take you to *Stalag Luft* Three."

During the initial body search, when Rick and Steve first parachuted in, the German soldiers paused and looked up when they heard the B-17 crashing and exploding in the distance. In doing so, one of them was distracted and overlooked something important.

Despite the casual meeting with the suave captain, the Americans were blindfolded and their hands bound. They were put into the back of a truck with two armed guards and told to keep their mouths shut. Except for fuel stops, they were jostled the rest of the day and all night over washboard mountain roads. The guards ate aroma-rich meat sandwiches they didn't share with the dog-hungry prisoners and conversed in German. From the little that could be deciphered, it was mostly about women. Rick's and Steve's thoughts were centered on their growling stomachs and where and how the Germans got the sandwiches. They daydreamed about Chicago delis.

The truck stopped around midday. They were taken off and brought into a long, one-story building. Orders were given, and they were led to small, windowless cells. The blindfolds were removed and their hands untied. Additional soldiers stood outside the cells with pointed rifles. The cell doors slammed and a key turned. The Germans closed and locked an outer door, the lights snapped off, and the Americans were in total darkness.

After the blindfolds came off and before the lights went out, Steve and Rick saw through blurred and blinking eyes that the cells had cold-tap only washstands, porcelain-only toilets, a single, low-wattage bulb in the ceiling and a cot with a straw mattress. The cell walls and door were solid steel with a small slot window in the door and a row of tiny air holes above that. This was solitary confinement at its worst.

In the morning after a disturbed sleep, Rick was brought out first and nearly blinded by the light. He was told to sit at a small table and given a tray with a cup of brackish water, a piece of stale bread and a dish of what looked like gray gruel. Thirsty and famished, he gagged it all down under the watchful eye of a middle-aged German guard and was immediately returned to the cell. Steve repeated the routine.

They saw that the twelve-by-twenty-five-foot day room that contained the cells had the one door they came through the night before and a high window approximately three feet wide and two feet high with three bars. They immediately saw that removal of the middle bar would leave enough room to slip through. They also saw that there were four cells, and they were occupying the ones on either end. The doors of the middle two were ajar, and the cells appeared to be empty.

Later that day, the men were questioned separately in a nearby room by a bored lieutenant who chain-smoked while either tapping a pencil on his shaved head or moving tiny, faux animals around his desk. Steve thought: *Where did they find this nerve-ending?*

To Rick, he was an oily loser dispatched to the boondocks by superiors who had given up on him. The lieutenant tried the tired game of asking each of them to inform on the other: "If you tell me what you and your partner were up to, I will see to it that your sentence is reduced. If you cooperate fully it is likely that we will have you moved to a neutral country like Switzerland, where life is, shall we say, more pleasant."

Wild horses would not make them implicate each other, and they said nothing. But from a tactical perspective, Steve and Rick responded appropriately to the classic Prisoner's Dilemma: Informing by either or both captives is the least advantageous solution. Seeing that his transparent game wouldn't work, the lieutenant began asking questions and got closely-matched answers:

"Were you parachuted in on a spy mission?"

"No, we were on a routine bombing raid and were shot down."

"Where is the rest of your crew?"

"We don't know; they jumped before us."

"What was your target?"

Name, rank and serial number were given.

"From what base did your mission originate?"

Name, rank and serial number again, and so on, until the lieutenant gave up and had them returned to their cells. There were two benefits to the meetings: Some good laughs later and seeing green and sky through the two interrogation-room windows was a lift to their spirits and increased the motivation to escape.

Each successive day was slightly better. Klaus, the paunchy, avuncular guard was not a Nazi. He had boys their age in the Wermacht, one on the Eastern Front and another in occupied Denmark. With a wry smile, Klaus said he wished both were in Denmark.

Steve and Rick were now allowed to walk in the room for fifteen minutes after their meals. One day while Rick was walking, Klaus went out and locked the outside door. Rick went to Steve's cell and opened the slot. It was the first time they had spoken in fourteen days. "I have a hacksaw blade. They took my medical kit but missed the escape kit. We need to get Klaus out long enough to start sawing. I'll find a place to hide it so we both can work on the middle bar." He heard Klaus returning and closed the slot.

Klaus liked and trusted the Americans. They liked him and were thankful for the fruit and vegetables he was able to bring them every few days, but they were not shy about using him. After another ten days, Klaus chatted with them for a few minutes then left them alone for sometimes an hour.

He knew as long as he could hear them singing everything was okay. Klaus didn't know that Americans liked singing so much. They were awful, Steve flat and Rick off-key, but they were game and belted every tune they knew as loud as they could. Klaus, sitting in the next room listened to the muffled songs through the thick door, shrugged his massive shoulders, smiled and puffed on his pipe. Rick started sawing again, and the more the saw screeched the louder he sang.

There was just enough room to slip the thin blade under the cell doors. Then it was inserted under a sock in the side of a boot. The thick bar was unforgiving, and they seldom got an hour total of filing a day. Sometimes five minutes, sometimes thirty, often nothing when Klaus was grumpy over duties he was given by superiors that he thought were beneath his dignity.

Finally, they got through the bottom of the middle bar. As strong as Steve and Rick were, it was impossible for them to bend the bar. Pockets filling with filings, with enough residue and dust to hide the break, they went to work on the top of the bar. Being high and hard to reach, their arms ached from the strain. Making things worse, it was difficult to maintain a purchase on the blade and keep the cut level.

Klaus was more uneasy as tensions increased in the building. Impatient voices issued brusque orders. Something was brewing, yet to their surprise no one else came to see or further interrogate them. Rick said, "Klaus, you seem unhappy."

"*Ach*, SS are here wanting lancers for the Eastern Front. I am afraid they take me. I am too old to march. I also hear they take you to *Stalag Luft* Three, maybe a few days."

The blade dulled, and their fingers were raw, chapped and leaking blood in the cracks. Klaus's morale worsened. He needed to talk more, mostly about his First World War trench fighting, "*Wahnsinnig*, we killed each other for nothing. Now it's the same thing all over." Opportunities to saw decreased to little or nothing, as the frustrating days accumulated during the second month of confinement.

Then, in a welcome change, and against regulations, Klaus let Rick and Steve out of their cells at the same time for recreation. "Stand by the window, boys, get some sun."

The best part of the view was the lack of a perimeter fence. For the past week, Klaus left the cell doors unlocked during the day, and they took turns sawing. When their fingers gave out, they walked, exercised or lay down on their cots. Klaus only locked their cell doors at night.

Rick and Steve sang themselves hoarse, hacked at the bar and got through. Then they gently tapped around the glass making it easier to knock out. A little later, Klaus unlocked the outside door and came in. "Two days we move out. They don't tell me where we are going. I hope it is not east. They take you to *stalag*. If it was close, you would be there now. The camps in this part of Poland are for other purposes." Steve and Rick glanced at each other, both thinking: *What does that mean?* "I do not know why they brought you this far south into Poland, *verrückt*."

The plan was in place, and tonight they were going out. They took the mattresses from the empty cells, put them in their own cells, shaped them like their bodies and pulled the blankets up high. They hid in the empty cells. Klaus came in at ten, looked through the slots and thought they were sleeping. He locked their cell doors and the outside door. The bar came out of the window, the glass was gently removed and they quietly wriggled out. It was September 29, 1944.

24

"You fight Nazis, too, with us?"

The moon was a pale sliver with Venus brilliant fifteen degrees northwest. And in a rare alignment, Jupiter hung in the sky beyond and below Venus. The Americans knew that Venus was in the western sky so they walked east through woods and fields trying not to crack a twig. They'd stored scraps of bread in their pockets and found a stream where the water was fresh. Not many words passed between them, just a nudge when one of them had to answer nature or thought they heard something other than insects of the night. Since they were friends who didn't need to be talking all the time, being quiet was not a problem

They walked through the forest all night wading creeks, climbing hills and catching catnaps for a few minutes in turn. During a brief stop at a brook, Steve whispered, "I'd eat those freakin' crickets live if I could find them."

"Fried with apple sauce," Rick whispered back. "Why do I keep thinking about apple sauce? I don't even like apple sauce."

While walking the next day, they twice listened to what they thought were German patrols with gruff voices and barking dogs and lay flat and unmoving until the sounds ebbed. At dusk, they came close to an open, marshy area and saw in the distance a sprawling compound with watchtowers, circling searchlights and an unpleasant odor like burnt charcoal. They wondered what it was since Klaus said no *stalags* were east of the jail. They didn't stay around to find out, and under a thick cloud cover inadvertently struck out in a more southwesterly direction.

Near daybreak the next morning they came upon an unlighted farmhouse and barn. Fortunately, the two watchdogs were off hunting rodents in the woods on the north side of the farm. One was a standard Schnauzer named 'Rat' because she was a good ratter. The other, a Lowland Sheepdog called 'Pon,' a nickname derived from the Polish abbreviation for his breed. In another break, the lone sentry was relieving himself on the far side of the front porch.

Stomachs long emptied and now cramping, parched and used up, they quietly entered the barn using the file to slip the door lock. They heard and smelled animals moving in their sleep or rummaging in their stalls. They bumped into a homemade ladder, climbed into the loft, flopped in the hay and slept as though narcotized.

An hour later, Rick woke up to a loudly whispered, *"Dzień dobry, Amerykanin. Cześć, Amerykanin"* and sat up blinking and disoriented.

Am I dreaming in the cell? When a cow mooed he remembered where he was and shook Steve. "We're being paged."

Rick called, "Friend?"

From below, *"Tak."*

With nowhere to run they climbed down the rickety ladder to see three men and three women armed, but with their weapons pointed toward the floor. One woman and one man were missing fingers; another man had only half an ear, a damaged eye and a raised, purple connecting scar. The three men looked like they would fare well in hand-to-hand combat.

Two of the women appeared robust enough to deliver a baby in the fields, nurse it, strap it to their backs and go on working. The third, introduced as Magda, was tall, full-bodied, attractive and sullen. Later, the Americans learned that when Magda worked in the barnyard the partisan men came out to watch, especially when she wore shorts and a brief top.

Piotr, the steely leader, spoke fractured but easily understood English, "I have cousin in Chicago, is funny fellow. He said he moved Chicago so he could keep voting after he die." Knowing Cook County politics, Steve and Rick had their first good laugh since they left Foggia. The other partisans may not have understood, but they joined the merriment. Even the animals in their stalls, stimulated by the talk and laughter, contributed. Steve thought it sounded like 'Old MacDonald Had a Farm.'

Rick said, "I read there are nearly as many Polish people in Chicago as you have in Warsaw." The leader translated for his comrades, and they reacted with surprised looks.

Piotr and the others led the Americans to the farmhouse where they met Flora and George, an elderly couple who owned the farm. The house was redolent of home cooking and appeared to have been built around a large kitchen that had a wood-burning stove and a working fireplace. Flora introduced their hulking, mentally-limited son Gwidon who stood in a corner. She said proudly, "Gwidon make farm work, he is strong boy." Gwidon, who looked to be in his mid-thirties and resembled his mother, blushed and lowered his pleasant-faced gaze.

"Gwidon sleep in barn, take care of animals," Piotr said. "He heard you but thought he dreamed. Woke up, hear snores, climb ladder, come down get me. Good job, Gwidon." Gwidon looked at the floor. "I climb ladder, shine light see American uniforms go down so you not shoot me. Call you."

Piotr motioned to one of the partisan men. "Gabriel, fix barn lock good, double lock."

The sturdy, full-bosomed, matriarchal Flora, helped by her husband George, sat the famished Americans at the kitchen table where they consumed ravenously: thick bread and butter, cheese, eggs, sausages, and creamy milk. When they finished, Flora handed the leader a jug. *"wódka?"*

It was the last thing they wanted, but knew it would be impolite to refuse. The jug was passed with *"na zdrowie"* before each gulp. Mercifully, the jug emptied after the second knee-buckling round, and the Americans were saved from total debilitation. Rick explained that they were fliers captured after they were shot down and later escaped.

Ruggedly muscular and clearly not a man to be trifled with, Piotr looked to be in his early forties. He had a naturally commanding voice, a fierce mustache, a bristling head of coal-black hair and dark eyes that never left you. "We are fighters, how you say, partisans, resistance, underground. We fight Nazis who stole our land, killed our people. You fight Nazis, too, with us?" Rick and Steve nodded.

"We do not kill Nazis, except sometimes. If we do, they take revenge kill many hostages, not worth it. You understand?" Again they nodded. "We blow up bridges, block trains with broken tracks, help escape *więzienie* like you, slash truck tires, sand in gasoline tanks, everything." As Piotr spread his arms wide, the other partisans grinned. "They catch us." Piotr made a finger slash across his throat, stuck his tongue out and pulled an imaginary noose upwards around his neck, shouldered a mock rifle and staggered backward from the fusillade to his chest.

The voluble Piotr went on, "Next Russians come. We help kill Germans then we fight Russians because they stay and rob us of our land, like always. America only friend of Poland." Rick and Steve didn't volunteer to join a battle with the Russians who were currently fighting the Nazis as America's partner, Uncle Joe Stalin and all that propaganda. It was now a hot war with the Axis, and it was widely accepted that the Allies were not likely to beat Hitler and his partners in destruction anytime soon without the Red Army swarming west at their heels.

Two more men came in from a raid. One of them, a reticent Hungarian guerilla named Andrik, had fled north with an Arrow Cross bounty on his head just ahead of pursuing Nazis. The other was a smart, tough, corded Russian Jew called Lev who spoke facile, Russian-accented English and several other languages. He told Rick and Steve that he was a doctoral student who escaped Stalin's pogroms in the late 1930's and walked west into Poland where he lived in the Warsaw Ghetto until the Nazis invaded. He trekked south at night and hid during the day until he found work on the farm where they were now living. Lev looked toward Flora and George and opened his arms. "Flora and George took me in and saved me."

His black-browed and fatigued eyes suddenly shimmered. "When the Nazis started killing Poland's Jews I joined the resistance group that sprang up here around Piotr. When the Russians come west into this part of Poland I will leave and go to Palestine where we will build our own country and defend it."

Rick mentioned the Balfour Declaration. Lev, delighted with his awareness, clapped him on the shoulder. "Yes, that undergirds our legal rights, and we will make it live."

Prodded by the group, they told their own war stories. That they spoke briefly and without embroidery impressed the partisans who disliked any kind of self-aggrandizement. When asked, they spoke of their parents in Chicago. The partisans lit up. "Ah, Chicago, Marta and Pawel go to Chicago."

"Are you married, boys?" Piotr asked with a grin. "Are your wives in Chicago?" When the group learned that their wives were American Army nurses stationed in Italy they smiled agreeably.

Lev asked, "Do they know you were not coming back yet?" Rick and Steve shook their heads no, and the group was somber.

"You say you walk east to avoid Germans," Piotr said. "You came to wrong place, Krakow, west of Krakow, here, Nazis everywhere. We do not avoid Germans. We seek them out. Try not let them see us. This is southwest Poland. Big prison in Oswiecim, Germans call Auschwitz-Birkenau near here."

"We may have seen it," Steve said. "Is it close to a wide river?"

"Yes," Piotr answered, "Vistula."

Flora's husband, George, a taciturn man with a weathered face and a compact, sinewy body had left briefly and now came back into the kitchen. He asked the Americans if they needed to rest. Flora took over. "No cellar tonight, George, they sleep in beds. Take upstairs, tomorrow they go to cellar." They slept eighteen hours.

Stefan, a serious young man with cascading black curls, a Botticelli face and Popeye forearms was the armorer. He brought the pair through a disguised door in the cellar wall under the kitchen into a tunnel; and then quickly through another false door off the tunnel that opened to a room lined with arms-laden shelves. A small generator provided light and power for the machines Stefan used for repairs.

He gave them razor-sharp, five-inch knives in leather sheaths. He pointed to his throat above the Adam's apple, said, "Here," and made a thrusting motion with a forefinger followed by a twist. Steve and Rick got the idea.

Next, they were given pistols and extra clips followed by two grenades each. Like the deadly knife demonstration, Stefan showed them how to handle the weapons and then mimed their use. For the pistol, he pointed a forefinger up the back of his neck to the base of his skull and made another point to the tip of his nose.

Four fingers were extended to show the time from pin-pulling to grenade detonation. He pulled the imaginary pin, brought his right arm back and followed through on the overhead motion like a major league pitcher. Then he quickly ducked, squatted deep while bringing his brawny arms over his head, and yelled, "Boom." Steve, of course, knew the drill, but wanted Rick to learn it, or at least be refreshed.

He gave each of them a roll of black tape and a coil of attenuated but strong rope and showed them a few knots for tying up people. Steve asked whether he had rifle grenades. "No, they are hard to get. We had one and lost it in a raid that went wrong." Rick and Steve agreed later that not only was Stefan a professional armorer, he was also a born teacher.

When Stefan concluded his lessons, Piotr joined them and showed Steve and Rick the rest of the tunnel system which went from under the back of the house north fifty meters to another large cellar under the barn floor. Here were the sleeping quarters for men and women and a ladder up to a concealed trapdoor in the corner of the barn floor above.

Just before they reached the barracks door, Piotr showed them the entrance to a long, branching tunnel that extended twenty meters into the woods beyond the barnyard's southeast perimeter. After looking around and being shown their cubicle, they exited the sleeping quarters and entered the outside-access tunnel. A flashlight's beam revealed how the partisans had reinforced the tunnel walls and ceiling with timbers. Piotr lifted a hatch covered with leaves and twigs fastened to the lid, and they looked outdoors. He explained how to locate the hatch using identifiable trees and other conspicuous landmarks.

On the way back to the house through the tunnels, he said, "We build tunnels and *baraki*, how you say, barracks? Warning system, sentries give alarm when Nazis come from town five kilometers northeast toward Oswiecim.

"SS major, soldiers come to farm maybe one time a week for food and vodka. We take good care of them. Germans leave few Deutschmarks, no value to us now, maybe someday. They like Flora and George, remind them of grandparents. Nazis want our food. Need Gwidon to help. Don't take him away. Nazis not like," and Piotr tapped his head. "Shoot, gas those people."

Rick asked, "How far is Oswiecim?"

"Thirty kilometers northeast, maybe a little less—we work hard here, more in summer with crops when not on raids. In winter we fix barn, house, shed, barracks, George's truck, build up tunnels with wood and large stones for base."

"How often do you go on raids?" Steve asked.

"Maybe five-six times in one week, try every day."

"How come the Nazis haven't figured out that you're here on the farm?"

"They close circle, come closer. Soon will be big attack. We get ready for long time, will need your help. You know combat on ground, close to enemy?"

"Yes."

"Oh, you told us in kitchen."

25

"*NA ZDROWIE*, TEREZA. I LIKE YOUR ASS AND THROAT BETTER THAN DOGS, TOO."

Piotr wanted to test the Americans, and a few days after their arrival he led a night raid. Tereza, the fourth person in the group, came back from a foray the day before. She had a sprinter's body, was snub-nosed and pretty with cropped blonde hair and a dazzling smile of conspicuous sincerity. Piotr slung a submachine gun over one shoulder and a packet of explosives over the other. Both Tereza and Piotr wore black.

Piotr had previously suggested that Rick and Steve always wear their American Army outfits. In case of capture they should say they were shot down and were lost trying to find German authorities to whom a proper surrender could be made. When Germans were near and capture imminent they should hide all weapons in the weeds, leaves, whatever and come out smiling saying '*sich ergeben!*' with hands held high. They sort of knew the routine from prior training but were grateful for the reminder. Their respect for Piotr's practical wisdom grew by the hour.

"There is bridge on tributary, like canal of Vistula, Germans use to supply Auschwitz coal, started using past week. They move around, how you say, *trasa*, route, yes route, try to fool us. We blow it tonight. Andrik say Germans only at east end. We go west end."

No path to a destination was linear. They vectored roundabout, sometimes stopping and circling, never moving in a straight line more than one-hundred meters. No talking was allowed, and they were expected to never make a sound. Any kind of coughing, sneezing, throat-clearing, belching, farting drew a reproving glance from Piotr who had the stealth and self-possession of a Plains Indian.

They went on hands and knees the final forty meters. The Americans were assigned to monitor the two points from which interlopers might emerge. Tereza and Piotr crept under the west end of the bridge. They could hear the Germans guarding the eastern end talking and joking. Listening from his location, Steve thought: *Keep yapping, assholes, and you won't hear them.*

Rick heard a truck in the distance over the sound of water rushing through the canal. *What the hell is that, and what's keeping those two. I mean, let's blow the fucking bridge.*

They came out moving rapidly, but noiselessly. Piotr hooted softly like a night owl, and the four met at a pre-arranged spot near a spreading tree. "We have two minutes before charge go off, follow me."

They stepped gingerly until the muffled blast echoed through the woods. When the timbers crashed into the canal, the four broke into a single-file run with Tereza guarding the rear. Rick thought: *Shouldn't Steve or I be back there?* He soon found out why Piotr used Tereza.

A German patrol with barking dogs ran in hot pursuit. Steve thought: *How the fuck could they find us so soon?* They changed direction and gained some distance. But the

Germans let the dogs loose, and louder barking warned that they were catching up. They knew they couldn't outrun the dogs and looked for trees to climb. But it was too late, the powerful, snarling, bare-toothed German Shepherds crashed through undergrowth just behind them. Steve drew his pistol, started back to help Tereza and saw that she stood unflinchingly. The lead dog leapt at her throat, but Tereza had her pistol aimed and shot it through the heart. The trailing dog bounded, and she shot it through the snout. The four ran again, and after wading across a stream they heard the patrol going off in a different direction, perhaps fooled by the echoes of the gunshots. Like the trip out, the return was circuitous and enervating.

When they got back to the farm and relaxed over food and vodka, Tereza said, "I like dogs. I don't want to shoot dogs, but I like my throat and ass more than dogs."

Piotr raised his cup and said with a wicked grin, "*Na zdrowie*, Tereza. I like your ass and throat better than dogs, too." Tereza smiled her incandescent smile as everybody roared. Rick noticed that Andrik seemed not to hear Piotr's joke. He stared at Tereza adoringly, and Rick wondered what that was all about.

26

"Sweet Mother of Christ."

At a meeting in a cellar room the next day Piotr mentioned that their radio operator was killed in a raid a few weeks back, "We have no one who," and he tapped his forefinger on the table.

"I'm a radio operator. Where is it?"

Piotr motioned to Gertrude, a rotund but easy-moving woman Rick and Steve first met in the barn. She quickly returned with a small suitcase and opened it. Steve looked it over. "Okay, if it works. How are the batteries? Can I turn it on?"

"Good, almost new," said Piotr. "We can't use here, Nazis hear us, always listen from truck. Take it to woods, move around each day, far kilometers. We talk to command near Warsaw, get information know what they need us to do here. I write code name, frequency, message. Steven, Richard, go send it, yes? Wait reply then run different way. Don't come back for few hours. We, as Americans say, back in business."

They walked south six kilometers through the Carpathian foothills. While taking turns lugging the radio and admiring the lush forest's abundant plant life, they heard animals rustling in the bushes. They were now used to standing stock still or lying down for minutes at a time, hoping the noises they heard weren't German patrols. This time they saw a brown bear forty meters away foraging on its hind legs and looking ten feet tall. After pulling their pistols and carefully stepping a few hundred meters away from the bear, Rick quietly said, "Highest pucker factor since the Germans caught us. I'll bet bullets would bounce off that brute."

After fifteen uneasy minutes of quick-footed hiking, Steve opened the case, turned the radio on, found his frequency and transmitted Piotr's message. The men sat on a fallen tree trunk drank water and ate the sausage and bread Flora had packed. The silvery birch-tree leaves reflected dappled sunlight around them as they waited for the reply. It soon came. Steve thought: *Good fist* as he copied.

Using landmarks seen from vantage points, a compass and Rick's solid dead-reckoning skills they descended toward the farm. A little under a kilometer from the foothill base they paused fifteen meters beyond a shaded glen. The forest around the glen was dense, and the men were naturally cautious as they watered the bushes. Just as they started out again, they heard a "Psst" type of sound and dropped to their knees while drawing pistols and wishing they were deeper in the woods. Nothing more was heard, and they decided it must have been the wind soughing through the leaves or a bird or ground animal accidentally mimicking a human expression.

Just as they started walking, they heard it again from the woods across the glen, louder this time, more urgent. Steve and Rick looked at each other, squinted and shrugged their shoulders. *What the hell should we do, run, call them out?*

They pulled their pistols again. Rick opened one palm to Steve who nodded. Rick shouted, "Drop your weapons and come out into the clearing with your hands up." *Jesus, I sound like a movie cop.*

Two bedraggled, barefoot men stumbled out of the woods. They tried to raise their hands but got only one hand chest high. One of the men held the other up. The stronger of the two croaked in foreign-accented English with British intonations, "Please do not shoot us."

Rick thought he sounded a bit like Henrik, his Danish friend from Northwestern. In the highly unlikely case that it might be a ruse, the Americans stayed out of sight. The emaciated men's sunken eyes stared out of black-ringed sockets. Their tattered prison-like garb hung like scarecrow's rags that had been picked at and shredded by angry birds. The Americans had never seen anything like this and didn't know quite what to make of it.

"Who are you and what do you want?" Steve asked. The weaker of the two unfortunate men sank to his knees and put his clasped hands before his chest in a pleading gesture.

His partner said, "We escaped SS, help us please" and keeled over as his companion rolled into a fetal position.

Rick and Steve approached them with guns drawn. Infantry combat had hardened Steve making him suspicious of anyone unknown. "Lie on your backs with your arms out to the side." The two cadaverous escapees stank, their feet black and their body skin soot-like with some small patches of white where ulcers and other festering sores were most visible. No flesh, just bones were felt as they were searched for weapons. As they put their guns away, the Americans were torn between pity and repulsion. They took the men's upper bodies in the crooks of their arms and gave them sips of water. "Let's not give them too much, might make them sicker."

Rick asked, "Where did you escape from?"

"Auschwitz."

Rick put the more incapacitated man on his back, pulled his arms around his neck and grasped his forearms. "Wrap your legs around my waist, if you can." He couldn't. Steve carried the radio in one hand, put the other man's arm around his shoulder, held his forearm fast and supported most of his weight. With muscles burning like fire they made the border of the farm without stopping. Neither of the men weighed more than eighty pounds, and their dead weight made the load feel twice as heavy, especially in the last three-hundred meters.

Gwidon, who had the hearing and senses of a fox pursued in the hunt, heard them coming and alerted Piotr and the others. The men rushed out, relieved the Americans and carried the sick men into the farmhouse. When Flora saw them, she whispered to herself over and over, "Sweet Mother of Christ. Sweet Mother of Christ."

They laid the two men on a rolled-out rug on the kitchen floor. Lev, with tears streaming down his face, cut away their remaining rags. "We will make them well, and I will take these two Jews to Palestine with me."

Two of the partisan women gently sponged the men. Before placing cloths over their loins they noticed that even their genitals were shriveled, and they mentally recoiled at the sight of the numbers tattooed on their forearms. Flora and George held their heads and spooned a few teaspoons of broth. Piotr said, "The fucking Nazi *jad* will pay for this and all the rest."

Steve gave Piotr the radio message and he smiled. "Now we have new plans. Thank you, boys, now have food, rest, we have big job tomorrow."

The next morning Coos, the Dutchman and Arne, the Dane, both of whom spoke English, were strong enough to talk a little from the cots they were lying on. Arne said, "We were on a work detail outside the fences in swampland when a riot broke out on the far side of the camp. The SS guards collected the workers and herded them inside the fence. We were working beyond a low mound and ducked when the roundup started and were missed. We crawled then walked away, heard patrols with dogs in the distance but managed to stay upwind of them. We wandered for three days living on berries and were ready to lie down and die when we saw the Americans."

Coos spoke for the first time. His voice quavered, and the words were barely audible: "Those that are not gassed are told 'Labor makes you free.' They work you to death, and if you cannot work any longer the SS guards shoot you where you fall." Then he dropped off with the semblance of a sad smile on his hollowed-out face.

27

"Stuff Nazi with Grenade."

The partisans fixed their own food under Flora's supervision. They then ate in shifts so that no more than four, plus Flora, were in the kitchen at any one time. Gabriel and Agnes talked and laughed as they milked cows in the barn. Two sentries signaled loudly. Gwidon fed the pigs and went rigid when he heard the warning and a distant rumble. He put two fingers in his teeth sending out an ear-splitting sound that resembled a shrill train whistle in the night. People in the cellar stayed put. The rest of the well-rehearsed partisans followed established procedures. Agnes and Gabriel dashed to the hidden trapdoor in the corner of the barn and down into the barracks. The breakfast four had already entered the cellar and headed toward the tunnel. Flora gathered the dishes and washed them while looking over her shoulders for any clues the partisans may have left in the kitchen. George, who was in the barnyard repairing the chicken coop fence, rushed to inspect the disguises on the trapdoor and the tunnel and barracks air vents in the corners of the barn floor.

Piotr and Tereza tramped at dawn high into the southern hills to check the integrity of the farm's water supply. As they neared the base on the descent, they heard approaching vehicles and the alerts and stayed out of sight well above the farm road.

Andrik and Gertrude mended the pasture fence. The Americans restrung brace wire for the grapevine posts. Four other partisan men and women shored up irrigation ditches and redistributed soil for spring planting. All were too far away to reach the cellar. So they carried their tools and took cover in the woods beyond the western boundaries. As always, they toted loaded pistols and knives. Stefan packed a grenade he'd fixed with a double pin lock.

Twin swastika flags fluttered above the front fenders of a long, low car with a corporal at the wheel and a sergeant next to him with a submachine gun in his lap. An officer, resplendent in his black SS uniform, lolled in the back wrapped in self-absorption while smoking a cigarette in a holder. The car rolled down the two-track dirt road and pulled up to the front door of the farmhouse.

An open truck carrying eight dust-eating privates parked behind the car. The soldiers hopped down, spread out, and six of them nosed around the farm. The driver opened the officer's door. He stepped out, arched his back, surveyed the area, removed the holder from its jaunty angle in his teeth, took the cigarette out of the holder, ground it out in the dirt, blew through the holder and put it in his shirt pocket.

He strode up the steps, across the porch, waited for the front door to be held for him and walked down the hall, boot heels pounding the floor. The corporal, accompanied by a private, searched the upstairs rooms while the sergeant, along with another private, probed the downstairs. Meanwhile, Flora washed, dried and put away several dishes. She turned while drying hands on her apron.

"Good morning, Major Herrmann, what brings you out this fine morning?"

"I just wanted to see you, *Frau* Pitulski."

"Oh, Major, I thought you loved me for my food." Flora hated being called '*Frau*.'

"No, it is really your vodka."

The bantering continued as the major sat and waited for coffee saved especially for him. Flora bustled about preparing a hearty breakfast. He asked in an offhand way, "*Frau*, er, Mrs. Pitulski, have you had any guests? We are looking for two escapees, possibly Jews, and wondered if they might have been seen out this way? Oh, we also learned that two Americans broke out of prison and may have come east."

"No, Major Herrmann, I see no one. George and Gwidon tell me if strangers near farm. I send George in truck to tell you if anyone come."

The Major sipped the aromatic coffee set in front of him. "I know you would, Mrs. Pitulski, and we would come to protect you from bad people."

One of the soldiers in the barnyard teased Gwidon with a rifle barrel prod in the ass. When he jumped, another soldier grabbed Gwidon's cap and made him scamper trying to get it back. George came out of the barn. "Gwidon, go to house get bread for soldiers." Other soldiers chased chickens around the barnyard imitating the squawks. George inwardly stiffened as one of the SS got dangerously close to the outside trapdoor.

Two more soldiers entered the barn and flirted with Magda who sat on a low stool in her brief shorts milking the goat. "Will you milk me, *schatzi*?" They checked the stalls, climbed into the loft and prodded the hay, all the time sneaking looks at Magda's long legs and abounding chest.

Back in the kitchen, Major Herrmann swallowed and wiped his mouth. "Mrs. Pitulski, we are planning a meal for a visiting general, and I wondered if we might have a large pig and a sheep for roasting, some vegetables and perhaps a few chickens dressed and maybe a little vodka, say six bottles of your best?"

Flora felt an extra heartbeat as the sergeant and private went down into the cellar just as Gwidon burst through the back door into the kitchen with Rat the Schnauzer at his heels. He bent forward awkwardly toward the major and then looked to his mother. "Mama, Papa want bread for soldiers."

Flora waved him toward the pantry. "Get bread, Gwidon, tell Papa to come in. Take dog out with you."

"*Kommen sie her, klein hund,*" and the Major stroked the dog's back before letting it go with Gwidon.

"Oh, I am sorry, Mrs. Pitulski we will also need bread, possibly seven or eight loaves, the kind you bake with the crust dusted with a little sugar, and of course the usual cakes and pies. The general will be pleased."

George came in wringing his cap, bowed to the major and was told by Flora what to prepare from the barnyard. Flora said, "Major Herrmann, George will bring food and vodka in truck tomorrow. And could you, Major, spare us few liters petrol."

"Of course, Mrs. Pitulski; be there by ten tomorrow morning, George. Thank you for breakfast." He laid some Deutschmarks on the table. "Oh, by the way, Major

Schroeder was out here last month, and he mentioned a handsome *fraulein* named, is it Margaret?"

"Yes, Major, no her name is Magda. She has worked for us long time. Good worker."

"She is not a Jew?"

"No, Major, a Catholic."

He stood, bowed to Flora, faced the door, clicked his heels, said *"Heil* Hitler" and marched out.

The sergeant and corporal had rounded up the soldiers, and they sat in the truck chewing on chunks of bread and playing catch with Gwidon's cap. The small caravan of fear pulled away laying down a dusty smokescreen out of which flew the cap, landing and skidding through the dirt.

Gwidon cried when he learned that his pet pig was going to the hated Nazis. Chicken heads were lopped off and the birds plucked, gutted and stuffed for roasting. Men and women worked all evening under Flora's supervision harvesting by moonlight and preparing vegetables, baking bread, cakes and pies, bottling vodka. Flora said, "Every dish we make for them, we make one for us, except pig and sheep. Only four pigs and three sheep left now.

"I am sorry Rat did not bite off Major's fingers. I could bake and send to his general as sausages." Flora flopped over a chicken for stuffing. "Too bad we not stuff chickens with poison."

George said, "Stuff Nazi with grenade, pull pin." He picked up the Deutschmarks and flung them onto the table in disgust. "Cheap Nazi *bękurts*."

Because of the work needed to keep Major Herrmann happy, Piotr postponed the mission scheduled for that night until the following day.

When George arrived at the German mess hall the next morning the SS cooks made him slit the throats of the pig and sheep. They didn't mind doing the job; in fact they liked doing it. But it gave them more pleasure to make George do the slaughtering because they knew he hated it. He and Gwidon raised the animals from newborns and had become attached. On the drive back to the farm, George murmured *"Bękarts. Bękarts. Bękarts."* and bit his first knuckle until it bled.

Andre and Coos couldn't climb the cellar stairs to the kitchen. One by one, Gwidon carried them out onto the porch and fresh air. They sat while Flora and other women fed them sips of soup, bits of bread soaked in cream, dibs of mashed vegetables and for dessert a few drops of vodka. Lev said, "Even Jews need alcohol, sometimes."

A narrow brook ran through the farm, and years before George and Gwidon partially dammed it creating a small pool. When the sun shone, the pool water warmed. Everybody bathed there in mild weather, and George had fashioned a gate in the dam to release the bath water and refill it for the next users. Arne and Coos, who were average-size men, could now walk with assistance, and they were brought to the pool wearing shorts that the women had made for them. The water soaked the dirt out of their pores, helped their sores to heal and relaxed them for a long nap when they were taken back to their cots. Their minds and bodies were slowly healing.

That night, Rick and Steve lay on their cots in an adjacent cubicle listening to Piotr and Tereza who were clearly oblivious to the sound effects of their lubricious lovemaking. Steve whispered, "Our wives probably think we're dead and have hooked up with Colonel Blimp and General Fartass." Rick's mid-section ached from trying to suppress a burst of laughter.

Upon recovery, he whispered, "You caught me by surprise. Instead of counting the days since we escaped, I was counting Tereza's orgasms." Then it was Steve who had to stifle the laughter.

28

"THE SS PURSUERS AND THEIR DOGS WENT DIRECTLY EAST."

In mid-morning, Lev collected Steve and Rick from their work in the barnyard, and the three met Piotr on the front porch. "You go west twenty kilometers, take radio." Piotr fetched a crude map out of his pocket, unfolded it and pointed. "Cross canal here. Lev knows where." Piotr's thick finger traced the map. *"Linia kolejowa,* I mean, what is English, Lev?"

"Rail line."

"Dziękuję. Rail line here, maybe one-half kilometer before crossing river; wait for train at two o'clock. Get there before one meet two men from Wachowiack group." His finger stabbed the page. "Cross meadow here to three-trunk birch tree. Lev knows password, 'Greta.'

"You know cryp English, Steven?" He nodded. "Code message here, this cryp code." He handed Steve two scraps of paper. "If Germans come, eat paper. Blow tracks, stop train. Wachowiack men have explosives. They come back with you. Do not fight Germans. Set fuse, get out. Stop five kilometers, send message, move fast, circle, double back. Lev leader tonight, do as he say. Leave after dark, my friends. Thank you."

Lev glided through the forest like a lynx, fast, silent, potentially deadly, traversing hills like they weren't there. Rick and Steve struggled to keep up, not quite back to top shape after their long confinement in the German jail. Lev was also lynx-eyed, seeing all possible dangers like fallen tree trunks and sinkholes in their path. Like Gwidon, he was rabbit-eared, hearing sounds unheard by the Americans, halting the patrol with a raised hand and standing statue-still for minutes at a time, breathing inaudibly.

When they paused for water, Lev whispered, "I like the silent forest at night, but still many soft sounds like animals sleeping and mating. Day is better; woods are like a big concert."

Steve made straps for the radio with the help of Gabriel, one of the hardest-working of the partisan men. Since the country was lower now, and they had to crawl at times, Steve strapped the radio to his back. They emerged from the forest, silently cursed the full-moon night and crept across the meadow toward the birch tree under which sat the two Wachowiaks with pistols pointed at them. From fifty meters away, Lev gave a low owl-hoot that sounded much like Piotr's signal from the bridge-blowing raid. A similar sound drifted back. At twenty meters, he said a between-the-teeth, "Greta." No other verbal greetings or introductions this night, only nods. Lev whispered to them in Polish while Steve unstrapped the radio from his aching back. He then indicated by pointing to his crotch that he had to pee, and Lev waved him away.

Steve walked a few steps up the tracks, heard a sound coming in his direction and slipped into the shadows. Lev also heard it and hoped Steve did as well. A helmeted

German soldier, rifle on a shoulder strap, walked on the ties down the middle of the tracks. When he came even, Steve stepped out, the soldier heard him, but too late as Steve pressed a nerve in his neck, and he went limp as a sack of wheat. Steve caught him under the armpits and dragged him off the tracks into a gully. Lev came over, gagged him with cloth, taped his mouth and eyes and trussed him head and foot with clever knots that would have given Houdini trouble. The soldier never saw their faces. Lev stuffed the German's ammunition clips into a small knapsack and put the rifle strap over his shoulder.

During this action, Rick helped the Wachowiak men set the charge. The five men regrouped. Steve picked up his radio, and with Lev in front crossed the meadow at a fast clip. They climbed a mound that oversaw the tracks two-hundred meters away. From this high vantage point they could also see more of the curving tracks to the west, shiny rails reflecting the moonlight. The unmistakable rumble of a long, heavy freight train came through the night air. Rick quietly asked Lev, "What kind of freight does it carry?"

"Munitions, other supplies, Jews."

Steve and Rick looked at each other as the charge blew, taking out five feet of track. The freight train engine tore around a curve too late for the engineer to see the blast, but since the brakes screeched he must have heard it. The engine skidded against locked brakes for about two-hundred meters, slowed, hit the gap and lurched to one side with the eardrum-bursting sound of tearing metal. Several freight cars also derailed, but like the engine didn't tip over.

The SS guards must have been warned or were expecting trouble. The doors of one freight car still on the tracks rolled open with an abrupt and resounding boom, and a dozen SS with dogs jumped to the ground. Lev said, "We must go in two groups. Rick, you go with him," pointing to one of the Wachowiak men. "Steve you and the other go with me."

Steve said, "Sorry, Lev, we told Piotr, Rick and I don't split up."

"Yes, all right, you go with the radio and meet at the farm. You can find the way?"

"We'll find it," and the two groups moved out. The Americans headed southeast, Lev and the Wachowiaks northeast.

The German Shepherds sniffed around, found the bound-up guard, and the SS called for assistance. The dogs smelled some more and soon pulled toward the meadow. The pursuers went directly east until they reached the observation spot on the mound where the dogs nosed around, barked and strained at their leashes. The partisans had a twelve-minute lead.

"I once read somewhere that dogs get confused if you go back over their own trail," Rick said. "Let's cut west a little then go back across the meadow at least for a ways then head southeast again." They did that and it worked. The dogs barked in the distance, and it sounded like the entire SS party was following Lev and the Wachowiaks.

"By the way, Steve, be sure and show me how you put that German guard on the ground."

Unlike the incursion at the bridge with Piotr and Tereza, the SS didn't release their dogs. Lev and the Wachowiaks simply outran and outmaneuvered them. Josef Wachowiak had a javelin arm and good luck. He threw a grenade from a bluff on a hill. It caromed off a rock adding twenty-five meters in distance before exploding in a hollow far below. When the SS went off in the direction of the blast and the partisans lit out the opposite way, the race was over.

Steve and Rick stopped five kilometers from the farm and radioed Piotr's message. They waited for the reply and then walked in. Piotr waited for them alone on the front porch, and Steve gave him the return message. Piotr asked, "Where is Lev?" Meanwhile Lev and the two Wachowiaks had come out of the woods on the opposite end of the farm with Pon and Rat trotting on each side of Lev.

He answered, "Lev here." They went into the kitchen. Flora shooed the dogs out and fed the men by candlelight while Piotr debriefed them. Josef Wachowiak was the eldest son of a famous partisan leader. Paul, his cousin, was a look-alike, tall and blonde with white teeth.

Rick thought: *Ski instructors in another life*, and asked Piotr, "What is the advantage of stopping the train? Won't they just fix the track, and the train arrives a little late?"

Piotr washed down bread with vodka. "You are true, Richard. We do anything to hurt Nazis. I tell you, we cannot kill them. They shoot too many innocent people in town. So we *odwrócić* . . ." and Piotr looked for help.

Paul Wachowiak said, "Divert."

"Yes," Piotr continued with an appreciative grin. "Anything to slow, stop supplies, coal, bullets, gas for Oswiecim ovens."

"But don't they murder the Jews on the trains anyway?" Steve asked.

"Yes, but to hold them off as long as we can something might happen," Lev said. "They escape from the train.

Russians come sooner. Germans leave, anything to slow the slaughter."

Paul Wachowiak, like his cousin Josef, had studied in England and spoke nearly unaccented English. "There is a smaller death camp near us. Our traps are set when the Nazis move out. And if our information is accurate, it will be two, maybe three months. Many will not reach the German border alive."

"Don't count too much on the Russians," Josef Wachowiak said. "They will do what suits their interests."

Lev smiled. "I know what you're saying. I learned that firsthand."

Josef continued, "When the Germans began a pullout from Warsaw in August, the resistance rose up thinking the Red Army would come in to help. They didn't. They sat across the Vistula and watched the Germans reinforce and shoot down thousands of our people. The Russians don't want a strong Polish government after the war. Stalin wants to run our country."

"We fight Russians again. We always do. Now we worry about Nazis," Piotr said. "Tonight, two of our people go to Oswiecim, put sand in Nazi truck tanks. No trucks, things slow down, same as trains. They cut barbed wire, go in depot, knock guard on head, pour sand. They run. Anna come back, she run good. Alfred too slow, bad leg, never should send him. Should send Gabriel, he is fast. Alfred begged to go. Lights come on, Anna say, 'Nazis shoot him in back.'" Piotr crossed himself.

Josef Wachowiak said, "Uncle Piotr, Paul and I will sleep two hours and then go home. My father needs us for a raid tonight on a Nazi munitions dump."

"Send your father, Josef, my sainted brother, my love and to your mother as well. You and Paul go with God." Piotr kissed them on both cheeks. Lev, Steve and Rick shook hands and wished them well.

29

"The Nazis came and took all the Jews away."

As they started to leave for bed, Piotr said, "Richard, Steven, wait . . . George talked to nun in town, helped many Jews. Sister Felicyta hide two Jews in convent, mother, daughter. Nazis come around, too much searching. Nazis shoot nuns who hide Jews, many in north killed. Need to send here, we have no room have no choice. Oh, room for one with Alfred dead, poor Alfred. His wife in barn crying, women try to comfort. Goodnight . . . oh, Steven, go back to woods with radio now *daleko*, oh, mean way far with Richard; send message to my brother that Paul and Josef on way home soon, thank you, boys."

On the way into the forest, Steve said, "This duty is getting worse by the day. Didn't we just leave the woods?"

"I wonder how far away the Russians are? They'd look very good along about now."

The next day was Saturday; the day George brought his farm goods to the outdoor market in town. George left at four in the morning in order to get a good place. Gwidon and Gabriel helped pack the boxes and load them onto the truck. Gwidon could not manage communications with customers so he did not go to market. George usually took

Magda along to help, but she was bedridden with pain and a high fever and this time he went alone, except for the Americans.

They were draped with potato sacks and hidden among the boxes under a tarpaulin. George dropped them off near a wooded patch a kilometer from town. He showed them on a crude map how to find the convent. "I stay in evening, have meal, drink with friends after market, like always. Get dark nine o'clock, we meet same place here, or other place I told you. I hide you under empty boxes. Rap convent door three times, wait, then three more, password 'Aloysius.' "

The part of town near the convent was asleep. The smell of rain was in the air, and the cobblestones were slick with morning dew. Steve and Rick kept tight to the buildings casting no shadows. As they neared the convent and saw the steeple of the nearby church, a light came on in the upper story of a house across the lane. They backed into a doorway until the light went out and it was dark again.

They knocked softly on the convent door.

". . . Who is there?"

"Aloysius."

Sister Felicyta, along with two other nuns, one aged like her the other a novitiate, smiled and inclined their heads approvingly as the Americans entered and doffed their caps. "Are you men Catholic?"

Steve said, "Yes, Sister."

"Are you American soldiers?"

"Yes, Sister."

"God bless you."

"Thank you, Sister."

Sister Felicyta was a handsome woman with an intelligent face and long, expressive fingers. In precise, Polish-accented English, she said, "George told you that we have two Jews who must leave for their own safety and for ours. We have hidden them for over two weeks. The SS or Gestapo come frequently and search. They have not found the hiding place, but they will. When they do, we will be shot and the two Jews, a mother and her child, will be taken to Oswiecim and gassed. We know of these things. How soon can you leave with them?"

Steve continued doing all the talking, "A little before nine o'clock tonight, Sister."

Sister Felicyta frowned. "It cannot be sooner?" The other older nun seemed to shrink.

"I'm sorry, Sister Felicyta, but George cannot meet us in the woods with his truck until that time."

"Very well, come with me."

They were led along a dark, wood-paneled corridor. Voices in prayer could be heard beyond the walls. "The Priest is away tending his flock. He is busy as many are sick and weak. Do you know that the Priest is the incarnation of Christ on earth?"

"Yes, Sister."

Many doors were unlocked as the hushed procession proceeded, descending stairs, opening more doors until they entered a modest chapel in which the only light came from votive candles. Sister Felicyta halted the group in front of the altar where they bowed and prayers were said.

They filed behind the altar. Sister moved what Steve thought was a rood screen. She knocked softly once and then three times in rapid succession on what appeared to be an engraved wood wall. They heard a lock being turned on the inside, and a small door in the wall, cleverly designed to resemble part of the wood wall, opened. Since the bottom of the four-foot-high faux door was two feet above the floor, they had to step up and in while ducking their heads.

A low-wattage bulb lit a svelte, dark-haired woman of medium height standing as though at attention with a willowy child who looked to be about five at her side. The novice turned on a brighter lamp. Sister Felicyta said, "Doctor Hellifield, these men are Americans who have come to take you and Sarah to a new and from what I know is a safe place. We will leave you now to make your own introductions and acquaintances. It will be a long day, so we will bring food for you soon and again later. Good morning."

Sarah smiled and made a small curtsy. "Thank you, Sister Felicyta, and thank you, dear Americans for coming to help my mother and me."

Steve and Rick were bowled over by the poise, presence and sparkling intelligence of this exquisitely-featured blonde and blue-eyed child. Rick thought: *Would the SS actually kill this little angel? . . . over my dead body.*

"I am Jean Krol, and you now know my daughter, Sarah Krol. We both, for reasons you will learn, use my maiden name, Hellifield. Let us sit at this table and please tell us about yourselves." She switched on another lamp revealing two cots and a small dresser along a side wall.

"I'm Rick Butler and this is Steve Millen. We were shot down over Germany, captured by the Germans, put in a jail, escaped and found a partisan group. We try to help them, I guess until the war is over."

Sarah, who was a full intellectual partner, asked, "Do you have family in America?"

"We're both from Chicago where our parents live," Steve said. "Our wives are army nurses still stationed, as far as we know, in Italy."

"Do they know that you're here in Poland?" Jean asked.

"No, and they probably think we're dead." Sarah shifted uncomfortably in her chair, and Steve knew he had said too much with a child, even a very smart child, present.

"I'm sorry you have no contact with your wives," Jean said. "It must be very hard for you and for them."

"We miss them," Rick said. "We'll be meeting at nine tonight with the owner of the farm where we're staying. We'll go there in his truck, and you'll be under the care of the partisans or resistance as they're also called."

"Are there other Jews there?" Sarah asked.

Should I tell her? He looked to Rick who gave an assenting grin and blink.

"Yes, two escapees from Auschwitz."

"I never heard of anyone getting out," Jean said. "How did they reach the farm?"

"Rick and I found them in the woods about a kilometer from the farm. We brought them in. They are not well, but seem to be getting stronger."

"I will help them."

"Oh, there is at least one more, a man who escaped the pogroms in Russia and made his way to the Warsaw Ghetto. He left there after the Nazis invaded and eventually joined the underground group Steve and I are with."

"Do you mind me asking who the leader of your group is?"

"With respect, we were told to never use names of other partisans. I know the leader will introduce himself to you."

"Of course, I should have intuited that."

"Don't you want to go back to your own army?"

"That's a good question, Sarah. Steve and I would like that, but we seemed to have landed in the midst of many Nazis, and we believe we probably wouldn't get back. We think we'll help more in the war to stay here and fight the Nazis with the underground."

The same knock on the door was repeated. Jean opened it, and the novitiate they met before and another novitiate entered with two trays of food and set them on the table. Jean thanked them, and they left smiling. Sarah and Jean arranged the plates, cups and bowls, and the four enjoyed an early lunch of hearty vegetable soup, bread and butter. Sarah entertained the men with word games she had learned and endless questions about America.

When the table was cleared, Rick said to Jean, "Now please tell us how you and Sarah came to be here."

"Excuse me, Mother, I'm sleepy."

"Of course, precious, we were awake so early."

Sarah got up from the table, pushed her chair in, came around and put her arms around the men's necks and kissed their cheeks. She went to her cot and lay down. Her mother covered her with a small blanket, kissed and hugged her, and soon she was in the deep sleep that only children can find.

The men began to whisper. Jean said, "No need to be quiet; she's good for at least two hours, and an earthquake would not wake her."

"I believe that Steve feels the same way I do. We hope someday to have daughters as wonderful as Sarah." Steve smiled.

"I don't believe I would have survived all this without her companionship and positive outlook. She is so full of good. I am blessed. Now . . . where do I start? At the beginning, I suppose." Jean steepled slim fingers under her chin.

"Obviously, I am British. My father, Robert Hellifield, is a surgeon and a Christian. My mother, Leslie, is a chemist of some renown. Her maiden name is Mendelson, and she is Jewish. My father and my husband said that I look like her. If that is so, I am a lucky person."

Rick thought: *She must be beautiful.*

"I am Jewish as is Sarah."

"I noticed that Sister Felicyta called you Doctor Hellifield," Steve said.

"I was interning at King's College Hospital in 1937. I met my husband, John Krol, at a social function. He was a professor at the London School of Economics. We married a few months later. Sarah was born in 1939 here in Poland. John was Polish. Like me, his father was a gentile and his mother Jewish. Again, like me, John is a Jew. Sarah looks like John, tall and fair."

Steve thought: *Jean has a voice that could talk you off a ledge.*

"At all events, we enjoyed a marvelous life in London. I received my certificate to practice general medicine. John was made a department head, which was unusual given his age. And I became pregnant with Sarah. Oh, I hate talking about myself."

"No, please go on," Rick said.

"In the summer of 1939, John received a letter from a cousin here in Poland saying that his parents were unwell. John's brother was an officer in the Polish Army stationed in the northern part of the country, and his parents were distraught over their physical ills, the separation from their sons and their belief that war was coming. John and I decided to make a quick trip. My parents were against my going, particularly since I was pregnant. But I wasn't going to let John go alone so we came, thinking the so-called 'Phony War' would continue for at least another year. Then shortly after we arrived the Nazis invaded and we couldn't get out."

"Do your parents back in England know where you are?" Steve asked.

Jean rubbed her brow and half-smiled through a small sigh. "We were able to maintain contact by mail until the Nazis began another round-up of Jews. That had been going on since the war began all across Poland, and it became more intense in southern Poland in nineteen-forty-two. Mail was cut off, and we've had no contact in nearly three years. I worry about my mother and father and also my brother, Ian, an RAF fighter pilot who, thank God, survived the Battle of Britain. The last I heard he was flying bomber escorts over Europe.

"I know you must be wondering where my husband is, and I'm coming to that. John's parents did much better once we got to them. Sarah was born, and she gave them new life. They had quite a good support system in their neighborhood, relatives and friends. But, of course, there's nothing like your own flesh and blood. John was able to get a teaching job at his own university, and I practiced on the side.

"As I mentioned, a huge campaign against Polish Jews happened in nineteen-forty-two. It came fast like a summer squall. Hundreds of shetls were decimated. A few days before this calamity, John, Sarah and I went on a two-night camping trip in the Carpathian Mountains. When we returned and drove into the street it was empty. A neighbor's dog that was never out except on a leash was wandering about. John said, 'Something's wrong.'

"He drove to the next street where we could enter his parents' home from the back. A man John knew, a Christian, was walking nearby. When he saw John, he said, 'The Nazis came and took all the Jews away. Everybody is gone.'

"It was so quiet as we went into the house. The Nazis had rummaged for money and jewels. John was like I had never seen him. His eyes stared. We heard a car in the street. Two men in plain clothes, probably Gestapo, got out and started going through the houses. John's father had a pistol. We, John, excuse me . . . John told me to take Sarah and hide in an attic closet.

"We heard the men come in the front door. There was an exchange of gunfire, seven, eight shots then silence. I told Sarah to wait in the attic closet with the door closed and say nothing. I went down to the front hall. The two Gestapo were shot dead. John was hit in the chest and abdomen. He was dying. I tried to cover his wounds with my hands to stop the blood. It was hopeless. He said, 'Leave me. Take the money in the closet. You and Sarah drive away fast now. Use the Hellifield name,' and he died in my arms."

Jean put her head down and shook with sobs. Sarah sighed and turned over. Steve went and covered her and gently stroked her hair. Rick came around the table. He patted Jean's shoulder and said what he hoped were comforting words. Jean sat up, smiled, wiped her eyes and blew her nose. "I'm sorry. I haven't cried in a long time. I guess I needed that. Thank you for being understanding."

Rick said, "It's good to get things out."

Jean arched her back, then settled into her chair with a slight groan and smiled. The Americans wondered why she groaned, but since she also smiled they didn't think more about it. For her it was a little release, as she thought to herself: *These are quality men. Sarah and I couldn't be in better hands. I think they will get us out of this and back to England.*

"Oh my, I can't tell you how much it means to have you both here to help us. I've watched you two. You're like brothers, finishing each other's sentences. Have you known each other long? Do you ever disagree?"

"A few months, we argue sometimes, but Rick always wins because he's a first lieutenant and I'm only a second lieutenant." They all had a good, air-clearing laugh.

"Since I started it, let me finish the story and get us back to why Sarah and I are here. Leaving my husband was unbearable, but I fixed him as best I could and hoped he would be found and given a proper burial. I quickly changed my clothes so that Sarah wouldn't see the blood, stuffed a few more things into a bag, ran to the attic for Sarah who stood there like the little trooper she is. Then . . ."

"What about the money?" Steve asked.

"Oh yes, the banks were unreliable so John kept our money and papers behind a panel in the attic closet. He built it as a boy, and unless you knew where it was you wouldn't find it. I had no time to go to our apartment, so Sarah and I got in the car and drove north to a mountain town I'd once seen. She asked me in the car where Daddy was, and I told her he would join us later.

"She saw that I couldn't stop my tears. And soon she said, 'Daddy's not coming, is he?' I had to say no. She cried for a long time, doubly so I'm sure for her grandparents, and I could scarcely see the road through my own tears. When Sarah stopped crying, she said, 'Don't worry, mommy, I'll take care of you.' It all sounds strange, I know, coming from a three-year-old, but she spoke in complete sentences and could reason by the time she was one."

"She is amazing," Rick said. "So what happened next? Were you pursued?"

"Fortunately, no Nazis came after us. We drove up into the Carpathians, found the town and went into the only hotel. The owner, Mr. Auttenberg, was front desk clerk, town mayor, ran the post office and more. He knew immediately what we were and the danger he might face. I had my physician's license which showed my maiden name. He looked at it, then skeptically at me, smiled and whispered, 'My wife and I are hidden Jews, too. You and your daughter will be safe with us.'

"The only doctor in the district was Jewish, and he had fled the Nazi roundup. They badly needed a doctor in the area, and I'd learned enough Polish over the past few years to get by, so I fit in quite nicely. Mr. Auttenberg was a polymath, could fix anything got things done without fuss. He had my car painted and found new plates, made identification papers for Sarah and me that fooled the Germans who came around.

"His wife loved books and was a teacher who ran the little one-room schoolhouse that had all the grades. Mr. and Mrs. Auttenberg, that's all we ever called them, had Sarah in kindergarten at three, said she was the smartest person she had ever known. We . . ."

"Franz was smart, too." Sarah hopped out of bed, kissed her mother, smiled at the men, dug at the corners of her eyes and sat down at the table. "I'm hungry, Mommy."

"I think Sister Felicyta will send food soon, sweetheart. I was just telling Steve and Rick about the town."

"Franz was my best friend. His father was German and loved beer." Sarah made a rounded form of her belly and grinned. "Franz's father ran a ski school. Franz taught me to ski. He was two years older than me, but didn't seem to mind. We had good times hiking, reading, talking. I miss him and Mr. and Mrs. Auttenberg."

"Please go back and make up your bed, Sarah." She immediately did so and neatly, all the time singing softly to herself.

Steve said, "Jean, Sister mentioned the facilities."

"Yes, you will need to slide the screen about two feet to the right, close the door and slide the screen back into position. It's the door on the left of the chapel as . . ."

"I have to go too, Mommy. I'll show Steve the way. He can stand outside." Everyone smiled at that one.

The bathroom was across a corridor. Steve looked in and was surprised to see a wooden stall within the bathroom, the kind with the flushing mechanism in a wood box near the ceiling. "I'll be fine, Steve, you can wait in the hall." Steve did as he was told. Sarah locked the bathroom door, and he heard the stall door creak as she opened it. Soon

Steve heard the cranking, booming flush. He heard Sarah washing her hands, then unlocking the bathroom door. She came out saying, "I'll wait here for you."

They heard voices in the chapel. It sounded like Sister Felicyta and at least two men, whose voices were unmistakably German-accented. Sarah put a finger to her lips. Steve thought: *Who's in charge here?* He took her hand, they went into the bathroom, left the door unlocked, turned the light off and felt their way into the stall, also keeping that door unlocked. He stood on the toilet seat, squatted and lifted Sarah onto his lap. She read what he was doing and put her arms around his neck. With hands free, Steve slid the dagger out of its sheath, pulled the pistol from inside his jacket and released the safety.

I hope when he doesn't see legs he'll leave. If he doesn't and opens the stall I'll kill him with a knife to the throat. Or I'll shoot him, leave Sarah here and go out and try to kill the others before they find Rick and Jean. He could feel Sarah trembling slightly.

Rick told Jean to get under the cot in case there was gunfire. He turned out the lights, drew his pistol and stood with his back to the wall beside the door. The voices were on the altar just outside the door, Sister Felicyta and a German man.

"What is this screen?"

"It is an altar screen depicting events from Christ's life."

"How can you believe in a Jew as your savior? What is behind this screen?" Rick and Jean could hear it sliding. Rick took the knife out ready to follow Stefan's advice on where to thrust it.

"What is this wall all wood?"

"It is an engraved wall of wood at the rear of the chapel."

"What is behind it?"

"An outside brick wall at the back of the convent." The German tapped on it.

"It does not sound like brick."

"We had it studded a few inches from the wall so it would not warp from moisture."

That's thinking on your feet, Rick thought.

Steve and Sarah heard the bathroom door open and saw the light go on for a few seconds. Sarah's arms tightened around Steve's neck, but her breath was held as was his. After a few shuffling steps the light went off and the door closed. *I'm glad the Nazi bastard didn't have to take a leak.*

Jean and Rick heard voices and footsteps retreating. An urgent voice said, "*Kommen*, Schramm." Fast steps sounded. The outside door at the far end of the chapel closed.

Steve and Sarah waited a few minutes and returned. He replaced the screen while Sarah gave the familiar soft knock. Rick asked, "Who is it?"

"Sarah and Steve."

When they entered and closed the door, Sarah whispered, "Oh, Mommy, I saw Steve put his knife away. He was going to stab the Nazi but he left. His name was Schramm." Sarah lowered her voice and growled, "*Kommen*, Schramm." Jean and the Americans shared a smile, and Sarah laughed knowing they liked her impersonation.

After a few minutes of chatter, mostly from Sarah unwinding, the coded knock came on the door. Steve and Rick pulled their pistols and knives and stood on each side of the door. Jean led Sarah to her cot and motioned for her to get under it. Jean turned off the lights and went under her cot. Rick said, "Who's there?"

"Aloysius," was the reply in Sister Felicyta's voice. Steve turned the lights on, both men put their weapons away, and Rick unlocked and opened the door.

Sister Felicyta and the church sexton, brittle as old brown paper, accompanied Father Wozniak, a tall, angular, determined man. "Good morning, Doctor Hellifield. Hello, Sarah, Gentlemen. Your staying here is endangering many religious. I ask you to come to the church where only the sexton and I will be at risk if you are found. Please follow me. Thank you, Sister."

Jean and Sarah thanked Sister Felicyta and gathered their things. Father led them along a hallway, down a steep flight of stairs and across a clammy passageway which the Americans assumed to be a tunnel between the convent and the church. The sexton used a key from a jangling ring to open a large door into the basement of the church, and finally another key opened the door to a room that smelled of candles, polished wood and old books. "I think you will be safe here. Food will be brought soon. I wish you well as you go with God. Sarah, you get prettier every day," as he patted her shoulder.

"Thank you, Father Wozniak."

They sat on extra pews that had been stored in the room. Sarah leafed through a hymnal that she took from the back pocket of a pew. Steve asked Jean, "So how did you and Sarah finally get here?"

"We . . ."

"Now, Sarah, please read the hymnal and let Mommy tell the story. I may get stuck and forget something, and then you can help me remember. Will that be a good plan?"

Sarah smiled. "Franz said I talk too much."

"There were some tight moments when the Nazis came around, but it wasn't too often. We stayed in the town almost two years. Sarah loved school and being with children of all ages."

Sarah looked up from the hymnal. "I learned from the big ones, some bad words, too."

"I practiced around the area and enjoyed the work and the people. We rented a small house from the Auttenbergs. They took care of Sarah when I had to go on night calls to people who needed me. It all worked out fine until one Sunday about two weeks ago when Sarah and I drove out to have a little picnic and see a mountain view we liked a few miles away. When we came back a man, a patient of mine who lived on the outskirts, waved us down. He said, 'Don't go back to your house. The Nazis are in the town. They took the Auttenbergs away and are looking for you and Sarah.'

"We never learned how we, the Auttenbergs, were found out, likely a collaborator. The SS, the Gestapo are relentless in tracking people down. They, of course, knew who we were, photographs and papers in his parents' house where John was . . . our apartment. That reminds me: For some reason, possibly a premonition, when Sarah and I went for the ride I took our money and papers.

"The man, Mr. Nedza, was a local handyman. I think he was Czech by birth. He hid our car in his shed, took us into the house, and his wife, who was also a patient, made us a meal. At midnight, he drove us here hidden in his truck. He is Sister Felicyta's brother, and he knew she helped Jews hide from the Nazis. He was a very brave man to do that. Some day when this awful war is over we will come back and thank those who helped us, won't we, Sarah?"

"Yes, and I will marry Franz." Everybody laughed, and Sarah giggled happily because she knew she had told a good one.

The sexton arrived with lunch and helped lay it out with trembling hands. It was simple, and it was gobbled up. When they finished, Sarah climbed up on Steve's lap, put her head on his chest and fell fast asleep. "Sarah loves to look at a picture of her father I have. You could be my husband's brother, strong resemblance."

The hours passed, and it was time to leave for the meeting with George. Father Wozniak drew a clear map showing the best route to the rendezvous point and which streets to avoid. He touched each of their heads, and said in his comforting voice, "God is good. He will show you the light and the way."

Since they needed to move at speed through the shadowed streets and alleys, Rick put Sarah on his shoulders, and they stayed close to whatever cover they could find. Steve led and put his hand up whenever a sound was heard, a dog barked, a light went on, or when things didn't look right. But, like all small towns, there was welcome after-dark vacantness. To their advantage, cloud cover obscured the otherwise friendly moonlight. Near the edge of town, a scurrying rat the size of a small cat froze them for an instant next to a row of garbage cans.

As a light rain fell, Steve carried Sarah in his arms so that Rick, with his unerring feel for direction, could lead them through the woods. Fifty meters later, Rick's hand shot up. They moved up into a knot to see the lights from George's truck, another vehicle and the unwelcome sound of loud conversation among three men.

"So why are you on the road so late, George? Isn't your wife waiting all warm in bed?"

"I had a meal with friends after market."

"I think you had more than dinner, George. I smell something a little stronger. Do you have some for us. It is cold out here chasing around after rodents and Jews." Sarah's fingers dug into Steve's shoulders.

Another voice, "Thank you, George, please next time bring a full bottle." He went to the back of the truck and lifted and looked under several boxes. "You don't have any more under these empty crates do you, possibly some schnapps?"

"No, *Herr Oberst*."

"Jurgen, George called me *Oberst*. If I was one I wouldn't be here. Good night, George. *Heil* Hitler." They soon heard a car turn around and drive away in the direction of town. George drove off toward the farm road.

"There is a second meeting place," Rick whispered. "There is always a second meeting place, this way."

One of the crates in the back of George's truck was big enough for Sarah to fit under. Jean and the two Americans had to deal with all sizes of boxes piled on top of them. Before George placed them, Rick put his hand over Jean's head and Steve put an arm across her back to reduce the weight. George unrolled a tarp and pulled it over the boxes to ward off the cold. It was November 24, 1944.

Piotr and several other partisans were out on raids, and most of the others had gone to bed early. Lev waited on the front porch for the sentry's signal that the truck was on the farm road. He called to Flora, and they went into the yard and followed the truck back to the shed. Lev and George removed the tarpaulin and lifted the boxes. After the last one was picked up, Sarah stood smiling and adorable in the light from a kitchen window. "I smell cow manure. This must be the farm." Everybody laughed as Flora held out her arms. Sarah went to her, and Flora lifted her off the truck. *This is the grandchild I have always wanted.*

George and Gwidon had built a hiding place behind a wall to the rear of a heavy armoire in one of the upstairs spare bedrooms. Flora wouldn't hear of Sarah sleeping in the cellar, and she wouldn't separate Sarah from her mother, so the two had a snug bedroom, with a place to hide if the SS or Gestapo came calling.

After Sarah had a snack, Jean and Flora put her to bed. Once she was asleep, Flora sat with her in the room while Jean went to the cellar with Lev who was the interim caregiver of the two escapees.

"Arne, Coos, are you awake?"

"Yes, Lev."

"I have brought Doctor Hellifield, who is a British Jew running from the Nazis. Her daughter, Sarah, is upstairs with Flora. You will meet her tomorrow, a charming little girl."

Lev held a light so they could see Jean. She smiled at them, said hello, then checked their pulses, and shined her penlight into their eyes, ears, noses and throats. She pressed their necks, chests and abdomens. She told them to sit up, took a stethoscope out of her black bag and had them breathe in and out.

"You are both doing better than I expected. Tomorrow, we will do further examinations and begin some light exercises. Do you have appetites?"

"It is getting better, Doctor Hellifield," Coos said. "Arne eats more than I do."

"Now go to sleep. I will come to you in the morning, and if it is not too cold we will go outside and walk a little. Good night and be well." Coos and Arne had their best sleeps since they were brought to the farm.

Then Lev brought Jean to Magda who was moaning in pain. Jean sent Lev for water and examined Magda while asking some questions. Jean took a pill from a vial in her bag. Magda swallowed it with water brought by Lev and was soon asleep. Over the next several days, Jean cured the malady.

Gwidon adopted Sarah. He grew up isolated on the farm, never going to school nor having childhood friends. Sarah was his first pal. He carried her on his shoulders, and they played horsey. He introduced her to all his animal friends, showed her how to milk the cows, feed the pigs and goats, muck the stalls and tend to the barnyard. Sarah petted the sheepdog Pon while he was eating, and he nipped at her forearm tearing the skin. Jean fixed the slight wound, and Sarah learned that you never touch an animal while it is being fed.

Sarah also learned to operate the dam gate, open and close the cellar vents and warn Gwidon or other adults of approaching vehicles. Another of Sarah's positive traits was that she loved to work. There was not a lazy bone in her little body.

She became Gwidon's loyal assistant. He was the boss for the first time in his life, and he thrived in the new role. Flora anticipated that Gwidon's proximity to Sarah might make Jean uncomfortable. She assured Jean that despite Gwidon's limitations he was a moral person.

30

"Turn that damn radio off or change the dial."

Suzanne and Beverly tried in vain to find their husbands, but neither the military nor the Red Cross could tell them anything new. They continued to believe that Steve and Rick were alive and that someday they would be reunited. In November 1944, Suzanne and Beverly were transferred from Foggia to a nursing group under General George S. Patton's command. Patton's Third Army was fighting SS divisions across the south of France, with neither side taking prisoners. Casualties were high, and the American nurses worked twenty-hour days.

In mid-December, 24 German divisions broke through under-defended lines in the Ardennes Forest. British and American commands could have but didn't pincer the Nazi advance. Allied troops were driven into a headlong westward retreat forcing them to form a defensive line near Bastogne, a Belgian town close to the Luxembourg border. German armored divisions circled the Allies and clobbered them with artillery. It was a bitterly cold winter, and the Americans in particular took heavy losses. Bad weather prevented air support, and the situation looked grim. The German command pressed the Allies to surrender. General

Anthony McCauliffe, Commander of the 101st Airborne Division, famously replied, "Nuts."

Large segments of Patton's Third Army were ordered north to relieve 'The battered bastards of Bastogne.' Beverly and Suzanne's nursing group raced north with them. As they neared Metz, the truck driver switched the frequency to Armed Forces Radio. Bing Crosby came on singing, "I'll be seeing you/In all old the old familiar places . . ." and Suzanne came apart, shoulders shaking, spilling tears.

"What is it Suzanne? What happened?"

She said in a tremulous voice, "I'll be seeing you are the last words Steve said before he left." Then, thinking of Rick, Beverly broke down, and they both wept. Soon other nurses cried in sympathy, as Bing crooned the heartrending lyrics.

The truck stopped, as vehicles up ahead waited at a crossroads. The driver slid his cab window open wider. "What's going on back there?"

One of the less-affected nurses yelled, "Turn that damn radio off or change the dial!"

The driver shrugged, said *Dames* to himself and found another station. 'I'll be Seeing You' became the legendary romantic ballad of the Second World War. Suzanne and Beverly could never listen to it without weeping.

The combination of clearing weather and improved air support, plus Patton's hell-bent interdiction, broke the German offensive. The 'Battle of the Bulge' was over and with it Hitler's pipe dream of splitting the Allies and driving through to Antwerp and the North Sea. Patton's armored force sped south to resume their bloody clashes with SS elite divisions.

Beverly's and Suzanne's nursing group stayed north and tended to wounded Americans in a makeshift hospital in Luxembourg. Some doctors and nurses, on continuous duty beyond the breaking point, passed out and had to be carried off to rest before recovering and returning to the operating room.

Suzanne said to Beverly in the first break they'd had in sixteen hours, "This is the worst since Anzio, so many multiple wounds. At least here we operate out of the rain and not out in some shell hole with water up to your ankles. I need to run in place between operations to keep my legs and hands from shaking." She sipped some coffee, put the cup down and shuddered. "I guess the coffee's not helping.

"I can't forget that one young kid with his ear blown off and the open throat, his scared eyes. Our hands in there trying to stop the bleeding and keep him from drowning before the doctor came. I couldn't blink away the tears. I'm guilty to say I was glad he died and out of his misery. I despise this hateful war."

"The blood, the never-ending warm blood," Beverly said in a plaintive voice. "I wish to God I'd lost my sense of smell."

"When it's the absolute worst, and I feel I can't go on, I think of being in Steve's arms and our tender moments."

"I know what you mean. When I hit bottom, I escape to my times with Rick in Foggia. What a lovely name, like a bowl of warm pasta. I'll have the Foggia, please." Suzanne smiled. "What a miraculous place, at least on the happy side. You found Steve again, and I meet Rick after I messed up knowing him better in college. I was lucky to get a second chance."

After thirteen days, the last survivors were moved to hospitals in England or sent stateside. The nursing group moved east on a new assignment, as the American and British armies drove toward the Rhine and eventually into Germany.

31

"OTHER COUNTRIES IN THAT REGION WILL FIGHT YOU TO THE DEATH."

When Sarah was not aiding Gwidon with the farm work she helped her mother and Lev with Arne and Coos, the two Auschwitz survivors. Both men had teenage children who had been gassed along with their mothers at Auschwitz. Having Sarah around was at first bittersweet, but being the sunny child she was they soon surrendered to her cheerful company.

Arne was a physicist and mathematician who apprenticed with the famed Danish physicist Niels Bohr. Recognizing Sarah's intelligence, he taught her formative mathematics and found her aptitude to be exceptional. "Doctor Hellifield, when you and Sarah get back to England you must enter her into the best schools so she can fully develop her talents."

Coos had been a biological scientist with a special interest in botany. On calm December days, with Lev supporting one of Coos's arms as needed, Sarah joined them for short walks on the fringes of the woods where Coos educated her on the intricacies and magic of nature. Like Arne, Coos found Sarah to be an apt pupil with a facility for asking the right questions. Jean would often go along, and they were a happy group sometimes stopping to cut winter savory for Flora's kitchen.

Later when they were alone. "Mommy, you and Lev like each other."

"He is a good and kind man."

Dieter, a brash, handsome Sudeten German, joined the partisan group. Steve and Rick knew how careful Piotr was and never questioned Dieter's background, what other partisan groups he may have been with and why he was recruited. In the first planning meeting that included Dieter, the Americans were surprised by the fervor of his vitriolic anti-Nazi rhetoric. Then Dieter laid into the Americans telling them in front of the others how dangerous their presence was. "It is all well and good that you feel safe from harm here, but if we are caught sheltering you we will all be shot and all you will suffer is a return to a *stalag*."

Steve thought: *I wonder how he knows about stalags?*

Piotr's eyes bore into Dieter as he said in an irritated tone, "I took you in. You know special code from my cousin. You worry about own skin, Dieter. Americans stay. If you not like, be free to leave and join partisans with no Americans. We have Jews here. Are they danger for you? We get shot havink them, too. This farm not like some others, we are Poles who care for all people. Next time, take complaint to me alone. You understand?" No answer.

Fist pounds on table then a rough-voiced, "Dieter, do you understand me?"

Dieter acknowledged the question by slowly lowering his head and saying a barely heard, "Yes." Rick looked up, and his eyes met Steve's.

Later, Rick said, "I don't like the guy, but I guess if Piotr vouches for him."

"I think if Dieter didn't agree, Piotr would have taken him outside and beaten the shit out of him, or kicked him off the reservation. Never saw him that pissed."

"Maybe he doesn't trust him. I know I don't."

"Me either. I was standing inside the porch door last evening, and Jean was sitting out there alone in her coat. Dieter walked across the yard, went up on the porch and tried to put the make on her. I was about to go out when she told him off good in a quiet voice finishing up by saying that if he ever bothered her again she would tell Piotr. Dieter mumbled something and walked away."

"She'd be better off telling Lev. It's obvious he's crazy about her and would kill Dieter with his bare hands if he knew about it."

"I wouldn't want to get in a scrap with him. Bite your ears and nose off. Reminds me how they used to say in the Navy no matter how tough you think you are never get in a fight with a small, southern guy. Bite your nuts off before giving up."

Arne and Coos took meals with the rest and walked around the farm helping with simple chores. Thanks to Flora's cooking and Jean's ministrations weight was gained, sores healed, eyes looked less sunken, their skin regained some color, their voices were almost back to full strength, and they were nearly self-sufficient.

The other partisans were going through a healthy stretch so Jean had a little more time. And when Sarah was busy helping Gwidon or Flora or getting educated by Coos and Arne, she and Lev took walks and talked about their lives. Once, when they were out of sight, she let Lev hold her hand. The next time, he held her, rubbed her back against the cold, and she lifted her lips to his. How good it was for both of them to feel a body in close contact. In Lev's case it was passionate love, and Jean felt his ample stiffness through their winter clothes. Although for her it was no more than love felt for a close friend and pent-up sexual need, she did not withdraw her lower body from the contact.

A week later when they walked at dusk Lev carried under his arm a sleeping bag he had fashioned out of blankets. Jean knew what it meant, and she throbbed in anticipation. On an earlier walk they'd seen a protected, mossy indent under a shelf of rock, and now they crawled into it. Without talking, all clothes came off, and they slipped nude and shivering into the well-padded makeshift bag. The naked bundling soon warmed them, and they kissed and caressed tenderly. Jean's nipples hardened against Lev's chest, and he pulsed against her. Breathing became more rapid as they kissed deeply, and his tongue tip flicked against her throat and breasts. She fondled him in places that made him want to scream with pleasure. They adjusted, and Jean was filled and pleasurably distended. She reached down, and her thumb and forefinger grasped the thick root of the hardness within her. Her hand came away and with the other caressed Lev's body. They soon found a rhythmic intensity that delivered an extended state of bliss.

Several more ardent interludes followed. Lev had told Jean of his dream to go to Palestine and help build a Jewish homeland. Now he wanted her to marry him. "You and

Sarah and I will go together. We will be a happy family, maybe more children, yours and mine."

"I love you, Lev, but it hurts me to say that I am not in love with you. You are a marvelous lover, and you have made me very happy. I respect you and your dream and hope you will fulfill it. Sarah and I, God willing, will go back to England. That will be our home. I want Sarah to know her grandparents, my parents, go to fine schools and become the person in full I know she will be.

"After this," Jean opened her arms, tears filled her eyes and her voice broke. "I will not expose her again to the dangers of war. And there will be war, Lev. Other countries in that region will fight you to the death. But I know you will prevail."

"I am a persistent fellow, Jean. Maybe before we leave here you will change your mind and love me more and go with me to Palestine." Jean ended the sexual relationship and was beyond happiness that Lev was a big enough man to remain her dearest friend.

He also stayed close to Sarah. She was fluent in Polish, and to Lev's delight used a few mispronunciations in her English like "goink" and "sayink." Sarah asked Lev to speak only Russian to her, and given its linguistic nearness to Polish, she picked it up quickly. She also requested that Arne and Coos talk with her in Danish and Dutch. Coos was amused by her questions from books read in school: "Do the Dutch really wear wooden shoes? Have you skated on the canals? Do you know Hans Brinker? Do you own a windmill?" Sarah asked Dieter for help with Czech and German, and he brushed her off.

Sometimes Sarah felt a little sad or lonely. If her mother was busy helping partisans with health problems, or Gwidon was working with his father, or Flora was busy she would go to Steve or Rick for a quiet talk, a little game or a hug. "If I ever go to America could I visit you?"

"Of course you'll visit me. Your mother gave me your grandparents' address in London, and I gave her my parents' address in Chicago. I know Rick did the same." Then they joined hands, spun themselves silly around the yard and fell into a belly-laughing heap.

32

"*HÄNDE HOCH ODER ES KNALLT.*"

The next day Piotr talked with the Americans, "George hear in town Nazis movink Jews out of Auschwitz-Birkenau back to Germany, Russians comink. Need to tell my brother, go with radio, check trains going west. Look *odległy*, um, way far beyond tracks where you meet Wachowiacks. There is underground group out there, big man." Piotr spread his arms wide side to side then top to bottom. "I met once few years back and not remember name, my brother knows him. I do not think you see them. If you do, may know 'Greta' password."

Rick and Steve went on a deep mission without other partisans for the second time. Flora fixed food and gave them long underwear she and the other women made. Stefan checked their firearms. Lev drew a map with landmarks over forty kilometers west. "Many more Germans closer to Czech border, patrols, more checkpoints."

Rick and Steve left at 0500 under thick clouds and light snow. They talked little, and when they did their frosty breaths framed the words like dialogue balloons in comic strips. They had learned from Piotr, Tereza, Lev and others how to track their way silently like Indian scouts. A fox, long-tailed and red-coated, crossed their path fifty meters ahead. The fox paused, gave them an appraising look and scurried into the woods. Steve said, "I doubt we'll see people in red jackets on horseback chasing Reynard."

"Reynard, that's good. I don't know why these things stick in my mind from classes I've taken, but I think it was Oscar Wilde who described fox hunting as 'The unspeakable in pursuit of the inedible.'"

"I like that, but how do you come up with this stuff? I love to read but forget everything, must be stupid."

Around ten kilometers out they ate something, set up the radio and Steve sent Piotr's message. The answer came back quickly and more information followed. "Hey, Rick, Josef and Paul Wachiowak are coming back to the farm, but it didn't say when or why. Think we should go back and tell Piotr?"

"I hope I'm not wrong, but I think we're too far out. We'd better finish this job and hurry back. Want to try them again and ask the question?" Steve tapped out the question and didn't receive a reply.

"Think one of us should go back?" Steve asked.

"No, if you and I are going to get out of this shit alive, it's going to take us sticking together and watching each other's backs. Besides, you'd probably get lost without me."

"I guess you're right, and incidentally, fuck you." Rick laughed.

It was too cold to lie on the ground so they walked all day, through the night and into the next day, stopping only for eating, checking the map and dozing while leaning against a tree. In the early afternoon they found a sunny, grassy spot in the middle of a meadow and lay down for a snooze. They knew it was exposed, but the winter grass was high, and they couldn't keep their eyes open.

A horse's snuffling woke them an hour later. They saw a girl in her mid-teens, astride an old plug, holding a rifle that was pointed at them. She had a broad body and face and flaxen pigtails hanging down to her waist. She spoke in a deep, mature, intelligent voice, "You do not look like Nazis. What are you?"

"Americans, Greta," Steve said.

She waggled her rifle. "Do not move until I tell you to. I know no Greta. Where do you live in America?"

"Chicago."

Her expressive eyes widened. "I know of Chicago. You cannot fool me. I have map of Chicago my cousin sent, name streets in Chicago with Polish names."

"Komensky."

"Pulaski."

"Cermak."

"Where is Polish Village Chicago?"

"Avondale."

"Cermak is Czech, but I believe you. Sound like American relatives, visited us. They came from Chicago and had same strange 'a' sound in speech you say in Pulaski and Avondale."

She put the rifle across her lap. "Come. Walk in front of horse."

Steve thought: *Between this and the first meeting in the barn with Piotr, it's saved our asses to be from Chicago.*

An hour later, after following a twisting path west through the woods, the girl stopped, cupped her hands and gave a low but penetrating birdlike warble. After walking for a minute more, three previously unseen men holding rifles stepped out of the woods. The girl said, "Americans."

The horse whinnied and defecated, and the group moved on with one of the partisan men holding his nose with the forefinger and thumb of an elaborately inverted hand.

They soon reached a farm similar in scope to the Pitulski's, and the girl gave the familiar warble. Her father, the local resistance leader, an adamantine mountain of a man came out of the farmhouse front door, crossed the porch and stepped down into the yard.

Steve thought: *Good tackle for the Chicago Bears*, and Rick was reminded of the foraging bear back in the forest.

The girl again said, "Americans."

The leader's greeting was level-eyed, bass-voiced and firm, "Where you come from?"

"Partisans southwest of Oswiecim," Rick said.

"How you find?"

"Walked, we were shot down, escaped from a German jail."

"What does leader look like?" Steve slashed a mustache across his upper lip and stuck ten fingers above his head.

"Ah, met him once know brother." He pointed north and Steve grinned.

"Son of brother's name?" Steve knelt in the dirt, supplicated, crossed himself and drew a nimbus over his head. The skeptical leader was finally convinced.

Steve should've been an actor, Rick thought.

The leader pointed to Steve's radio. "Our radio broken, will you send messages? You do code?" Steve answered yes to both questions. They entered the house and were taken into the kitchen. The girl sat passively next to her even-more-broad-beamed mother. Stalwart partisans of both sexes ringed the room. They looked like a nice group to have on your side. The mother and girl got up, went to a cupboard and brought out a jug and cups. They poured vodka and passed it around. No one drank until the leader looked to the Americans, raised his cup and said *"na zdrowzie."* All the rest said *"na zdrowie"* and drained their drinks.

Like the farm of Flora and George, the leader's property was small, efficient and self-supporting. The Americans didn't know where the partisans hid when the Nazis came, if they did come. And they didn't ask. They had a filling meal with endless rounds of vodka at a long, rustic kitchen table. Slightly thick in the tongue, Rick and Steve told their stories and the partisans told theirs with the daughter interpreting as needed.

The mood was light with the leader holding court, telling some earthy jokes and slapping his wife's considerable behind as she walked by. Seeing the American's drooping eyes, the wife cracked her hands, motioned everyone up, told Rick and Steve to *sikać* outside, brought them to couches in a parlor and put her hands together at her temple in a sleeping pose.

The wife shook them at first light. They slept eleven hours covered in thick blankets. After breakfast, they met alone with the leader and a squat partisan whose wide, impassive face resembled an Easter Island statue. His neck was wider than his head and anchoring that muscle mass was a body shaped like an oil drum with stove-pipe arms and legs. Steve thought: *Don't think I'll challenge him to a wrestling match, break my back in a bear hug.*

"Here are radio messages, important," the leader said. "We go west far, send messages see tracks you asked for, watch trains. I also show Nazi cave. We find what they hide."

The two partisans and the Americans walked west on a cold, clear day, keeping inside the woods, but within sight of the lowland grassy meadows along a tributary of the Odra River. The leader signaled, and they moved farther up into the foothills and paused. Steve set up the radio, found the correct frequency and sent the leader's messages. They waited for the reply, but none came and they resumed the hike.

An hour later, the leader motioned for them to stop. He moved ahead alone with quiet, athletic foot plants. After about forty meters he dropped, went on all fours and disappeared into the undergrowth. A few minutes later came the same low warble used by his daughter.

The Americans followed the leader's lieutenant, as they walked silently in single file until they saw the leader prone looking through field glasses. He waved them up the escarpment; and like him they clambered the last ten meters, until the four lay parallel at the edge of a cliff. Far below, a long freight train was stopped on a curve, and they could see people moving about on the side of the tracks nearest them.

The leader passed the binoculars to his lieutenant who scanned the scene several times, shook his head and handed the glasses to Rick. Armed SS guards stood next to the tracks. The freight car doors were open, and bodies were being tossed into a ditch beyond the tracks. Rick passed the field glasses to Steve who observed for a half-minute and asked the leader what was going on.

"Nazis know *Radziecki*, uh, Soviet Army near. They send Jews from Oswiecim to Germany. Ones who die are thrown out of cars by other Jews. They do this or are shot. Same thing Oswiecim, SS make Jews take their own out of gas chambers and put in ovens. That is smell near Oswiecim."

I wonder if they made Coos and Arne put their own families in the ovens, Rick thought.

"Can we blow the tracks?" Steve asked.

"Will do no good, they fix tracks. We must save explosives for when Nazis flee Russians. Then we blow tracks and roads, airplane fields, kill Nazis. We hope war is over before too many more Jews are gassed." Rick and Steve thought of Jean, Sarah, Coos and Arne and how they could save them.

"Now I show you somethink else." The prodigious leader, who had the grace of a gymnast, flipped over, rotated head to heel and crab-walked backwards five meters from the cliff's edge. The others emulated his moves with varying degrees of success. They stood and descended from the high outlook. When the savanna was near, they could hear the train chugging away from them in the distance. They reached a narrow point in the tributary and crossed by holding onto the branches of a fallen tree. Rick looked down at the rushing water full of ice chunks: *You'd freeze to death out here in the cold if you fell in.*

They came to the train tracks and crossed them. At this point, the tracks headed northwest, east of the Czech border, toward Germany. Steve thought: *I used to love the trains and the sound of the tracks clicking below. Never feel that way again.*

They slogged across frozen marshes and up into hills that were steeper on the north side of the tributary. Lowering clouds formed, and a biting wind blew a freezing drizzle that stung like sharp needles on their faces. Footing became difficult as ice surfacing the snow made the path slick. The Americans pulled their caps down and scarves up while the partisans soldiered on, hardened to the cold, necks open, hats pushed back on their heads. The humongous leader and his thick-bodied lieutenant moved nimbly, and the Americans had to break into an occasional trot to keep up as the drizzle turned to snow.

Steve suggested another transmission attempt, and the leader said no, the Nazis are too close. The pace slowed, and the leader frequently held his hand up. They stopped thirty meters from a dirt road barely wide enough for two vehicles to pass. After listening for a minute or so, trying to hear above the wind and snow rustling through the few remaining oak leaves, they crossed the road in quickstep and trudged up a sharply-inclined, densely-wooded hill.

They climbed north for a thousand meters and then west for about five-hundred. Soon they stopped near another crest. The leader edged forward, lay down and motioned the other three up. The road they crossed earlier snaked through the valley below them. Above them a white-tailed eagle with wide, slotted wings soared on the updraft searching for its prey.

The eagle beat its wings and flew out of sight as a large van came along, pulled off the road and stopped. The driver and the man sitting in the passenger seat were gray-clad German soldiers. They got out, swung open the rear doors, let a ramp down, and two more soldiers came out of the truck and walked down.

The four lit cigarettes and talked, occasionally gesturing toward a higher place that was out of sight to the four men watching from above. It appeared from the group dynamics that one of the Germans was an officer or at least a noncom. Soon, they ground out the cigarettes. The four tramped uphill through the snow, paused for about a minute and disappeared inside.

Soon, the four partners in theft came out single file, each carrying a crate. They climbed the truck ramp and quickly reappeared to repeat the process. On the second trip down the hill one of the soldiers lugged a head and neck sculpture. Rick thought: *Possibly a Rodin.*

Another German stepped carefully down toward the truck carrying an uncrated painting in each hand. All four worked nonstop, and some of the bulkier crates required a two-man carry. On one of these, the lead man slipped. The crate dropped and careered down the path like a runaway toboggan, accompanied by *"Kamel, Scheiße, Trottel"* and a few more choice maledictions.

Following the mishap and recovery, thoroughly enjoyed by the four watching from above, two Germans descended gingerly each carrying what looked like violin and cello-sized cases.

Rick whispered, "It's obvious they've hidden stolen loot, mostly artwork in a cave. I guess they're taking it away to store someplace else."

"Nazis come here before, always bring things in," the partisan leader said. "We go down, stop them before they take all away."

Steve asked the leader, "Why did they pick this place?"

"Good cave, short truck ride to railroad, Silesia close to Germany."

"How did they find the cave?" Rick asked.

"Informers, we will find and hang or shoot later. Many Poles fight Nazis; help Jews, but not all. Some spy and steal. Take advantage of war, people hunted like animals, bad." He spit on the ground.

He described the plan: They would, under the cover of thick snow, and the sound of the idling truck, capture the Germans, steal the truck and hide the contents. "Do not kill Germans, unless you will be killed."

"Do you have a place to hide the stuff until the Russians come?" Steve asked. "And can we get the truck there without being stopped by German patrols?"

"Yes, ten kilometers southeast of farm. I know back roads."

They picked their way down the hill and set up, the partisans situated above the truck away from the path to the cave. The Americans dashed into the woods across the road. They waited until the four Germans finished clearing out the storehouse and were having cigarettes before raising the ramp and locking the back of the truck. They heard one loud-voiced German say in answer to a muffled question, *"Ja, meisterworks."*

The partisan leader shouted in a voice that could start an avalanche, *"Hände hoch oder es knallt!"* The German sergeant went for his weapon, and the partisan leader's bullet whined just over his head snapping through branches in its path. All four Germans raised their arms to the stretching point. Further orders put them face down on the ground with hands stretched out in front.

While the leader's second in command stood watch at the truck, the leader and the Americans secured the Germans' weapons, blindfolded them, tied their hands behind their backs, taped their mouths, got them on their feet and marched them up the hill to the cave opening. They removed a lashed-together canopy of branches, leaves and twigs cleverly fastened to the wood-door opening by hidden twine. The leader relieved the sergeant of his key ring. He unlocked the massive padlock on the door. Rick and the leader entered. Steve guarded the prisoners sitting on the ground outside. One of them struggled with his bonds, and a sharp jab of the pistol barrel to the back of the neck ended that.

With flashlights casting mean shadows, they crouched through a narrow passage and came to an undisguised inner door. One of the keys opened that lock; and they entered what seemed to be a natural cave, deep under the slope of the hill. The room was lined with shelves, and thick wooden pallets covered most of the floor. The temperature was moderate with comfortable humidity, an ideal room for storing valuable objects. All of the smuggled goods had been removed.

The two men exited, and Rick suggested that Steve take a look. Just as he emerged, they heard a motorcycle approaching from the west. There wasn't time to get down to the truck so they waited. The partisan lieutenant hid in front of the van with his face disguised by a pulled-up scarf. When the motorcycle stopped and the engine turned off he stepped around the van loudly ordering, *"Hände hoch! Hände hoch! Mach schnell!"*

The motorcycle had a sidecar in which sat a German soldier. The driver was aggressive. He dove to the side and rolled while trying to extract his weapon. The lieutenant pitted the roadway on each side of the evasive target.

Taking advantage of the *pas de deux*, the sidecar occupant raised a machine pistol. The lieutenant shot it out of his grip, and it clunked on the roadway. The soldier raised two quivering hands over his head, one dripping blood.

While Rick and the leader covered the Nazis at the cave mouth, Steve rocketed down the path, scarf up to his eyes. He quickly had his pistol muzzle at the back of the driver's head and disarmed him. The partisan lieutenant lifted the sidecar passenger out of his seat and threw him face down on the road. The two were blindfolded, bound at the wrists, a cloth was tied around the bloody hand, mouths were taped, and they were guided up the hill by pistol barrels pressed into their backs.

The six Germans were frog-marched into the cave where they were hog-tied and all six roped together in a circle facing each other. The doors were padlocked and the keys thrown deep into the woods. Rick said, "They'll live. Their buddies will come looking for them in a few hours, and are they going to catch heavy shit from the brass."

They wheeled the motorcycle across the road, slashed the tires, bent the spokes and pushed the bike out of sight into a deep hollow. Those keys were also tossed where only a miracle would find them. The lieutenant kept some of the Germans' weapons and ammunition. He smashed the rest against a tree and flung the shells into the woods.

Steve and Rick rode in the back of the van with the leader driving and his lieutenant beside him. Fortunately, there was a sliding window between the cab and the storage area. The Americans could see the road ahead and had enough light filtering in to make out the inventory. The truck was packed to near the roof with crates. The two uncrated paintings, the sculpture and the string-instrument cases were propped on crates near the front. They took the paintings down for a look.

Steve angled one painting to get more light. "My mother loved the impressionists. She had books she showed me when I was little. I can't see the signature, but I'll bet those haystacks are by Cezanne."

"No, Monet. He did the haystacks, lots of them."

"Are you ever wrong?"

"I thought I was once, but was wrong about that."

Steve laughed. "And never in doubt either."

"Well, all you had to do was go down to the Chicago Art Institute and see for yourself."

"Remind me when we get back. I'll hop off the train at Union Station, not even stop for a beer, go right there. Christ, I'm thirsty wouldn't a beer go nice right now?"

"Those Germans weren't very thoughtful. The least they could have done was bring a few. I hear the country's one big brewery."

"Let's look in those violin cases back there . . . Jesus, look at that wood, like a honey color. There's a label under that hole. I can't read it in the light. Think it's a Stradivarius?"

"If it is, it's worth a lot of dough."

"The case must be expensive, too. Look at the purple fur inside. Wonder who they stole it from?"

"I'm sure some unlucky bastard who probably got shot trying to hide it from them. I hope the leader knows how to avoid Krauts. He sure can't avoid potholes. I don't think this new turnoff is even a road." They held the paintings on their laps. The sculpture wobbled between Rick's ankles. *The only ride bumpier was the kidney-cracking PT-Boat.*

"I doubt if the Russians get their mitts on these they'll ever give them back."

"I don't know, but for sure the Nazis wouldn't. I wonder how much shit the Nazis stole?"

"Lots . . . I was just thinking about Josef and his cousin. They're probably at the farm. What do you think is up?"

"Maybe it's about the Russians and how we meet up with them. They'll be shooting everything that moves."

"And some things that don't. They've been fighting Nazis for what, four years?"

"The leader can drive. I think we're going through just woods now, and this is a big rig."

"My ass is broken. If he turns this thing over, your ass and mine will be dead under these crates."

Rick reached through the window and tapped the leader on the shoulder. "How much farther?"

"Five, six kilometers." Rick and Steve shook their heads as the leader made one more wild turn, the truck tilted sharply, the crates threatened to crash on their heads, and the bucking-bronco climb up into and east across the foothills continued. The two Americans were now standing with their arms outstretched trying to contain the piled-up artwork. They feared for the two uncrated paintings that were now unprotected, and the Rodin bust rolled and bumped against their feet.

I thought the half-track was bad. It was a Sunday drive compared to this.

"Don't these two madmen ever stop to piss, eat a live squirrel?"

"I can't stop thinking about a chocolate milkshake."

"And a burger, couple of beers, some bratwurst."

"The day games, Cubs, Bears, those bars near Wrigley."

They ascended higher; it grew colder, and the crates slowly shifted toward the back doors. Then, suddenly, they leveled off and stopped with a jolt that made the Americans grab for a handhold. Rick went to the cab rear window. "Open the back door slowly, the crates shifted." They checked the two uncrated paintings, and although the frames had some dings the canvases seemed okay. The putative Rodin was smudged, and when Steve rubbed the surface with his sleeve it looked undamaged.

They climbed up, reached over the stack toward the rear of the van and held the top crates while the two partisans opened the rear doors. Everything stayed aboard. The leader said, "We hide them here."

"Where?" Rick asked.

The leader pointed. "In cave, Roman and I hunted in woods as boys. We know all caves, Nazi cave, this cave, many."

Now the Americans had one name, but in the spirit of this particular partisan group they didn't use it to address the tight-lipped lieutenant. The leader walked a few steps, cleared away some brush and leaves, and there was the opening, just big enough for the leader to wiggle through. "Hello, any bears and wolves inside?" He cocked his head, cupped his ear and chuckled to himself.

The Americans took the crates off the truck, lay down at the opening and pushed them through. The partisans pulled the crates inside the cave and stacked them. The cave was not as clean, wide or deep as the last one, but roomy enough to hold all the goods. When they finished and disguised the opening, Steve asked, "Do you have any food or water?"

Roman pulled a half-loaf of thick-crusted bread out of his jacket pocket, tore it into four pieces, and they champed like famished dogs. The leader grinned. "No water, *wódka*," and pulled a small flask from his pocket. The bread was gamey, so the burning vodka hid the taste, wet their throats and offered a slight lift.

The leader said, "I think I not tell Russians, will tell Polish government when Germans and Russians leave Poland."

"Do you think the Russians will leave?"

The leader frowned. "If they not leave, I tell Russians and hope they do not steal and send all back where it came from. Maybe some is theirs stolen by Nazis. Can't leave in cave too long, will rot.

"Now you are closer east, take truck few kilometers, hide in woods walk back. We go home. You are good men. Go with God." They hugged the Americans and kissed their cheeks. Then, lugging the German guns, they walked down the hill without a backward wave of hands.

"Do you want to drive this thing, ever drive a truck?"

"No and yes, but you drive, you're the pilot, I'm only a radio operator."

The truck lights pierced the gathering gloom; as Rick moved the van slowly through the forest, fumbling with the shift, cursing the clutch and the whole lousy world.

"Watch out for the boulder." Rick jerked the wheel left and then quickly right scraping paint off the side as the truck lurched against a tree. "First, I almost died when you crashed the plane. Now I know I'll die the way you're driving."

"Well, fuck me, if you're so good why don't you try it? And what's this, *I* crashed the plane bullshit?"

"No, my chances are bad with you, but they'd be worse with me driving." Rick smiled.

They found the bare semblance of a path and poked along, dimmed headlights reflecting the dense snow. The cab had minimal heat, a thin, lukewarm stream that was no help to the inside of the frosty windshield. As Steve rubbed at it, they came over a slight rise and gathered unwanted momentum on an unexpectedly long and steep downhill run. Rick tapped the brakes, and the bulky van swung sideways, bounced off a tree trunk and resumed its skid down the slope. Steve said, "Holy shit, I hope there's no cliff down at the bottom of this ski jump," and he thought of his buddy Lou, the half-track driver.

Fifty-meters-out-of-control later, Rick saw a big rock in the path and spun the wheel hard left. The truck swung sideways, the rear end bashed a tree, peeled away, careened off the path, pitched down a small hill, sideswiped another tree and slowly rolled over, as if in slow motion, ending upside down with all wheels spinning. The back end settled at an angle against a dangerously small tree leaving the dizzied occupants sprawled against the cab roof. Rick still hung onto the steering wheel. "I think I tore my arms out of their sockets. You'd better get the hell out before I land on you."

"I take it all back," Steve said. "You didn't kill us."

"Let's get out of here in case this thing catches on fire."

Steve threw his weight against the passenger-side door and it opened a crack. Then he got his feet against it; and it squeaked open enough to let them squeeze out, jump to the ground, lose their footing and roll through the snow into a deep gorge below the truck. The precariously balanced truck was above them, and its weight shifted ominously in the snow. The tree bent like a bow and its agitated branches released a shower onto them.

The deluge of soft ice and wet snow soaked their heads, and they realized the hard way that they'd lost their wool caps in the rollover. While fearing the truck would break loose and crush them they had to scrape and claw out of the ice bowl they were skating around in, fish around the cab to find the caps and the radio which had been under Steve's feet. "I'm glad it was the ice not the radio that conked us."

As they stumbled and struggled up to what they thought was a path, Rick said, "I think we're far enough east from the cave, maybe a couple of kilometers, so that someone finding the truck won't connect it."

The tree snapped, and the truck plunged into the gorge they just vacated. "Nobody sees it down there," Steve said. "I wonder how many lives we have left?"

"We're nowhere near nine yet."

"Speak for yourself."

"Nobody but an animal who likes art finds that cave either. Let's try to get some direction and find the farm. I'm soaked and my feet are frozen. I hope Jean doesn't have to cut off our toes and fingers."

"I'm more worried about my privates, unless the cold has shrunk me into a girl."

"Why don't you get on the horn and contact Armed Forces Radio or somebody and report two Americans lost on a Polish mountain in a German truck."

"Sounds like a bad joke."

"It is a bad joke. After that spinout, I haven't got a hint which way is up or where."

"What happened to your bump of direction?"

"My body's covered in bumps, and direction's not one of them. Anyway, according to the leader we headed east so let's keep going the same way."

The snow turned again to freezing rain making the footing more treacherous. The radio was busted in the truck turnover, along with the compass, and the flashlight's beam was thread-narrow. "Hope we don't run into the bear."

"He's too smart to be out in this, probably in a cozy cave making cubs with mama bear."

"Maybe they're having cocktails and enjoying the artwork."

"Let's hit the next bar we see."

"I think we missed last call. I never thought I'd say this, but I'd take a cup of coffee."

"Or cocoa, remember after skating?"

"After this, I'll never go on ice again, even for hot chocolate."

The joking around didn't last long. Soon, the only sound, except for the occasional sit-down spill and wet slide into a defile accompanied by the requisite string of curses, was the incessant crunch, crunch, crunch of boots on ice and snow. They were nearly out on their feet from hunger and overexertion when, seven hours later, they staggered onto the farm road.

The freezing rain and snow stopped, the clouds cleared, the temperature dove, and a three-quarter moon shone some helpful rays. A sharp north wind blew the congealing cold through their stiff clothes and icicle-filled hair under the damp, snow-crusted caps. After being struck by the full burdens of winter, they could barely put one benumbed foot in front of the other. When they got near the farm's perimeter they tried the code whistle, but their cracked and unfeeling lips couldn't form the necessary embouchure and only air came out. To avoid getting shot by the ever-alert partisan sentries, they broke the rules and shouted the verbal code. A guard answered, raced over, saw their state, and bolted to the house.

Shadows from a flickering candle danced across the faces of partisans in deep discussion at the kitchen table. The sentry burst into the kitchen, and the candle blew out. "Help freezink *Amerykanins* on road." Four of the bigger men ran out, put Steve's and Rick's arms over their shoulders, and supported their weight. Lights were switched on, and the group surrounded the door as they were brought in.

Jean said, "Lay them down in front of the stove on a blanket and strip off their clothes. Get more blankets, my bag and warm water, some small towels or clean rags." Gabriel, Tereza and Agnes raced upstairs and quickly came back with armloads of blankets and Jean's medical satchel. Two of the men went to the sink, pumped water into a bucket and hung it on a hook over the fire.

"It's good their extremities are white not black," Jean said. "They have frostbite, but I don't think it's dangerous, we'll see. Now everyone kneel down around them, get down close and blow on their skin, especially their toes, fingers, lips, ears, noses. That's right, keep doing it all over. Is the water warm yet? We don't want it hot."

Flora said it was warm. "All right, dip the rags into it, wring them out a little so they don't drip and bring them to me." She first draped the warm cloths over the most vulnerable parts of their bodies. "More rags, cloths anything." Some of the men stripped off their shirts and dipped those. "Good, now keep going. Take these rags and dip them again . . . too hot. Take the water off the fire, and put the bucket on the floor. Add a little cold water and stir it . . . good. See their skin is getting a little color. We can't stop the warm-water cloths. They have hypothermia. Let them drink a little warm water. Add a small amount of vodka to the cup, George . . . that's enough. Now stir it in. Just little sips, men. Urban, Jerek, please put your palms over their ears. Don't press or rub."

The treatment went on for another hour while both slept. They had long since stopped shivering and chattering. Jean applied lukewarm cloths now, the skin got redder, and she and Flora gently massaged their toes. "Gertrude, Lev, massage their fingers, very soft pressure." After another fifteen minutes the curative measures ended.

"Now please get some clean, warm clothes and we'll dress them, no boots, just thick socks. We need wool hats to keep their body heat in." The men were now able to sit up and also stand while they were helped to dress. Other than the occasional mumbled "Thank you," they both were too depleted to speak.

"Some of you men go to the cellar and bring their cots up here. They need to sleep in front of the fire. I'll stay with them and drowse in a chair. Thank you all. You've done a wonderful job."

Jean fed the fire with logs cut by Gwidon. Both men spoke out in their sleep, and she stroked foreheads and felt to see if fingers, toes, noses and ears were warm enough. She pulled the caps down over their ears. They both woke up when George and Flora came into the kitchen at five o'clock. Jean said, "I'm taking Rick and Steve upstairs and put them in bed for more sleep. One will use my bed the other yours if that is acceptable." They happily agreed.

"Can you walk?" They sat up with groans and stood. Each took a few steps, moving like sharp pebbles were underfoot. "It will take a few days before your feet get back to normal. Now you need more sleep. Can you climb the stairs?" They murmured something in agreement. It was difficult for them, but they made it and slept until dusk.

Sarah came downstairs a few hours after the men went up. "Mommy, why is Steve in your bed? Were you in there with him?" The partisans at breakfast howled; and Sarah did a little jig, tickled she said something that made everyone laugh.

33

"WE LEAVE BEFORE NAZIS COME, REACH RUSSIAN LINES."

Around seven in the evening Jean checked on the men in their beds and found them healthy enough to come downstairs and eat. George and Flora worked at the sink. Piotr came in to talk with them, "Jean say you frozetbite in storm. Not so bad up north."

Steve asked, "Did Josef and Paul come down?"

"They signal sentry, say they want meeting away from farm and left. Urban run in to tell me, run back, other sentry cover for him. Dieter and I met ten kilometers north at place we both know. They say we have traitor here, but not who it is. I know from look you think Dieter is traitor. I do not think Dieter, but," and he shrugged.

"How do they know there is a traitor?" Rick asked.

"Before they tell me we hear Nazi patrol west, dogs way off coming to us. They run północny, oh, north, we run back to farm. Never know why they think this."

"What are you going to do?"

"We leave before Nazis come, reach Russian lines." Stefan came into the kitchen. "Stefan, everybody at farm, do count?"

A few minutes later Stefan came in with Lev. "Magda's not here."

"Do women know where?" Two different partisan women had seen her sneak out at night through the tunnel in the past few weeks and said nothing.

The second of them who saw her leave confronted Magda the next day. "I had to go help sick relatives and swear I will not go again. You know Piotr lets no one off farm. Please do not tell him." And now, fearing Piotr's wrath, the two women kept quiet.

"No," Lev said. "She was gone after the meal, maybe in the night through the tunnel."

George stopped tossing logs into the stove and turned toward Piotr. "I should have spoke before but did not think too much. Magda went with me to town last week to help in market. See her talking long to SS officer buying dried fruit. I see at farm once, ordered us to bring food, not Herrmann. When German left she touched his arm. I asked her what she was talking about with German so long. She said, 'Oh, nothing, just food.' I did not like her touching his arm, should have told you, Piotr. I am sorry."

"It is all right, George, we thought she was good person. Stefan, Lev get everybody armed now, grenades. Bring me machine gun. Richard, Steven can you fight?"

They said that they could.

"I know Germans, always plan, wait until ready, will not come before early light tomorrow, if they come. Lev, put four guards corners of farm all night, another far down road, change them at eleven o'clock. We leave at two o'clock, everybody with light pack, guns, ammunition.

"Now, boys you see?" Piotr extended his arms high to low then side to side. They nodded. "Nazis ship Jews west, north from Oswiecim?"

"We saw what was probably a trainload," Rick said.

"How you know?"

"The train stopped for a while, and dead people were being thrown out of the cars."

Piotr shook his head in disgust. "Any big Nazi troops go west?"

"Not that we saw," Steve said.

Piotr ran a hand through his hair. It sprung up like wire. "Anythink else?"

Rick said, "We saw Nazis take crates, mostly artwork we think, from a cave the leader knew about and put it in a truck."

"Did you stop Nazis?"

"We locked them in the cave and took the truck to another cave up in the hills the leader knew about. Then we ditched the truck and walked back."

"You did good job. Now get more sleep. You will need it. We wake you at one."

After the Americans went down to their cots, Lev, Stefan and Dieter came into the kitchen. Flora, George and Tereza were already there, cooking. Lev said, "Guards on the way."

"Everybody has gun and grenades," Stefan said. "Here is the machine gun loaded, extra clips, grenades."

"I talked with some of our people," Dieter said. "They think we're safer here instead of running alone through the woods."

"Maybe Nazi just wanted Magda's body. She wants him and money, doesn't tell," Flora added.

Piotr scowled. "We not risk her not telling."

"Do you think Nazis too busy running from Russians to bother us?" Tereza asked.

"If Magda tell Nazis we have Americans or Jews they come," Piotr said. "They ship Jews from Oswiecim to Germany so they can kill more. Nazis have no sense when they want Jews. Now listen, if Nazis come they come with big trucks, many men. They have no way here except road. I do not believe they will sneak into farm through woods. They like big force. We have lookouts. Tell everyone to sleep with clothes, gun next to bed. If Nazis come on road we have time to scatter or fight here. We not kill many Nazis for long time, too much revenge. Now they are on run and will taste our bullets. Now go to bed, sleep and be ready. We meet at six. George, are keys in truck?"

"Yes, Piotr."

Jean listened briefly at the top of the stairs. *I must somehow get Sarah out of this. I hope Rick and Steve are up to a fight or a run for our lives. Lev will help us, Piotr. Are Coos and Arne strong enough?*

Steve woke at five-thirty and shook Rick. "I guess they didn't clear out. Let's see what's up." He stood. "Feet are a little better."

Rick got up and walked in place. "Less sore, but I wouldn't want have to walk too far just yet. Remind me when we get back to Chicago to move to Miami."

All partisan fighters not on sentry duty met in the barn. Piotr asked, "Does anyone want to leave?" Nobody raised a hand. "Good, no one is allowed to leave; you caught Nazis torture, learn where we are. I decide we stay here, Russians comink maybe before Nazis. This is market day, George, right?" George said it was. "I not like sayink, but you must go so Nazis not suspect and come looking. Find out what you can. Bring pies and cakes to Herrmann. You bake, Flora?"

"Always, Piotr. Tereza, Agnes and I made last night for George to take to Nazis. I do not like George going alone. May I go with him?"

"Have you gone with him before, Nazis see you?"

"No, Piotr."

"I am sorry, Flora, you cannot go now may get them thinking. George go alone; right, George?"

"If you say, Piotr."

"Now everybody on watch and listen: when Nazis come, get out of cellar and barn, wait in groups of three inside woods, groups spread out over whole edge of farm two-hundred meters apart. Talk who goes where, pick point. Tell Lev who will make map. We will have . . ." Piotr crossed his arms pointing in opposite directions.

"Intersecting fire."

"Yes, *dzięki*, Steven."

"They not have enough men to cover us all. If they come for you wait until close then shoot them and run east. Stay in woods, try to find Russians. If Nazis do not come for you, shoot them in barnyard. They need rifles, Stefan.

"George, try to get petrol from Herrmann. We may need truck for Jean, Sarah, Arne, Coos cannot run fast. Get breakfast now. Others help George, Gwidon get food and load truck, everybody do farm work pigs, cows, chickens. George, look around town, anything new, see if Germans leaving?"

"Yes, Piotr."

"Richard, Steven, Lev, Dieter, me stay inside buildinks, fight from here draw them off you. We will kill the Nazis, God willing. Oh, Stefan, you stay around here, bring ammunition. Get bags ready now."

Piotr asked the four who would fight from the buildings to wait, and the rest of the partisans left to perform their duties. "Now, what are your ideas?"

"Two of us should be in the front upstairs windows of the farmhouse," Steve said. "I suggest Rick and myself. One in the barn loft and another inside the truck shed. All of us at the high points can throw grenades down on the Germans and also have a clean field of fire. The man in the shed needs a submachine gun."

"That will be me. I like plan, Steven, you know combat."

Dieter said, "Lev, if you will take the barn loft I will go down the road and roll grenades under the trucks."

"Good, Dieter. Also have other man on road bring grenades," Piotr said. "Ask Stefan for submachine gun. You will be low, need to spray after grenade before you run. Go east, do not come back here. No matter, we all run from more Germans coming soon."

"What about Flora, George, Gwidon?" Rick asked.

"They hide in woods with others who protect them, take them east to Russians. They come back to farm after Germans leave."

"Jean and Sarah, Arne, Coos?"

"They must stay in cellar until we kill Germans."

"But won't the Germans know about the cellar from Magda, if she does go over?"

"Yes, correct, oh, hiding place behind room where Jean and Sarah sleep, I forget. Kitchen stove pipe go through, some heat. We keep them there."

"Does Magda know about it?"

"No, only me, Gwidon, George, Flora."

"Could Gwidon have told Magda?" Steve asked.

"No, he forget, not talk good. He hates Magda. She *flirtować*, tease him with body, poor Gwidon."

"What are you going to do, Piotr, when this is all over?" Rick asked.

"Tereza and I find small farm like this, just right size. Raise many children. That is all."

34

"I do not believe you, Schnitzel."

Most everyone in town knew the Russians would arrive any day. Individuals and small-store owners came early to George's truck, and he was sold out well before noon. Since it was winter, supplies were lean, mostly eggs, yogurt, other milk products, bread and pastries. A few German soldiers stopped by and were disappointed Magda was not there. George saw no officers.

Just as he finished loading the empty boxes into the back of the truck he saw Magda slip into the passenger side and scrunch down. George got in. "What do you want, Magda?"

"Please take me to farm, George."

"I cannot, Magda. Piotr will not take back people who leave farm. Go with Germans. You dressed for them with clothes they bought, high shoes, tight dress."

"The German major . . ."

"Herrmann?"

"Herrmann's gone, too; no Schroeder's his name. Said he would take me to Berlin, big house, nice clothes, diamonds, servant. I go to meet him and he left. Soldiers laugh, say, 'He tell all girls they go to Berlin. That is how he gets you in bed.'"

"You tell Schroeder about farm?"

"Nothing, I swear, George. He asked if we hide Jews. I say no. He say, 'I do not believe you, schnitzel.' Schnitzel stupid name, I hate him." She also hated him because he was a pervert who made her pose naked while he pleasured himself. But she was snarled in a web of her own making with no way out.

"Schroeder asked if we hide Americans. I say no. He gave me look like question, eyebrow up. Please take me, George," through torn gasps and tears.

"I cannot take you. Try to find Russians, maybe save you. God help you, Magda."

She got out and walked down the street without looking back. *Maybe find Russian major, swing tits, poor Magda.* A car came around the corner and pulled up beside her. A man in a suit and hat hopped out, pincered Magda's arm as she started to run, pushed her into the back seat, jumped in beside her, and the car roared off.

Gestapo, now she will tell. Why not arrest me?

The local Gestapo officials were fed up to the teeth with being told by Major Herrmann that no one but farmers lived on the farm. But now Herrmann was gone, and they were intent on finding out for themselves or by asking SS units to investigate. The Gestapo did not know if the farm was populated by partisans. Nor did they know whether Americans or Jews were there. Frustrated by numerous fruitless searches over a wide area of southwestern Poland for the two Auschwitz escapees, for Dr. Hellifield and her daughter, and the two Americans they suspected as much and were determined to know one way or the other.

Magda did not consciously disclose secrets before and after her intimacies with Schroeder, but she inadvertently slipped and hints were dropped. The manipulative Schroeder drew her out more than she realized at the time. The Gestapo considered detaining George, but knew that had he gone missing, anyone of interest at the farm would have fled. They did know that Magda had come to town to go off with Major Schroeder. *That rascal Schroeder, all he thought about was bumsen.*

The man in the back seat grabbed a handful of Magda's hair, viciously pulled her head back and repeatedly slapped her face. "You will talk now, yes? Or you will talk later, but you will talk, yes?" When she didn't answer, he put one hand around her throat and squeezed. When he released his grip she gulped and coughed. Her hair, matted with tears, hung over her face. They arrived at Gestapo headquarters, formerly the town hall and police station, now commandeered by Nazis who enforced security for the surrounding area.

Magda was rushed into the building with one arm painfully doubled behind her back. She was shoved through a corridor, down a flight of stairs and thrust into a dark room. A harsh, overhead light flicked on revealing a flat raised table covered by a soiled white sheet and two wooden chairs against the wall. A woman with impassive eyes in a hatchet face came in. She ordered Magda to strip and lie on the table for inspection. Following that humiliation, the woman told Magda to dress and then left the room and locked the door.

Soon a male Gestapo agent entered smiling and closed the door. He spoke to Magda in kind tones apologizing for what she had been put through, explaining that enemies of the Reich were about and how they needed Magda's help to find and punish them. "If you answer my questions truthfully, we will give you a sack of gold coins." He hefted an imaginary sack in his hand. "And you will have safe passage to a place where you are not known and where you can start a new life, but only if you are truthful and tell me all you that you know. If you do not cooperate, well, I shall be forced to turn you over to less sympathetic persons, and you will not like that, will you, Magda?"

Magda's throat ached, perspiration ran down her sides, her heart raced and her feet felt numb. "May I have water?"

"Of course, Magda, anything you want. Would you like food, possibly a pastry?"

"No thank you, just water." Since associates were listening, the water quickly arrived.

"Major Schroeder said you were a good girl, and he was sorry you could not go with him, but circumstances arose preventing that. Now, Magda, we know that the farm where you live is a refuge for many partisans and others. Is that not true?"

"No just the owners and their son and me."

"We are off to a poor beginning, Magda, but I am a patient man. We know that you have two Americans and four Jews at the farm. You do not deny that I hope?"

"I know of no Americans or Jews."

The officer furiously screamed, *"lügner, hure, schlampe.* You will tell me the truth or we will beat it out of you. Now choose." He walked over, and the full backhanded swipe whipped Magda's head to one side hair flying, knocking her off the chair and sprawling on the concrete floor.

After she got back to the chair, his voice returned to comforting tones, "I did not like doing that, Magda. But you forced me to lose my temper." Magda touched the side of her face, red from the blow. "I am a reasonable man who does not like violence, but I also do not like lies. Now please, Magda, you too must be reasonable so we may get along and get to the truth. Let us set aside the question of the Americans and the Jews, although we know that you have two Americans and four Jews, two escaped from Auschwitz. Would you like me to tell you their names? And you have two other Jews, a Doctor Hellifield, or is it Krol, and her child? But let us, in the interest of not confusing important issues, hold off on those questions for the moment. All I ask now is that you simply tell me the partisan leader's name. That is not much to ask, is it?"

"I live and work there with two owners, old man and woman and their *glupi* son, no more people."

The officer got up, walked toward Magda raising his arm. She shrank back. He lowered his arm and shrugged. "You will be sorry, you miserable *mose*," and he left the room.

Two men came in. One of them had a cigarette curling smoke in the corner of his mouth. They grasped Magda's upper arms in vice-like grips and dragged her into an even more stygian room without windows and with one chair. They jerked Magda's hands behind her and tied them to the back of the chair. This round of interrogation included no kind words and unabated torture. Magda was as brave as she could be. She revealed no partisan names, but said there were eight total. She did admit to seeing two Jews, not four. She said they left the farm in fear of being caught.

Despite the unceasing pain of the beatings, she could not bring herself to tell of Jean and Sarah. Jean had been kind, helping her through an acute medical problem, and she adored Sarah. Hoping to save herself, she rasped through broken teeth, lips, nose and bruised larynx of one American at the farm and said that he left a few days before with the two Jews. "We did not want the American and Jews there, the farmers told them to leave. We did not hide them." One of the Gestapo agents left the room.

While standing in front of Magda, the remaining agent barked in her face as spittle flew, "You will be shot for harboring Jews and an American." Full of hate and mustering her last shreds of willpower she kicked him square in the balls. He doubled over vomiting and then hopped around holding himself and yelping. The cries brought the other agent back who ruthlessly beat Magda about the head and neck with a truncheon.

Body covered in bruise and burn marks, one eye swollen shut, suffering from excruciating internal injuries, barely conscious and nearly dead, Magda was dragged into a courtyard, propped up on a stool against a wall without a blindfold and shot by rifle fire. After she fell, the volatile Gestapo interrogator who conducted the first inquisition took a Luger out of his trench coat pocket and put a bullet through her brain. Although the *coup de grâce* was unnecessary, he believed it to be bad form not to follow established custom. The Gestapo section left the town a few hours later with one of the three remaining armored SS contingents fleeing west from the Soviet advance. Magda's crumpled body lay next to the tipped-over stool, the last victim of the local Gestapo's theater of cruelty.

35

"If I die, Piotr, I die with you."

George drove home thinking all the way about how soon the Nazis would raid the farm. *Nazis burn farm, kill us for hiding Jews, Americans. Russians not like Poles. Where can I take Flora, Gwidon? Petrol tank near empty, woods cold.* Since it had been snowing during the past few hours, George was glad that with Steve's and Rick's help they fixed the makeshift wooden plow, reattached it with heavy wire and tightened the rusted struts and bolts. He couldn't risk banging the plow so he kept it about four inches above the ground. The old truck could make it through that much snow but not much more.

The sentries gave the safe whistle as George, spattered by snow and chilled by icy wind flying up through holes in the floorboards, passed them. The worn-out truck clanked and wheezed, as he patted the wheel and eased the cranky throttle in and out. The emergency was the only functioning brake he had left, and shifting down was problematic since adjusting the clutch for what always seemed to be the last time. The tubes and tires had more patches than rubber. But George loved the crumbling wreck and talked to it like an old friend in trouble. He felt lucky when he saw fellow farmers trundling to market in antiquated, horse-drawn wagons.

Everybody within hailing distance came out and cheered, as they followed the puttering truck into the yard. It was like the return of the conquering hero. They all but hoisted George onto their shoulders; Flora embraced him, Gwidon beamed and George smiled bashfully. Piotr said, "In here," and they filed into the barn.

George had traded for tobacco, a rare wartime commodity. He filled and lit his pipe, and they passed it like Indians around a campfire. Some of the women took puffs.

"I see Madga," and everything stopped as though a shot rang out.

"And?" Piotr asked as he handed the pipe back to George?

"Her Nazi leave town, Herrmann, too." He smiled. "I sell his cakes and pies." Flora massaged his back. "Magda wanted to come to farm. I say, no. She said she not tell of our Americans and Jews. I believe her. She said her Nazi major asked if we hide Americans and Jews. She say no, but he look at her like asking question. She is too stupid to know lies. I say find Russians, and she walked down street. Gestapo car came, took her. Will make her tell, did not stop me." George opened his hands. "Should I have brought her back, Piotr? Now Gestapo has Magda. They make her talk."

"You did right, George; either way they will come; today, back truck into shed. Get petrol?"

"I asked soldiers, they laughed."

Gwidon tugged at George's sleeve. "Have petrol, Papa."

"Good boy, Gwidon." He remembered. "I bring Major Herrmann big birthday cake Flora make in summer. He gave extra can if we run out. Gwidon hide in shed rafters.

Get can, Gwidon, put petrol in tank. Not much there, maybe four, five liters." Sarah came into the barn. Gwidon took her hand, and they skipped off singing a simple folk tune.

Piotr said, "Does everybody know duty? Be ready like that," and he snapped his fingers. "Now is time to kill Nazis. If questions see me, Lev, Dieter, Tereza; we meet in better tomorrow, go with God . . . and shoot straight."

Ten days earlier, the Nazis decided to establish a line farther west against the Red Army advance. Many battalions of men and large stores of materiel had already been moved out. One of the remaining sections of the Nazi garrison was scheduled to break camp later that day and now learned of a temporary diversion. In better, less-pressured times they assaulted with overwhelming force. Now they were hurried and short-handed. Magda's courageous lies under torment and in the face of death deceived them into believing that the partisan numbers were far less than the actual strength.

The detachment was one of two left from the remnants of an SS armored division. Only two soldiers had been to the farm on Major Herrmann's scrounging expeditions. Both were privates, and their superiors considered them dolts who never should have been in the Waffen-SS. Neither was involved in searching the farmhouse and barn and had been occupied chasing chickens and making sport of Gwidon. An officer asked them:

"Who was at the farm?"

"An old man and his *frau*, their *dummkopf* son and a *fraulein*." He raised his eyebrows and smirked knowingly, recalling that one of his comrades described Magda's physical attributes on the ride back to the base.

"How many buildings?"

"A house and barn."

"Oh," the other private added, "a little shed."

The SS attack force was told to storm and burn the farm and kill all inhabitants. The phalanx included one truck containing twelve men and two open-style armored personnel carriers or half-tracks, each carrying six men and a heavy machine gun. The mobile force totaled twenty-four and was a kilometer from the farm road at three in the afternoon.

An additional, eight-man SS patrol operating nearby was tasked to trace the farm's perimeter and shoot partisans fleeing into the woods. Steve anticipated this and spoke to Lev about it. Lev told the five partisan groups to guard their rear by positioning one man each up in a tree with a rifle and grenades. Lev also communicated Steve's advice that everyone else in the woods should be prone and remain silent using hand signals only.

The partisan sentry nearest the farm road entrance heard the SS vehicles approaching and signaled his closer-in counterpart who passed on the alert. Gwidon let loose his ear-shattering whistle. Fifteen partisan men and women, along with Flora and George, waited in the barn. On hearing Gwidon's warning they dashed in five directions to the edges of the farm. Gwidon was supposed to go with them, but he misunderstood and stayed put. His parents didn't miss him until they reached their position. George had to be restrained by other men from going back for Gwidon. The SS patrol was now five-hundred meters from the partisans in the woods. Threatening clouds rolled in on gusting wind, snow fell, dusk came early.

The Americans led Jean, Sarah, Arne and Coos upstairs from the kitchen to the bedroom sanctuary. The armoire was pulled aside, the hiding place opened, and they were ready to enter when the ever-adventurous Sarah said, "This is like hiding in the convent bathroom, Steve. Where is Gwidon?"

"He's in the woods with his parents."

"I hope they're safe."

Arne and Coos implored Piotr to let them fight the Germans. After questioning them about their experience he learned that they had been too young for the First World War and too old to enlist in this one and said no. Up in the bedroom they pleaded with Rick and Steve, who also said no, on the grounds that Piotr was in charge, and they would not countermand his orders.

Piotr and Tereza went to the truck shed. He had tried with all his persuasive powers to convince her to go to the woods. "If I die, Piotr, I die with you."

Lev ran into the barn, was surprised to see Gwidon, and said, "Come with me." They climbed into the loft, and Lev showed him again how to fire a rifle and arm and throw a grenade.

Snow clung to eyebrows, lids and the strands of blonde hair spilling out of his cap as Dieter hastened down the road, machine gun hanging from a shoulder strap, grenades jostling on his belt.

The lead SS half-track turned onto the farm road. Urban, the partisan sentry, a small, well-made, quick man edged around out of sight behind a wide-trunked, roadside tree. He had prepared a thick branch stripped of twigs now balanced vertically in meaty hands too big for his body. When the slow-moving half-track reached an opposite point, Urban stepped out smartly, thrust the sturdy limb into the track and receded into the forest. The track dislodged enough to make the vehicle spin sideways, run off the road and bang into a tree. Soldiers tried to fix the track and soon gave up.

As he ran and reached a crest, Urban heard pursuers gaining. He went over the rise, veered left, dropped to the ground, rolled into undergrowth, waited until they were nearly upon him and shot the lead SS in the chest. The man following turned to run, and he was shot between the shoulder blades. Urban listened for other chasers, got up and made certain the Nazis were dead. He waited until the convoy moved out; and decided to re-track, cross the road, follow from back in the woods and distract the assaulters from the rear when they attacked the farm.

Dieter whistled, heard the response and soon joined Jerek, the second sentry nearer the farm. They both had heard the distant gunfire and wondered what it meant. The German soldiers in the disabled armored vehicle crowded into the truck, and they headed down the road. Dieter motioned Jerek back into the woods a few steps. When he saw the convoy, he said, "You shoot the driver of the truck and I shoot out the half-track tires. Then we cut through the forest to the farm." Jerek killed his man and Dieter flattened one of the half-track's front tires. When a helmeted head popped out of the half-track turret Dieter shot it through the neck.

They ran as bullets cracked through leaves and underbrush around them. Dieter made it; Jerek didn't when a bullet impacted the back of his head. Three SS jumped from the truck and chased Dieter, but he had been a four-hundred-meter runner in school, had a head start, and easily outdistanced them. They became disoriented, lost all sense of direction in the snowy forest and tramped northeast away from the farm and north of the town. Their fate lay with the Red Army steamrolling west toward Germany, scouring the land. Dieter jogged toward the farm when he saw through the snowscape the distant, spectral figures of the SS patrol and followed them.

Planning to pick up their bodies on the way out, the Germans placed their dead just inside the woods along the road. The blinding snow formed a near-horizontal white curtain, as the north wind gusted harder. Jerek not only killed the truck driver, his bullet shredded the left wiper on its path through the now-spidery windshield. The replacement driver found visibility severely limited, but he could closely follow the half-track ahead whose operator struggled to keep the cumbersome vehicle with a flat front tire on the road.

Dieter knew from Lev's map the partisan locations in the woods at the edge of the farm. The SS patrol didn't know two things: Urban and Dieter were stalking them, and many partisans were already spread out in the woods. Implementing Steve's sage advice, five of them were now up in trees scanning in all directions. Those on the ground lay in the snow, sighting at three-hundred meters, ready to pick off Germans arriving in the barnyard. George had the foresight to bring a heavy blanket; and he rolled Flora up in it, adjusted her hat and scarf for maximum protection and held her against him.

Back in the upstairs bedroom, Steve said to Rick, "I hear a half-track. If it's like the ones I've seen it has a cannon or heavy machine gun that will cut us to pieces. I'm going to try and knock it out."

"You're a better shot than me from up here. Why don't I go?"

"I've used grenades and you haven't. It's better if you cover me." Steve smiled. "Unless you want to pull rank."

"No, I'll cover you. Keep your head down."

"I'll go out the back door, wave to Lev in the loft and Piotr and Tereza in the shed so they know what I'm doing. Go around the side, up into that little grove of trees above the road where it starts the turn into the farm and drop a couple on the gun."

Steve didn't know that the Nazis already had their troopers out of the truck and were preparing an assault from several angles. Their order was to wait until the machine gun opened up and then go in. As Steve ran up the low hill he saw SS troops coming his way, but they hadn't seen him. The half-track crawled around the bend. Steve pulled two grenade pins, waited two seconds and tossed them underhand toward the machine gun and ducked. One grenade was a dud that clanked against the armored hood and fell away. The other exploded on the hood blowing off the machine gun muzzle.

He slid backwards down the slope, jumped up and ran toward the farmhouse, unhealed feet on fire. Four of the SS were now off the road and in sight of the barnyard. They saw him and opened up. Steve ran low and zigzag while Rick rapid-fired his rifle from the upstairs window, drilling one of the SS through the gut and another in the thigh. As Rick leaned over to put down his empty rifle and grab Steve's loaded one, Steve vaulted up the front steps and rolled across the porch. Sizing up the situation, Piotr left the shed and came in through the back door. He opened the front door, pulled Steve inside, stepped out on the porch with his submachine gun and eliminated two SS who had turned their guns on Rick's empty upstairs window and never saw Piotr.

Piotr beat it through the house and outside toward the shed without first checking for SS. Three entered the backyard, ghostlike in the snow. Steve yelled upstairs to Rick. "Go to the back window and cover Piotr." By the time Rick got to the window, Tereza was kneeling at the shed door with her rifle aimed. She shot one SS dead, put another on the ground wounded and sent the third running for his life which ended when, from the barn loft, Lev got him from the rear through the left aorta. The wounded man tried to crawl away and was stopped by a lethal spray from Piotr's submachine gun.

The Germans retreated to their vehicles to consider a new plan of attack. Except for the horse's whinny, the chickens clucking and the pigs grunting, all was quiet in the barn. As the partisans returned to their posts in the buildings they heard gunfire from the woods to the west.

The SS patrol's members were now in a thirty-meter spread working their way through the forest in a northwesterly direction. Dieter shadowed the trailing soldier from a point deeper in the woods. The Nazi patrol heard the barnyard gunfire and headed toward the farm's boundary. The nearest sentry in a tree saw the Nazi Dieter was following and fired a round that deflected off his helmet. Helmet knocked back on his buzzing head, the soldier turned to run, and Dieter drilled him through the forehead.

The SS lieutenant leading the patrol recognized the situation, saw that they would be shot by snipers in trees or the partisans on their flanks and pulled his men back deeper into the woods. They double-timed east around the farm then southeast back to and up the farm road to join the motorized convoy near the farmhouse.

Dieter diagnosed the intent of the Nazi patrol. He whistled to the nearby snipers in trees and came down to the partisan cluster at the forest edge nearest the farmhouse. After a brief conversation and a series of signals passed along the partisan positions, he brazenly dashed two-hundred meters across the open field. About two-thirds of the way to the buildings, SS troops from the convoy spotted him and opened fire. Dieter cut back and forth through the deepening snow like the football striker he had been in school, as Lev blasted a covering fusillade from the barn loft door and Piotr and Tereza added firepower from the shed. The SS troops suffered casualties and backed off, and Dieter finished his broken-field run with a snow-spraying slide into the shed.

Steve and Rick wanted to meet with Piotr and the other partisans in the farm buildings. They pulled back the armoire, opened the wall and called to Arne and Coos to come out. Sarah said, "Can I come out, too?"

"No, you stay with mommy where it's safe," Rick said. "Jean, we're doing pretty well so far. I think we have a good chance to drive them off. You and Sarah should sit down and stay behind the wall covered by the armoire. We're pushing it back now."

"Thank you, Rick, we will."

"Can you guys shoot?" Steve asked.

"I hunted with my father," Arne said. "Show me how to use the rifle."

"No, but I'll help Arne find Nazis."

"Don't get in front of the windows, just peek out. If you see any Nazis coming your way, call us and start shooting by pointing the rifle outside, around the edge like this, and firing away. As I said, don't get fancy in front of the windows just stick the rifle around the window frame like I showed you. Rick and I will only be gone a minute or two." Steve looked out. "They aren't showing their faces now."

Rick and Steve ran downstairs to the back door. Steve yelled, "Dieter, what's going on in the woods?"

"An SS patrol, I think eight. We got one, probably seven. They're on the way back to the convoy. They will not be there for possibly one-quarter hour."

"How big is the convoy?"

"One half-track and a truck—Jerek knocked out the truck windshield and the driver. We flattened a tire on the half-track and got one SS. I don't know how many men, more than twenty, maybe thirty with the patrol. Jerek was shot in the head as we ran."

"Piotr," Steve continued, "we had to put Coos and Arne on the lookout. We'll put them back in when we go up. I think the Nazis will try a frontal assault using the truck and half-track to shield them. Once we draw their fire, the troops will spread out and try to surround us. I think Dieter should come over here and cover the upstairs back windows."

Lev said, "I think we need to cover the back window of the barn loft. We are more open there."

"Correct," Piotr said. "I send Dieter to barn and Tereza to house. We cannot let Nazis get close to throw, shoot grenades into buildinks."

"Steve knocked out the half-track machine gun," Rick said.

"Our next problem is rifle grenades," Steve said. "Shoot those guys first."

They heard shots. Rick and Steve looked through the front door window, saw Nazis coming into the front yard, two with rifle grenades, and raced upstairs. Dieter ran into the barn. Tereza sprinted the forty meters, rifle at port arms, from the shed to the farmhouse back door and up the stairs. Arne sat on the bedroom floor holding his left arm in his bloody right hand. Coos stood square in front of the window screaming, *"Godverdomme hoerenjong"* and shooting frenetically. Rick pulled him away from the window. Steve craned to see two Nazis running off and a third on his knees with his helmet resting on the ground.

"Sarah, stay back there!" Rick shouted. "Jean, come out here on your hands and knees." They pulled back the armoire and opened the wall.

Jean examined Arne. "It's a flesh wound, no bone was hit. I'll fix it. Bring him back there."

"I can walk."

"No, Arne, you can't stand up. I'll help you crawl."

Sarah said in her loudest voice, "Please teach me those bad words, Coos."

The wall was again closed up, armoire pushed back and weapons reloaded as the Americans sneaked looks outside. The wounded Nazi in the yard below was almost indistinguishable in the blizzard, but left a trail of fresh blood as he nearly crept out of view. Steve shot him dead. Rick said, "Jesus, I hate war, bombing, shooting people."

"One less guy to get patched up and shoot us, I guess I'm used to it. You think they're dead and they sit up and kill you. But I take your point."

Stefan ran in with a bag of ammunition, dropped some off to the Americans and then to Tereza. He ran downstairs and bravely continued his rounds by shunning the tunnel and running across the barnyard to Piotr in the shed and Lev and Dieter in the barn. Completing that business, he lifted the barn trapdoor and returned to the armor room for more ammunition.

After signaling their approach, the seven-man SS patrol, winded from slogging through deep snow, joined the convoy. The two groups combined now totaled twenty-four men. The lieutenant in charge of the patrol was a pragmatist. He had glimpsed the farm buildings from across the fields and knew that the odds against storming them were fair at best. He also told his superior of the unknown numbers of partisans in the woods who could have picked off his entire patrol from their perches in the trees and hidden locations in the forest.

The captain of the convoy was a pig-headed Nazi fanatic who had gotten his undeserved rank through an influential uncle who was a friend of Heinrich Himmler, head of the SS. He would not hear of a pull-out. "They hide Jews and an American. We will attack and kill them all."

Yes, and us too, you shithead.

Steve was right. The Germans would form up behind the truck and half-track, enter the barnyard firing, spread out encircling the buildings while launching rifle grenades from behind the vehicles and from within the half-track.

Since he was a small boy, Urban hunted and trapped with his father and brothers and knew how to listen and move. Snow-covered, he slipped through the forest like a Finnish soldier in all-white camouflage. Urban heard the idling SS vehicles and stopped eighty meters deep in the woods. He heard a code whistle and answered. Gertrude and Andrik, who had been stationed in the two posts nearest to the buildings, knew the patrol had pulled out of the woods behind them and surmised that they would join the main SS body near the farm house. Like Urban, they came to mount a rearguard action. Now there were three partisans behind the Germans, all armed with rifles, pistols, knives and grenades, ready to attack.

The lieutenant said to the SS captain, "We need to watch our rear, sir. These Polish know how to sneak up on you."

"By the time they get here, we will have reduced the buildings to ashes."

"Do you think we should radio the garrison in the town and ask for help?"

"We do not need help. We are SS. Moreover, they have already left the town for the new line. Just follow my orders, Lieutenant."

Rick knelt next to an upstairs window. "Let's flatten the other half-track tire, Steve."

"Right, and let's get the truck tires, too, and the driver. I'm pretty sure they can operate the half-track from inside. The snow's getting deep and drifting, maybe they get stuck. Shoot anybody carrying what looks like a rifle grenade. It sticks up from the end of the barrel like a thin pineapple or, I don't know, long pine cone. I'll go tell Tereza."

When Steve returned, Rick said, "They're revving the engines, probably coming."

"Tereza and I heard it. I waved it to Piotr and Lev who'll tell Dieter."

"Think the partisans in the woods will come in to help?"

"I hope so. They know from Dieter the patrol moved out."

The SS captain gathered his men behind the truck. "We will kill the Polish and the Jews. An American is with them. Kill him too. No prisoners. You have your assignments. Stay behind the vehicles. Wait for the signal to fan out. *Sieg Heil!*"

Jean finished disinfecting, stitching and bandaging Arne's wound. Sarah questioned Coos on how many Nazis he shot. "I do not know, Sarah, some ran away. The snow was too thick to see very much."

"Were you scared?"

"Yes, but I was angry."

"I heard you, Coos."

Jean said, "Sarah, let's all be quiet now so if Rick and Steve call us we will hear them."

The partisans in the buildings and those to the Germans' rear checked their weapons. Steve and Rick saw the half-track, covered with several inches of snow, chug into view. Although the tire treads were snow-packed, they could see them. The helmets of several moving, crouching soldiers were visible behind the half-track as its punctured left tire and the drifting snow made the vehicle swerve a few feet before the driver brought it back. Rick flattened the right front tire with a single shot.

"Hey, buddy, you're getting good at this."

"Wyatt Earp."

The half-track was still able to creep slowly. Then the truck came around the turn and entered the yard. "You get the tires, Wyatt, and I'll shoot the driver." On the word 'driver' Piotr's submachine gun opened up from a ground-floor front window, and the truck lost its entire windshield, the driver and the radiator, which belched a cloud of steam before emitting a dying hiss.

Steve joined Rick in targeting the truck's front tires and they quickly demolished them. Steve said, "I figured Piotr wouldn't stay in the shed once the half-track got started."

The truck was finished with no chance of moving in the deep snow. The half-track slogged ahead, track spinning, then catching a few feet of forward progress. Piotr saw helmets bobbing in the half-track's rear compartment. He ran out onto the porch and blasted away with the submachine gun. One helmet disappeared. A rifle poked out of a low port on the half-track's right side and shot Piotr in the left shoulder knocking him to the porch floor. He got up without his gun knowing he wouldn't be able to use it, pulled a grenade off his belt and ran toward the half-track with his left arm dangling. Miraculously unscathed from intense gunfire, Piotr pulled the pin with his teeth and threw the grenade aiming for the rear compartment, but it went long and exploded. Two SS troopers, thinking they were shielded from rifle fire by the half-track, inspected the truck's front end. The shrapnel killed one outright and fatally wounded the other.

Despite Rick's and Steve's covering fire, Piotr was mortally wounded by enemy riflemen in the half-track, and he died in the snow. Tereza saw Piotr run across the backyard and into the house. She ran down the stairs, saw him disable the truck, get shot, ignore her screams, run toward the half-track and die. Rick heard Tereza pounding down the stairs. He followed and grabbed her just before she ran through the front door to Piotr and certain death. After a struggle, Tereza went back to her post seething and bitterly repeating, "I want to die. I want to die."

Gwidon, up in the barn loft with Lev, grew increasingly anxious as he listened to the gunfire. Neither of them could see the action in front of the house. "I help Sarah. Me go Sarah. Germans hurt Sarah, where Mama, Papa?"

"We stay here, Gwidon. Mama and Papa are safe in the forest with the others. We will see them soon. Rick and Steve care for Sarah in the house."

Urban, Gertrude and Andrik crawled fifteen meters apart through mounding snow to advantageous firing positions. They were thirty meters back from the road. They decided not to strike until the SS rushed the barnyard.

Now the half-track stalled. The occupants in the front needed to open the hatch to use rifle grenades or have the troops in the back stand and launch them. Because of the fusillade coming from the farmhouse second story, no one wanted to volunteer.

The three partisans, now near the edge of the woods, saw two SS behind the truck preparing rifle grenades. They shot them down. The captain and lieutenant tried to scurry to the front of the truck and were flattened with bullets to their torsos. The highest-ranking SS left was a master sergeant, and he and the dwindling contingent now under his command were busy slithering under the truck.

A combative noncom in the half-track ordered that a rifleman near the hatch prepare a rifle grenade. Another in the rear compartment got the same order, "On my command, the hatch will open. You, Gruber, will come up and shoot the grenade through the front door of the house. Willy, you will fire through the front window next to the door. The rest of you will also stand with them and aim your rifles at the upstairs windows to distract or kill the partisans who are up there. Get ready . . . now fire."

Willy's rifle grenade misfired. Gruber's grenade was a lucky shot that crashed through the front door, slammed into the kitchen, rocked the wood stove, blew out the back door and detonated in the back yard harming no one. The stove door flew open, embers spewed out and pinwheeled around the kitchen igniting several small fires.

Stefan had come up from the cellar and was on the first stair to the second floor when the rocket grenade came through the downstairs hall. He missed being killed by a split second while bringing ammunition up to Rick and Steve. They were away from the windows patting their pockets in a search for more bullets and weren't hit by the rifle barrage that fractured the ceiling plaster and littered the room. Rick asked, "What the hell happened down there, Stefan? I smell smoke."

"Rifle grenade went through downstairs. I'll go look."

Gertrude and Urban ran forward each carrying a grenade in one hand and firing their rifles with the other. Just as they threw, one of the SS under the back bumper saw them and returned fire. Gertrude went down, Urban didn't. His grenade flew over the truck in an attempt to hit the half-track. It fell short. Gertrude's grenade exploded under the truck killing and wounding seven men. A few of the wounded crawled out and were finished off by Andrik, who was providing cover and now ran out to support the assault.

The half-track crew got the vehicle started, and it crept around the east side of the farmhouse, which had no side windows. Before it went out of sight, the soldiers in the back crowded against the near side to avoid the bullets poured down on them by the Americans. The half-track was too far from the house for them to throw a grenade. Andrik and Urban dashed for the half-track but dove into the snow when assaulted by rifle fire. Two SS had crept away to set up as snipers just inside the eastern edge of the woods, and they were now too far northeast of Steve and Rick's shooting zone.

"Steve, I'll tell Tereza the half-track's coming her way then go downstairs and check the damage."

Gwidon was in the burning kitchen and had the instinct to throw the bucketful of water he brought from the barn onto flames near the pump. Stefan ran over. "Give me the bucket, Gwidon and you pump." Gwidon frantically worked the handle and coughed in spasms. Stefan ran around choking, dumping water on the flames and slapping his sleeves to stop the singeing. Rick bolted into the kitchen and stamped around the floor preventing little fires from getting bigger. It felt like there were razors in his boots punishing his previously frostbitten feet.

Lev and Tereza saw the half-track come around the northeast corner of the house heading for the barn. Lev called Dieter from the back of the barn loft to the front. The snow-covered half-track was too far away to reach with a grenade. Lev said, "I'm going down the back around the barn and throw a grenade under it," and he took off.

Tereza detected an SS soldier, looking like a white apparition, come around the northeast corner of the farmhouse and sidle along the back of the building toward the kitchen. She couldn't get an angle on him with her rifle and realized that Lev couldn't see him through the thick flakes. She smelled the smoke, had seen Gwidon run from the barn to the kitchen with a bucket of water, and couldn't drop a grenade that might kill or injure him.

Tereza took out her knife, sat on the window sill, and when the SS was under her she jumped onto him while driving the knife down next to his clavicle and into his heart. She rolled in the snow, sprung to her feet, pulled out a grenade, and while high-stepping through the snow toward the back of the half-track, pulled the pin.

An SS in the rear of the half-track saw Tereza approaching and stood up with rifle pointed. Dieter's shot from the rear knocked him out of the truck, and he was dead before hitting the snow. Another SS saw Lev charge around the corner of the barn while readying a grenade, and before he could raise his rifle Dieter downed him, too. Lev and Tereza spotted each other. He threw his grenade under the left side of the half-track. Tereza tossed hers under from the rear. They turned, ran, and before the two grenades exploded belly flopped into the snow.

Shrapnel from one or both of the grenades penetrated the half-track's fuel tank, and it exploded in an orange fireball. The occupants of the interior compartment were trapped and burned to death amid frenzied, muffled screams. The occupants of the open, rear compartment jumped off and ran across the barnyard, two of them trailing flames and shrieking in pain. Partisans, using the intersecting fire prescribed by Piotr, brought them all down before they'd gone a hundred meters.

While this action was going on, Urban crawled through two feet of snow to get behind the position of the two snipers in the woods. They were gone, and he saw where they had hidden among the trees northeast of the house and how they had given up the fight and made tracks toward the town.

Andrik walked around the front and back yards kicking Nazis and then shooting in the head any he suspected of not being dead. Steve covered him from the upstairs windows. The SS were all dead or had run off before being shot. The battle for the farm was over, at least for now.

36

"Who will lead us now?"

Gwidon, Rick and Stefan doused the fire; and except for broken windows, some charred woodwork, and a few spots on the floor where embers stuck, the damage was fixable. The fire was controlled about the same time the shooting stopped. Gwidon raced up the stairs in time to help Steve move the furniture back and bring the group out of hiding. Gwidon knelt and hugged Sarah. "I'm glad you weren't hurt, Gwidon."

"Stefan, Rick, Gwidon put out fire."

They assembled in the barn where it was warmer. The outlying partisans were in the worst shape, and Jean told them to get into the stalls and hug the animals for warmth. The rest stood around the wood stove. One partisan said, "Where is Piotr, Tereza?"

"Tereza is in the front yard with Piotr who is dead," Andrik said.

Several partisans broke into tears, others hung their heads. Agnes said, "I will go help Tereza."

"Where is Gertrude?"

Urban joined the group. "Gertrude is dead as well. She threw grenade under German truck saving us." People groaned and bodies sagged. "She was shot, a brave Pole.

The ground is too hard to dig. Let us go soon and find safe place in woods to cover them with nature and pray."

Gabriel asked, "Who will lead us now?"

"Lev."

Rick thought: *Good move, smart move, always pick the natural leader.*

"Thank you, Dieter. Please be my second." Dieter agreed. The others crowded around them with pats on backs and spoken support. Some of the partisans who had grown up with anti-Semitic traditions no longer felt that way after knowing Lev, Jean, Sarah, Arne and Coos.

The animals in the barn, agitated from the gunfire, the large crowd and partisans hugging them, mooed, baaed, clucked and grunted in cacophonous disharmony.

While Jean circulated among the partisans checking for frostbite and dehydration, Steve asked Dieter and Lev if he and Rick could speak with them. The four went off to a corner of the barn. "Rick and I were just talking. Maybe there's more Germans in the town. We don't know where the Russians are. We need sentries down the road and around the farm to look for anyone approaching. I think we need to act like there's more trouble coming." Lev led them back to the main body.

"People, listen. Steve is an American Army combat veteran. He is right, Germans may come back, could be more in town. We do not know how close are the Russians. Let us guard the farm. We need seven sentries." Many partisan men and women raised their hands. "Talk to Dieter, he will tell you where to go."

Gwidon rushed into the barn holding Sarah's hand. He gathered his mother and father, who came out of the snow-choked woods in better shape than many of the younger people, in a huge embrace as tears ran down his cheeks.

"Gwidon and Stefan saved the house, put out the fire in the kitchen," Rick said.

They were encircled and patted while pointing at Rick as if to say, "Him, too." George's and Flora's wide smiles crinkled their eyes.

When Flora broke free, she said, "Gwidon, see to animals while Papa and I go to kitchen fix food."

Jean said, "Gwidon, please milk the cows. Our people need warm milk now."

"Jean is right, Gwidon, cows first."

"Yes, Mama."

"I'll help," Sarah said. "I'm a good milker."

A partisan yelled out, "Need vodka."

"Bring jug, George," Flora said, as she put a finger and thumb an inch apart. "Give each little, no drunk with Germans about."

One of the partisans stoked the barn's wood stove. Stefan got the farmhouse back door fastened on its hinges, and his forearm muscles bulged as he hammered the kitchen stove door flush. Agnes gathered several partisans to help Flora and George get the rest of the kitchen cleaned up and in working order. Two other handy partisans worked on patching broken windows, the front door and the upstairs bedroom ceiling.

Dieter and Rick found Jerek's body and carried it to the temporary burial site. Steve, Lev, Andrik and several others tended to Piotr's and Gertrude's bodies as best they could, wrapped them in sheets and carried them into the forest.

Tereza knelt in the snow shaking and keening. Andrik lifted and supported her, and they followed the somber procession. Other mourners included close friends of Gertrude. Gabriel, who had once studied for the priesthood, said prayers. Lev kissed the dead partisans' faces. Tereza, wailing uncontrollably, gave Piotr a final embrace, and the bodies were covered first with boughs and then with heavy limbs cut by Gwidon.

On Lev's orders, partisans in teams of two carried dead SS into another part of the forest far from Piotr, Gertrude and Jerek. No tears were shed. The stench of charred flesh from the half-track was appalling. Arne and Coos, having experienced the smell before, were excused from any outdoor cleanup and stayed in the barn helping Jean. That night the storm blew out, a cold snap set in, and the putrefaction became less nauseating.

Sleep was fitful for the Americans and most others in the barn-cellar barracks that night. Many partisans wept. Tereza was inconsolable in her cubicle, thrashing about, grinding her teeth and crying, "Piotr, oh, Piotr" over and over. Jean and Gabriel circulated among the bereaved trying to console as best they could. The next day Tereza would not eat. Jean tried to help her but to no avail.

37

"Do you know the whereabouts of . . . ?"

Although worn down from nursing without letup, and jittery from treating ghastly wounds, the two were promptly assigned to provide medical support for American infantry forces advancing east toward the Rhine. They were never far from the front lines and in constant threat of German counterattacks. American fighter planes, flying low-level ground support, thundered over them letting loose with bombs, rockets and machine gun fire on the Germans only a short distance ahead.

Suzanne and Beverly rode in the front seat of an ambulance speeding toward an aid station even closer to the action. From the top of a hill, and to their horror, they saw an apparently undamaged P-47 that was strafing a German truck convoy fly into the ground and explode in the valley far below them. The driver said, "My cousin's a fighter pilot. Told me about that, called it target fixation. Sometimes pilots are so concentrated on the strafing they lose sight of how low they are and pull out too late."

Whenever Beverly and Suzanne saw or heard of an American plane going down their thoughts went to Rick and Steve. They asked everywhere they went and to all, including the Red Cross, who might possibly have information, "Do you know the whereabouts of Lieutenants Richard Heydon and Steven Millen shot down over Blechhammer, Germany on August second, nineteen-forty-four?" No one could tell them more than they already knew, and they received no encouragement. Despite the heartache, neither lost faith.

38

"My friend and I know you from Auschwitz."

The last SS detachment had orders to leave the town with all deliberate speed and head west to a new defensive line. They didn't depart as ordered. The captain had a girlfriend in the town, and after the extended overnight goodbyes the dilatory leader arrived. The troops were packed into a truck and a half-track, and the vehicles rumbled in readiness as hopeful townspeople watched from between their window coverings.

The Nazis were about to roll out when a motorcycle with an empty sidecar roared into the town square and skidded to a stop. The tall captain stood ramrod straight in his immaculate black SS uniform. He lifted his goggles and looked down his nose at the late-arriving sergeant who dismounted and saluted. "Captain Hahn, the Russians are within ten kilometers and rapidly moving in this direction. I heard their cannon and there are many."

Now they heard and saw a large formation of Soviet fighters in four, star-shaped squadrons layered at different altitudes. The planes flew several kilometers north of the town heading west toward the main body of the retreating German SS division on the ground. Hahn thought of his fleeing comrades, some of whom he had known for years and the battering they were about to get. *Schadenfreude* creased his face into a slight smirk. *Better them than me.*

The captain, whose self-important mindtrip could justify his tardiness, snapped his fingers twice and called out, "Lieutenant Bauer come up here . . . is there news from the farm? Have any of our men returned?"

The obsequious Bauer saluted and, as was his custom, answered in stilted language, "No, to both of your questions, Captain Hahn, sir. We have had no radio contact. And I feel confident that the poorly-defended farm is secured and in order and our SS brothers are tidying things up before rejoining us."

"Since we are now going to the farm, I hope that you are right, Lieutenant. We will double our forces once we join them. I believe it is a fair wager that the Russians, or Soviets as they call themselves, will bypass the farm not knowing its location."

Captain Hahn was supremely haughty by nature and derelict in not heading west as ordered. But he was a more competent field tactician than the mulish captain who blindly led his men into eternity the day before. And now that Auschwitz had been abandoned, Hahn was pleased to be back in charge of an armored group, albeit a small one. He was also bitter at not having been promoted to major and determined to lead a victorious assault that would be rewarded by superiors.

Why would they promote imbeciles like Herrmann and Schroeder and bypass me? They knew I always surpassed my extermination quotas at Auschwitz.

Pairs of SS scouts scanned the woods on each side of the farm road prior to the convoy's approach. A silent knife to the throat from the rear killed the partisan sentry close to the entrance. The sentry nearer the farm heard the pair of scouts stalking him. He drove them into a defensive position with productive shooting and ran to safety. They didn't chase him. If they had, one of the partisan snipers in a tree would have been well-positioned to end the pursuit.

However, one of the scouts had a radio, and Captain Hahn learned that at least some of the partisans were still operating near the farm. The scout had not gotten close enough to observe the wrecked vehicles near the farm buildings.

Lev and Dieter, using additional, combat-experienced advice from Steve, issued new assignments. This time, only nine partisans hid in the woods surrounding the farm. All of them now perched in trees, with more of them closer to the road. Three other partisans, one armed with a German rifle grenade, waited under the tunnel trapdoor that opened into the woods southwest of the house.

Several armed and able partisans huddled by the cellar stairs under the kitchen waiting to fill the positions of fallen comrades. Lev wisely kept Flora, George and Gwidon indoors, and they hid in the cellar barracks.

Two partisan sharpshooters lay on the back edge of the farmhouse roof peak with favorable shooting angles. One of them held a captured rifle grenade. Another two were in similar positions on the barn roof. Andrik crouched in the rear compartment of the disabled German truck gripping a rifle grenade and hoping to use it. Rick, Steve, Lev and Dieter switched their previous positions and Tereza kept hers. Stefan successfully repaired a defective German rifle grenade, rushed upstairs and gave it to Lev.

The sentry who gave the warning was given a partner and dispatched to the woods to find the SS patrol south of the road and drive it toward the snipers in the trees. The partisans were unaware of the SS patrol that knifed the sentry on the north side of the road entrance.

Captain Hahn had fewer men under his command than the fatuous captain of the previous day. The German truck carried fourteen troops, the half-track six, and the two-man motorcycle with sidecar that brought news of the advancing Russians. With the four scouts in the woods along the farm road they totaled twenty-six.

Hahn was courageous in battle, or foolhardy, depending upon your point of view. If spunk was a trait, it was diluted by poor judgment. He elected to lead the attack, announcing that he would ride in the sidecar and man the mounted machine gun. Lieutenant Bauer was told to drive, a decision that filled him with terror. With the leaders out front in an exposed vehicle, the entourage departed the town at ten in the morning just as they heard the distant sound of Russian artillery. Once the Germans were out of sight the vodka poured, and the townspeople frolicked in the snow-covered streets.

Alerted by the rifle exchange between the sentry on the south side of the road and the SS scouts, all of the partisan posts near the farm buildings went on high alert and the others ran to their hiding places. One of the SS scouts on the north side of the farm road had commando skills, and he found a vantage point that afforded a view of the farm. The scout saw the disabled truck in front of the house and the burned-out half-track near the barn. He also noted that no SS were in the vicinity and radioed the news to Captain Hahn.

Advance Soviet scouts entered the town to showers of candy and other treats. A few of the locals spoke Russian and were only too happy to point the way toward the just-departed Germans. The scouts radioed back to their main force and then followed the Germans with other locals popping out of their homes to eagerly direct them.

Anticipating the likelihood of extreme danger to the rear, SS Captain Hahn figured that fighting the partisans and attempting to outrun the Russians was the best strategy. So they barreled on and soon turned onto the farm road. Fifty meters in, a keen-eyed soldier spotted the preceding engagement's disabled half-track shunted into the undergrowth and covered with branches. It was not a morale booster. Morale would have been further degraded by the sight of German dead from the previous day's battle, but they were covered by a thick mantle of snow.

Hahn stopped the convoy, got the men out of the truck, split the detail, and ordered them to file through the woods near the road. Unlike the ill-fated half-tracks in the first German raid, the more-advanced machine under Hahn's command was clad in steel protecting the troopers in the rear compartment from gunfire and shrapnel. As the imperious captain swiveled the machine gun and practiced his aim, the vehicles jounced along the rutted, snow-filled tracks.

Two-hundred meters in, a partisan sniper in a tree shot the lieutenant off his motorcycle. The front wheel crimped, and the vehicle spun and crashed into the bushes. Captain Hahn, who had not fastened his helmet chin strap, was thrown out of the sidecar, the helmet flew off, and his head slammed into a tree stump. He struggled to his feet, staggered back to the road holding his head and climbed into the front seat of the truck next to the driver. The formidable half-track now led the parade, and the machine gunner fired a short burst to test his weapon.

Shots sounded and echoed as partisan snipers in the trees on either side of the road eliminated two SS soldiers in the woods below them. One partisan was hit by return fire, fell wounded to the ground and died instantly when the impact snapped his neck.

The Soviet mechanized division now entering the town did not participate in the liberation of the Auschwitz-Birkenau death camp eight days earlier, but they knew of the horror. This force was assigned to kill retreating Nazis before they reached the new defensive line currently being established to the west.

The division split near the town with plans to re-form seven kilometers northwest. A force of four tanks, six armored vehicles and seventy-five infantry was assigned to engage the Germans who were now far down the farm road. The advance Soviet scouts stopped near the farm road entrance and waited for the larger force to join them.

The Nazi scout who radioed Hahn from the farm's eastern outskirts was told to rejoin the convoy. He felt an itch as he neared the road and removed his helmet to scratch. A partisan sniper in a tree shot him through the top of his head. The half-track machine gunner spotted the sniper in branches too low for safe hiding and riddled his body.

Gabriel, scouting on the ground, saw the SS convoy through the forest and ran back to alert the farm. Lev and the others were delighted to learn that the Nazi force was no bigger than the one they wiped out the day before. They were not pleased with the description of the half-track's steel-clad rear compartment and met briefly in the kitchen to decide how to neutralize it. Steve was called in from the barn and volunteered for the job. After listening to Tereza's pleas and seeing her grief-stricken face, Lev could not deny her the revenge she sought. He said he wanted Steve's rifle skills in the barn loft door and chose the capable Gabriel as Tereza's partner.

Steve told Tereza and Gabriel how he took out the other half-track's machine gun with grenades lobbed from the hillock above the turn into the front yard. They chose the same tactic. Lev wanted cover for them and told the group he would join the three partisans waiting to exit from the outside trapdoor and create a diversion across the road from Gabriel and Tereza.

The Soviet mechanized force rendezvoused with their advance-scout vehicles at the farm road entrance. Colonel Sokolov, commander of the group split off from the division, ordered that the tanks and armored vehicles be interspersed with soldiers in the woods near the road much like the Nazi plan only on a larger scale. Soviet scouts in the woods preceded the main force. Two men with metal detectors walked in the road ahead of the lead tank. They understood their vulnerability from snipers and missed mines, but were of a fearless sort.

The German convoy did not hear the Soviet vehicles approaching from the rear over the din of their own motors. An SS trooper in the woods did see them and boldly ran forward along the road to alert his people. A partisan sentry in a tree shot him dead before the warning was heard. The sentry then saw the Soviet soldiers with mine detectors approaching down the road in front of a tank. He reflexively raised his rifle and aimed while thinking: *Those are not Nazi gray uniforms*, and lowered his sights.

Gabriel and Tereza crawled to the vantage point, brought out their grenades and waited for the German half-track to reach a point below them. Before Gabriel could stop her Tereza pulled the pin on a grenade and jumped onto the hood of the half-track. She tried unsuccessfully to pry open a hatch. Either she didn't hold the grenade's striker lever down, or it was faulty and she died in the explosion.

Gabriel flipped two live grenades. Both blew but didn't penetrate the armor, disable the machine gun or the track and front tires. Lev's group was now out of the trapdoor just inside the woods. Andrik ran out and threw a grenade that exploded near the half-track but didn't disable it. Lev's group poured rifle fire into the half-track's tires, but nothing seemed to stop it. Like the day before, the half-track swiveled into the front yard ready to attack the house with heavy machine gun fire and rifle grenades. Soviet troops chased and killed Nazis fleeing through the forest, and the repeated crack of rifle fire resounded down the length of the farm road.

The lead Soviet tank came around a turn, and the gunner spotted the German truck ahead. Within five seconds the truck was on fire and a moment later the fuel tank exploded. The rear occupants of the German half-track saw the truck destroyed and told the driver to abort the mission and get out before they were blown up. The half-track picked up speed, crossed in front of the farm house and headed for the open field. A big Soviet soldier with a bazooka on his shoulder burst out of the woods nearest the house, ran across the yard, knelt and blew the top off the half-track.

The surviving SS who were able crawled out and ran. Dieter, Steve, Rick and Lev's group shot them all dead. Gabriel sprinted over to look down into the vehicle. He pulled the pin on a grenade, dropped it in and ducked away. *That is for you, Tereza*. Later, no one asked him how many dead or wounded SS he found inside the half-track. Soviet troops hunted down the rest of the Nazis and killed them with the exception of Captain Hahn who had jumped from the flaming truck and stumbled undetected through the woods holding his fractured skull.

The partisans in the woods survived by dropping their weapons and yelling, *"Polski!"* A few understandably trigger-happy Soviet soldiers took some potshots. Fortunately, they missed. The Soviet vehicles had access to a fairly flat detour around the burned-out German truck, and they soon lined up across the front yard.

Colonel Sokolov, a Russian bear of a man, came up out of the lead tank turret and climbed down. Rick thought of the actor Akim Tamiroff. Lev stepped up and said in flowing Russian, "Welcome comrades, I am Lev Rabinovich, a Russian national who is fighting the Nazis with the Polish resistance. We are happy that you are here and hope that you will accept our hospitality." The partisans gathered in the yard and on the front porch. Gwidon moved the armoire back, opened the wall and released Jean, Sarah, Coos and Arne. They watched from the upstairs bedroom windows.

A Soviet soldier brought Captain Hahn into the yard with a pistol to the back of his neck and made him kneel. He said to Colonel Sokolov, "Sir, I found this Nazi in the woods sitting on a log holding his head and thought he might have valuable information. Or would you prefer that I shot him now?" Swift justice was routine on the Eastern Front: Nazis captured by the Soviets were typically shot on the spot.

In addition to the one holding the gun on Hahn, many of the Soviet soldiers standing in the yard had relatives who were killed by the Nazis in Operation Barbarossa, the over one-hundred divisions, scorched-earth invasion of the Soviet Union in the summer of 1941. And many of the men who lived west of the Volga River had lost entire families. Some small children saved themselves by crawling under the dead bodies of parents and siblings. The bestial *Einsatzgruppen*, SS paramilitary death squads, accompanied the invading Nazi divisions and killed hundreds of thousands of Soviet civilians.

Arne said to Coos, "Look, it is Captain Hahn from Auschwitz. Come Coos we must have a reunion. Jean, please keep Sarah out of sight of the front yard until this meeting is over." They went down the stairs. Pistols, knives and other weapons were heaped on a hall table. Arne picked up a pistol, released the safety, and put it in his pocket. Coos took one of Stefan's stilettos, and they walked onto the porch.

Coos spoke German in a forceful voice, "Welcome to our humble farm, Captain Hahn." Gesturing toward Arne, "My friend and I know you from Auschwitz. We saw you shoot Jews in the head when they could no longer work. You would have shot us, too, but we escaped and these people," his arms opened wide, "saved us."

Arne spoke malevolently, "Captain Hahn, you herded our families into the gas chambers and then burned them in the ovens. I would show you pictures of our wives and children if we had them. But we do not have them, nor do we have our wives and children. You and your other SS filth killed them all at Auschwitz." The Polish partisans, the Americans and the Soviets stood riveted, and it was now so quiet they heard the wind sighing through the forest.

Arne and Coos went down the steps, across the yard and stopped in front of Hahn who looked up at them and spit out, *"Juden schweine."* Coos kicked him in the mouth knocking out teeth and Hahn onto his back. The Russian soldier looked to Colonel Sokolov who motioned him away with a head turn.

While crying, *"Arbeit macht frei"* in a voice strangled with rage, Coos lunged and drove the knife into Hahn's throat a few inches below the chin. Hahn writhed, his eyes bulged, his face turned purple and blood gushed from his mouth. Coos turned the knife and stepped away leaving the knife in Hahn's throat.

He wasn't dead yet. Arne took the pistol out of his pocket, knelt, jammed the barrel into Hahn's mouth to the cylinders and pulled the trigger blowing a hole through the back of his head. Arne left the gun in Hahn's mouth, and the two walked back into the house. No one who witnessed the execution of SS Captain Wolfgang Hahn would ever forget it.

39

"You are quiet, strong fighters. God bless you."

Soviet soldiers carried Hahn's body into the woods. They also picked up the rest of the dead Germans and placed them deep in the frozen forest. The partisans found their own and brought them to the temporary gravesite. Tereza's remains were wrapped in a grapevine covering with silent tears falling onto the cloth. As the wind moaned through the bare branches, Tereza's body was placed against Piotr's. One of her hands was enfolded into one of his. Tears flowed, prayers said and the boughs and logs replaced. No one wept over the deaths of Piotr and Tereza more openly than Andrik, the Hungarian national.

Flora said, "We have Father Wozniak come and bless them. Soon we take to town in truck, George, and bury them in the name of *Jezus Chrystus*, our Lord."

"Amen."

The Red Army soldiers welcomed the barn's warmth, and they shared the food that George, Flora and Agnes were immediately able to give them.

Colonel Sokolov was invited to stay the night and enjoy a meal. Other Soviet officers were with him in the kitchen. Jean and Sarah came in for introductions. Sarah greeted the

Colonel in fluent Russian and he was captivated. He knelt and opened his arms. Sarah ran to him and they embraced warmly. He held her at arm's length. "Oh, my little treasure, you and my grandchild Valentina would be friends. She is blonde and blue-eyed like you."

Colonel Sokolov studied English since early grade school and spoke it well. Over tumblers of vodka, Lev related their fight against the Nazis, how the Americans found the farm and Jean and Sarah's rescue. The Colonel asked, "What do you plan to do now that Fritz is no longer a threat to this region?"

"I am a Jew like Coos and Arne, the two who escaped from Auschwitz. They have nothing to go home to in Holland and Denmark and want to join me in going to Palestine. We wish to help establish a Jewish homeland."

Colonel Sokolov looked toward Jean and Sarah. They both started talking at the same time, but Sarah stopped and looked up at her mother as if to say, no you go ahead. "As you heard a moment ago, I am a physician. My husband, John Krol, was Polish and a university professor in England. We came here for a visit in mid-1939 and were unable to leave when the Nazis invaded. He was murdered by the Gestapo. Sarah and I escaped thanks to these and other people. We are both British citizens . . ."

"I am also a Polish citizen."

The Colonel and Jean smiled. "Yes, Sarah, you are. We wish to return to England where Sarah will know her grandparents. I will resume practice, and Sarah will go to school."

"Does Sarah have grandparents in Poland?"

"She did, my husband's parents, but they were taken away by the Nazis, and we fear they did not survive."

"Where did you learn Russian, Sarah?"

"From Lev, Colonel Sokolov," then she saluted thinking it was a good idea after seeing Rick and Steve do it when they first walked in to meet the Colonel. Sokolov was totally in love. "I can also speak Danish and Dutch. Arne and Coos taught me, and Polish."

"I'll bet you can."

Colonel Sokolov looked to the Americans. Steve nodded toward Rick who saluted as did Steve. "We went down over Germany, sir. We were captured, spent time in a German jail, a small jail, not a stalag, escaped and were taken in by these kind people. We hope to rejoin our units and help finish the war."

"Where was your base of operations?"

"Foggia, Italy, sir."

"I fear we cannot take you there." He looked at Lev and then Jean. "Or you and your friends to Palestine, or you, Doctor and Sarah to England. But we will do our best to get you to a safe place." He smiled and looked around the room. "Does anyone else want to leave Poland?" Lev translated into Polish. Everybody except Dieter and Andrik shook their heads no.

"Czechoslovakia, sir."

"Hungary, sir."

"We are going northwest, and I do not believe we can help with transport. If you wish, I will give you papers that should keep you out of trouble with other Soviet officials."

"Thank you, sir."

Along with other partisans, George and Flora listened while preparing food. They knew from the period when Hitler and Stalin divided Poland that the Russians mistreated people living in the eastern part of the country. After observing Sokolov, they decided he was a *dobry facet* who would not allow expropriation or abuse by his soldiers. George halted his work and approached the Colonel to ask in a nervous, halting voice, "Colonel Sokolov, sir, may I ask a favor of you?"

"Of course, and I hope that I can grant the favor."

"Would it be possible for one of your tanks to push the German vehicles into the forest?"

"Yes, we will do that."

"Thank you, sir, possibly far enough so that we cannot see them." Sokolov smiled at George and looked toward one of his officers who saluted and went outside. Soon, two tanks were heard warming up.

The weather also warmed up. The afternoon was mild under a clear sky, and the sun made the house and barn comfortable. Flora dispatched people to bring preserved vegetables and fruit from a cellar hiding place. On his mother's orders, Gwidon and a few men had already made ready a dozen hens for roasting. Alarmed by the diminished flock, Flora told George it was time to borrow his friend Tadzio's rooster.

While pushing the two German half-tracks out of the way, Russian tanks packed the snow in the back yard between the house and barn. A fire pit was uncovered and stoked with sacks of coal George had bartered for in the market. A plump pig and a large sheep were prepared, and their bodies with metal rods though them hung on tripods over the fire. When

Stefan made the tripods he welded handles onto the rods, and two big men wearing makeshift mitts turned them for even cooking. The dripping fat sizzled in the fire. Soviet soldiers gathered around inhaling the aroma.

In addition to his vodka recipe, George made summer wine. Flora told him that the wine would not be served until the Germans were gone. Gwidon and other strong men hauled the casks out of the hiding place behind a cellar wall and out into the back yard. The casks were tapped and the wine poured into mugs that were passed around. Plates were filled, and these made the rounds as partisans and Russian soldiers feasted on meat, vegetables, fruit and bread. The wine did not pack the vodka's wallop, but the high alcohol content made everybody merry.

Flora and George served Colonel Sokolov, two other Russian officers, the Americans, Jean and Sarah and Lev and Dieter in the kitchen. George placed a fresh jug of vodka on the table already groaning with food. The Colonel was a witty raconteur who could drain endless tumblers of vodka and never show it. They laughed until faces flushed and tears were wiped away. Before the stories became too ribald, Jean put Sarah to bed. Before going upstairs, she kissed everyone at the table.

When Jean came back to the table, Colonel Sokolov said, "Doctor Krol, my Valentina is bright, but Sarah is the most brilliant child I have ever met."

"Thank you. Sarah said to me before going to sleep, 'I love Colonel Sokolov.' "

Three Soviet soldiers approached Coos and Arne in the yard. One said, "We are Jews: Russian, Ukrainian, Latvian. Where will you go now?"

Coos had a good ear for languages. He had picked up some Russian listening to Lev teach Sarah. He told them of the plan to go to Palestine with Lev and build a Jewish homeland. The soldiers liked that idea. The Ukrainian said, "One day I may join you there." The other two agreed. They all hugged and wished each other well.

Urban had a concertina. He had not used it since the occupation. Now he brought it out and played expertly. Polish men and women danced and sang folk tunes around the fire. The kitchen group came out to watch. Urban played Russian folk songs, and the soldiers joined arms and circled the fire swiveling their heads. Two of them could squat and shoot one leg out at a time, Cossack-style, as the crowd applauded.

The fire dwindled, the concertina was put away, people stifled yawns and the numerous sentries were rotated and fed. Many of the Soviet soldiers were farm boys, and they didn't mind bedding down with animals or sleeping in the hayloft. Flora put Colonel Sokolov on the parlor couch. The other officers were given blankets and slept on the floor or sitting up in chairs. As Jean got into bed, Sarah half woke up. "Mommy, I think I hear guns."

"No, sweetheart, it is only Russian soldiers snoring."

"I wish I could snore in Russian."

After packing the few things they could bring and having some breakfast, the Americans, Lev, Arne, Coos, Jean and Sarah stood in the front yard receiving hugs, pats, kisses and endless good wishes. Steve and Rick were happy that Dieter came forward and shook hands. Although they didn't cotton to him at first, they had gained great respect for his skill and bravery. Rick said, "All the best, Dieter, you're a good man."

"I have learned much from both of you. You are quiet, strong fighters. God bless you."

Gwidon knelt, and with his face wet with tears, embraced Sarah. "Gwidon love you."

"Thank you, Gwidon, for teaching me to be a farmer. I love you. I'll miss you very much."

Flora embraced and kissed Sarah. "I love you, Sarah, and never forget you. In dark time you brought happiness. Please do not forget us."

"I never will. I love you all."

The seven, all with their own hopes, dreams and memories, were distributed among three armored vehicles. Soon the Soviet convoy rumbled down the farm road heading toward some of the worst fighting of the war. The partisans followed, waved their caps, cried and shouted hoarse goodbyes until the last vehicle was beyond their view.

40

Aftermath

Except for Agnes and Gabriel, who married and stayed on the farm to work, the partisans who survived the resistance left for their own homes and new lives. Just after the Soviets departed, some of George's friends found Magda's frozen body where the Gestapo left it and brought her remains to the farm. Soon, the bodies of Piotr, Tereza, Gertrude, Magda, Jerek and the other partisans slain by the Nazis were moved from their temporary forest resting places, placed in newly-made wood caskets and brought to town. Somehow, George's tumbledown truck managed to make several cheerless journeys. Townspeople pitched in and dug graves in the churchyard. Following an emotional mass presided over by Father Wozniak, the partisans were buried.

Life and work resumed on the farm. It was not appreciated that Soviet apparatchiks wanted a bigger share of farm production for less money than even the paltry sums the Germans had been willing to pay, but the owners' modest needs were met. Flora and George were politically astute survivors who kept a low profile and played the good communists as necessary. They had hosted an underground cell, while making the Nazi occupiers happy by providing food and vodka. Later, they used the same tactics with the Soviets, while keeping financial bribes at a manageable level. Agnes had been a teacher before the war, and now she home-schooled her children and kept them away from Communist indoctrination.

When the local bank became stable enough to exchange money, Flora and George took the deutschmarks they'd earned from the market days and Major Herrmann's quasi-confiscatory visits and exchanged them for zlotys. Using that money, along with their bartering skills and zlotys accumulated from Polish customers, they bought a used truck of more recent vintage, a second kitchen stove and new clothes for church on Sunday. Since the old horse died, they also got a small tractor.

Flora and Agnes expanded the bread and pastry business and found many new customers in nearby towns, places they dared not go to during the Nazi occupation. George and Gabriel traveled to local town markets every Saturday and brought back a pile of zlotys. As custom dictated, they were deposited into Flora's apron.

After decades of grinding work, Flora's heart gave out in 1954, and she collapsed next to her kitchen stove at the age of eighty-eight. Agnes was with her and tried to help. She saw that it was hopeless and went out to the barn to tell George. Gabriel and Gwidon were also there, and they started for the house in deep distress. Gwidon took his father's arm because senescence, years of stooping and other hardships of farming since childhood had bent him like a stunted tree on a windy shore.

As they were about to exit the barn, George said that his head hurt and he had to lie down. He collapsed on Gwidon's cot unable to move or speak. He either couldn't or didn't want to live without Flora. After fifteen minutes of hoarse, labored breathing, George gasped and died, with Gabriel, Agnes and Gwidon kneeling and praying next to him. Father Wozniak conducted that crowded service as well. George and Flora were loved and respected in the town, and they were buried in the churchyard alongside their compatriots.

Gwidon suffered greatly, and thanks to Agnes's and Gabriel's kindnesses he quickly recovered. Gwidon's help was indispensable around the farm, and he became a boon companion and mentor to the couple's growing brood. Above all he taught them to work hard, a shining trait of the Polish people. About a year before their deaths, Flora and George bequeathed the farm to Agnes and Gabriel with the proviso that they would always care for Gwidon, which they did with affection.

* * *

Thanks to the official papers given to them by Colonel Sokolov, Andrik and Dieter made it through long and arduous journeys to their homes. With Piotr as his hero, and ever the revolutionary, Andrik joined the Budapest underground in opposition to the Soviet occupation. He always told his friends that the experiences fighting the Nazis with the Polish partisans reshaped his life and prepared him for any successes he may have subsequently attained.

His shyness long behind him, Andrik grew into a tough negotiator and combative patriot. His inspiration was instrumental in the 1956 Hungarian Uprising. While leading troops, Andrik was killed in the streets when Soviet tanks and troops brutally crushed the revolution. Even though he'd had many romances, and later a happy marriage with children, his last thoughts were of Tereza, the unattainable woman who was the untouched love of his life.

Dieter, with his native intelligence and newfound social skills, learned largely from watching Piotr and the Americans, got into politics. He was a hero of the Prague Spring of 1968 and was jailed for months following the crushing Soviet reprisal. Later, in 1993, at the age of seventy-four, Dieter was instrumental in helping to establish the Czech Republic, four years after the collapse of the Soviet Union.

* * *

Luis Alvarez and Wes Trowbridge left Rick's B-17 together, separated and met again twenty-five years later at an Arizona reunion. It was there that Wes learned from Rick Heydon and Steve Millen that Luis had saved his life.

After wrapping them around each other, Steve pushed them out at three-thousand feet. After six seconds of free fall with the gale-force wind trying to pull Wes from his grip, Luis opened his legs, pushed Les away with his left hand and pulled the rip cord ring with the right.

Fortunately, Wes was upright, and the pilot chute did not entangle with his legs. The main chute deployed, Wes's body jerked upward, and his chin lay against his chest during the descent. Luis had a panicky few seconds as he fished around his own parachute trying to find the ring. He finally grasped it, pulled, and the pilot chute and then the main chute opened. By this time, he and Wes were far apart. Luis could still see Wes's chute in the distance and hoped that he would find a soft place to land and not hit his head.

Luis and Wes landed two kilometers apart. Luis was immediately captured and taken to a *stalag* where he stayed until liberated. Wes landed soft, avoided further damage but remained unconscious and in deep shock. The German patrol leader recognized Wes's condition and had him removed to a military hospital for treatment. He received competent care for three months after which he was kept in a prisoner-of-war camp for the duration of the war.

Following liberation, Luis connived and talked his way into returning to Sardinia to find his girlfriend, Nicla. She waited for him as promised. When Luis walked into her yard nearly a year after he last saw her, Nicla looked up from pumping water at the well and fainted dead away. They married, went to America, settled on the family farm in Southern California's Imperial Valley, raised four children and enjoyed a happy life.

Wes suffered from migraines and a general nervous condition. But, like many lucky men, he had a supportive wife, a successful career woman who found excellent medical care for her husband. Except for partial deafness in his right ear and limited peripheral vision in his right eye, he was nursed and loved back to his former, healthy self. Wes founded a car agency with two old friends from his hometown of Denver, Colorado, and they rode the postwar boom to success with two additional agencies.

Every crew member who bailed out of Rick's B-17 over Germany survived the war, and none died before the age of seventy.

* * *

On the ragged edge from hours of nonstop operations on grievously wounded soldiers, Beverly and Suzanne got a rare few minutes to lie on their cots. Their infantry division moved steadily forward under hellish Nazi bombardment near the front, just west of the Rhine. Howitzers boomed and mortars chuffed in the near distance. Shock waves from the explosions of incoming shells rocked their cots, spattered dirt on the bunker roof and filled the air with dust. Troops dashed around outside. Loud voices shouted orders. A jeep raced by horn blaring.

"So what are you thinking about?"

"Hoping we don't get killed, at least we aren't in foxholes like Anzio. I'm thinking the same thing you are, just a different person."

"I'll bet those two bad boys are in a London pub drinking pints with two little East End chippies, all bright red lipstick and fingernails. 'Buy me a pint, Luv?' "

"I'll scratch their eyes out."

Then they were quiet, not really up to talking about the pain and fear they both felt and unable to keep up the humor derived from what they knew might be false hopes.

The head nurse, Captain Rose Fratelli, came into the bunker. "Don't get up. I've just been reading your papers. Except for that brief vacation, if you can call it that, in Foggia, you two have been on the line for months, way too long. I see Anzio, the German defensive line, with Patton in the south of France, the Bulge now this mess.

"Some new nurses just came in, and I'm rotating you back to England for a little R and R." Suzanne and Beverly sat up with spreading smiles. "With luck you might not have to come back. Pack your gear." The two stood up and bent from the waist in ungovernable glee. "You're going by truck to an airfield near here and flying to somewhere in England, they don't know where yet. I know you're trying to find your husbands, but you'll probably have better luck tracking them down from there. You two are the best combat nurses I've seen. I'm putting you both in for medals." They saluted and thanked her. Then they had a three-way hug.

* * *

Colonel Mikhail Sokolov had no intention of exposing his passengers to the upcoming battles with the Nazis. He was determined to find an escape route for them. After reconnecting with the full mechanized division west of the town, they were ordered north-northwest in a feint designed to flank the new Nazi defensive line. In three days of nearly nonstop driving, the maneuver brought them to a recently abandoned German airfield now populated with Soviet aircraft.

Steve and Rick had ridden on hardpan roads in rigid, unyielding vehicles, but nothing like this. The other four, and Jean and Sarah in particular, were ill-equipped for stifling, fume-ridden, jolt-wagon punishment. Colonel Sokolov did all he could to make them comfortable. Despite the lack of complaining they were drained and sore in body and spirit once the airport was reached and they were released from their metal conveyances.

The seven were shown where to wash up, and following that refreshing interlude they were given a meal of thick soup and black bread in the mess hall. Curious Soviet airmen came by their table to ask questions. Except for those asking in difficult to understand ethnic dialects, Lev and Sarah fielded them all. All were enchanted by the friendly and gifted little girl.

Watching Sarah made Rick think of *The Bridge of San Luis Rey*. And that reminded him of Luis Alvarez, and he wondered where Luis was and how he fared. *Tough guy, I'm sure he's doing fine.* Then Rick's thoughts came back to the passage that described a fascinating woman. He couldn't remember the entire description only the final words, '. . . this strange, beautiful bird who lived among us.' *Sarah may be strange in the sense of being unusual, but for sure she is beautiful.* Sarah sensed that Rick was staring at her, and she gave him the most adoring smile.

A Soviet officer came to the table. The men around the table saluted him and moved away. The officer told the seven sojourners, in English, that Colonel Sokolov wished to meet with them and would they please follow him. They were led to a conference room in which sat the Colonel and another officer. Rick, Steve and then Sarah saluted. "Please sit down, my friends and introduce yourselves to Captain Mikhail Starkova of the Soviet Air Forces."

When that was completed, Captain Starkova said in American-accented English, "It is a pleasure to know you all. Colonel Sokolov has briefed me on your backgrounds and on your hoped-for destinations. I am pilot of a Petlyakov bomber. We are on the final leg of a flight to England. Along with my crew, we are transporting three, high-level Soviet Commissars, one of whom is joining us here, to a London conference. I have asked the Commissars whether they would be willing to let you fly with us and they have agreed."

Captain Starkova turned to Lev, Arne and Coos. "Not having papers, please understand that we cannot guarantee the nature of the reception that the three of you, being neither British nor American, will receive in England, but we expect that it will be helpful, and I will do all I can to make it so. I will definitely see that you are escorted to International Red Cross offices in London.

"Now, also understand that the trip will be long and hazardous. However, the aircraft has been specially adapted, and the cabin has seating and is pressurized and heated. We will make all efforts to circumvent German air space, but the mission is fraught with danger. Do any of you not wish to fly?" No hands went up. "Good, we leave in three hours at dusk."

"Captain Starkova," Rick said. "I think I can speak on behalf of the group in thanking you and Colonel Sokolov for your generosity in letting us fly to England with you." The Captain and Colonel smiled.

Steve asked, "Sir, may I ask whether you were educated in the United States?"

"That is an interesting question. My father, Aleksei Starkova, attended the Massachusetts Institute of Technology before the 1917 Revolution. I am honored to say that he was later a hero of the Revolution. While at MIT he made it his business to learn English–that is English spoken with an American flavor. He made it a rule in our home that everyone, from the time they were babies, to speak only English on alternate days. Since we learned from him, it was, of course, American English. My father was a taskmaster, and lapses into Russian were met with punishment. I hope when the war is over to join the diplomatic service and perhaps be posted to America."

The seven shook hands and several of them hugged Colonel Sokolov. Sarah gave huge hugs and kisses. The Colonel smiled, said his goodbyes and left to join his armored division and continue their mission to smash the Nazis.

In the final stages of the endgame, his division led the Red Army into Berlin, and Sokolov was made a general and a hero of the Soviet Union. After returning to Russia, he held a high government position, and later he and his wife retired to a *dacha* on the Black Sea near Sevastopol.

To avoid anti-aircraft batteries and fighter interception, the flight took a circle route north over Poland, high up into the Baltic Sea, west across Sweden and northern Norway, south over the North Sea and into England. The Commissars gave friendly greetings then huddled, talking among themselves for most of the trip. Steve and Rick chatted with Captain Starkova and other crew members. They asked the Americans a stream of questions and were fascinated by the men's stories and especially how Steve had to bail out on his first mission. None of the Soviet airmen had ever used a parachute.

They then slept on the cabin floor. Sarah stretched out on Rick's chest for a few hours. Then when he turned over and she rolled off, she went over to sprawl on Steve. Lev, Coos and Arne talked quietly in nervous anticipation about their plans and what kind of reception they might receive in England. Jean napped in her seat, lulled by the incessant drone of the engines.

Rick returned to his seat and thought of the last trip into England and how he wished there was a window so he could watch the landing: *Starkova's letting down now, must be over the North Sea. The weather seems better, no chop. Hope these guys have clearance from British air defense like we did on the last trip. Wonder if we'll land at Bury St. Edmunds?*

They touched down at six-thirty in the morning at an RAF airfield in East Anglia just south of Cambridge. Jean had attended the University. Because she had a sliver of a view, she recognized landmarks during the approach and pointed them out to Sarah who was now sitting on her lap.

"My parents, your grandparents have a second, sort of summer home south and east of here on the North Sea. You will love it there, Sarah. But it's likely we'll see them first at the family home in London, the house my brother and I grew up in. Are you excited?"

"They don't know me. Do you think they'll like me?"

"I know they will like you and love you."

Steve and Rick had their I.D.'s. When Jean got the money out of the hiding place in her in-laws house, she took her British passport and Sarah's Polish birth certificate. Military security at the airfield found this documentation sufficient. During the flight, Captain Starkova prepared temporary papers for Lev, Arne and Coos. The Commissars also vouched for them and asked for safe passage to London which was granted, with the understanding that the three would be accompanied by a military detail.

British intelligence had arranged transportation for the Commissars in a private railroad car. After tough negotiations with security, led by Rick, the seven were allowed to ride along with them. Lev, Coos and Arne were kept in a separate compartment with an armed guard. They were not happy with the memory-inducing categorization but understood it.

It was a glorious morning for the trip through East Anglia to London. Jean described the distinctive features and some local history with Sarah translating into Russian as necessary. The atmosphere in the railcar was electric as the train huffed and puffed into Paddington Station. The Commissars had luggage to retrieve and other transportation and security issues to contend with so farewells were said.

After emotional goodbyes, cloaked in steam near the hissing engine, the security detail escorted Lev, Coos and Arne to International Red Cross headquarters. Before they left, Arne said to Rick and Steve, "You two saved our lives. We will never forget you."

Coos said, "Jean, you nursed us back to health, and we will always be grateful. And you, beautiful Sarah, gave us hope and happiness. We will miss you very much."

Lev held Jean briefly. "I will love you with all my being until the day I die."

"I love you, Lev, be well and happy."

Lev, Arne and Coos were welcomed at Red Cross headquarters in London. British and American intelligence learned that Coos and Arne had been Auschwitz prisoners.

They were asked to discuss their experiences with war crimes investigators. The atrocities were delineated and responsible SS personnel at the camp were named. The intelligence staff helped them and Lev gain temporary asylum in Britain and steered them through a long visa-procurement process that led to an even longer and more wearisome trip by air, boat, truck, bus, rail and foot to Palestine.

Both Coos and Arne held academic doctorates, and British Intelligence retrieved their credentials from the Netherlands and Denmark. Arne's scientific reputation as an assistant to physicist Niels Bohr preceded him, and he became a faculty member of the Technion in Haifa. Coos joined the Daniel Sieff Research Institute, later named the Weizmann Institute of Science, as a researcher in the biological sciences.

Lev enlisted in the military, was commissioned shortly thereafter, and fought with distinction in the 1948 Arab-Israeli War for Independence. Following the establishment of the State of Israel, Lev entered politics and was elected a member of the Israeli Parliament, the Knesset. All three men remained friends, married and enjoyed happy, productive lives. They often talked with great affection and appreciation of the turbulent times they spent with the partisans on the Pitulski farm.

* * *

Jean wanted to call her parents, but every red telephone box had a long queue. She and Sarah saw a taxi dropping off passengers and hopped in. To Sarah's delight, her mother and the Cockney driver pointed out many landmarks and the bombed-out ruins on the trip across the city. Sensing from Jean's comments that she hadn't been in London since before the war, the driver pointed toward the dome. "I sang in the choir at St. Paul's during the blitz." Jean smiled to herself. *How many London cabbies have made that claim?*

"Are you scared, Mommy?"

"Not really scared, probably like you just a little apprehensive." She took Sarah's hand and patted it. "It has been a long time. I hope they're well, and my brother your Uncle Ian. Oh, it will be fine. They are strong people."

The Hellifield house was on the Chelsea Embankment, near the historic home of Sir Thomas More. It was a Saturday and both parents, Dr. Hellifield and Dr. Mendelson, were at home. Both were doing what they liked best, puttering in their garden diligently preparing the ground for spring planting.

They hadn't seen their daughter, Jean, in nearly five years and had no news of her for almost three years. They last knew of Sarah when she was two-and-a-half, and, except for early snapshot images, had never seen her. Letters sent to Poland went unanswered. Telephone calls never connected. Many inquiries were made to the International Red Cross and other agencies. The responses conveyed no helpful information. They had reluctantly and with resigned sorrow given up both of them, and their son-in-law John Krol, for dead at the hands of the Nazis.

As the cab came down onto the Embankment, Jean pointed. "Oh, Sarah, there is the Thames flowing right through the heart of London . . . and look, here we are. That is our house. I always loved that wide red brick chimney. Wait until you see the fireplace."

The cab was hidden from the yard by a tall hedge when it stopped at the curb with a slight squeal of brakes. Both parents looked up wondering who it might be. Jean and Sarah got out of the cab carrying their meager belongings, crossed the sidewalk and entered the path to the front door. Jean heard a rustle, turned to the left and saw her parents in the garden just as they saw their daughter and granddaughter standing hand-in-hand.

* * *

Rick and Steve had an English breakfast of eggs and scrape and started walking. Every G.I. they met was asked the whereabouts of U.S. Army headquarters. After rides on the tube and much walking they found it. After the usual waiting in lines, shuffling around and other bureaucratic frustrations, new uniforms, thirty-day passes and portions of back pay were issued. An officer inquired about what had happened since they were shot down, "There's nothing in the records. I read here that you two are up for medals, and Lieutenant Millen has been promoted. It says here, posthumously, to First Lieutenant."

"Do I still get it?" Steve asked with a grin. "Or do I have to die again?"

The officer laughed. "You'll get it. Come back tomorrow morning, and I'll have the paperwork and the new bars and more on the decorations. And be ready to be debriefed by Army intelligence. They'll want to know more about what went on in Poland. Before you get one of your medals, Lieutenant Millen, you'll have to listen to a speech from some general. Now, you asked first about your wives, and let's talk about that. Your best bet is to go to Army Nurse Headquarters just down the street on this side. See you tomorrow."

"The last entry we have is that they're with the First Infantry Division. You know, the one they call The Big Red One. I heard they crossed the Rhine a few days ago, the first Allies to do it, and they beat the Brits across. I'll bet Monty isn't happy."

"Can we get word to them?" Rick asked the lieutenant. "They've had no news from us for months and probably think we're dead." Steve thought back to his comment to Jean in front of Sarah at the convent.

"We'll try, but no guarantees, it's chaotic over there."

Steve asked, "Can you tell us if they're alive?"

"I can only tell you that neither of them has been reported KIA or missing or taken prisoner. We're way behind on where most combat nurses are. Many who've been in combat for a long time, like your wives, are being rotated out. They could be in Paris, here in another location." She smiled and shrugged.

After they left, Rick said, "Let's go get drunk."

"I'm for that. I'd like to fill a pool with beer and swim around in it guzzling."

"Let's first send telegrams back home. They'll be scared when the Western Union guy comes to the door, but when they read them they'll feel better."

"We'd better tell the Red Cross, too. Maybe they can get word to our wives. Let's see if the Red Cross can send the news back home, it may be faster." They set out on that mission and got the job done.

Their assigned quarters were on Baker Street in the Metropolitan Borough of St. Marylebone. Rick said, "Hey, maybe we'll see Sherlock." On the way down Baker Street from the tube station, they stopped in a barbershop for much-needed haircuts and treated themselves to barber's shaves. After that, they stopped in a pub for a few pints, had a good time chatting up the locals and then continued on to the converted hotel.

Rick finished showering and changing into his new uniform first. "I'm going to head out to find Sherlock's house. It's right near here. I think 221B Baker Street. How about I meet you at that pub in half an hour?"

Rick walked up Baker Street looking at the residences, stopping to peer into store windows and checking the house numbers. A car horn blast made Rick look up and he saw two American Army women across the street about a block ahead. Both were tall and slender, one dark-haired, the other a few inches shorter with light hair. He instantly knew it was Beverly and Suzanne. He dodged through traffic, got to the other side and ran up behind them. "Excuse me, can you direct me to the house of Sher . . ." He and Beverly fell into each other's arms. Rick quickly saw Suzanne's anxious, questioning look over Beverly's shoulder. "Steve's here. He'll be along soon."

"Where is he?"

He pointed. "See that hotel way down the street on the other side, the one with the white part on top? Room, uh, three-twelve."

Beverly turned toward Suzanne, and said through her tears, "Run, Suzanne, run."

People turned to watch the stunning American officer zip past them. Suzanne ran with her head high, eyes luminous, smile wide, honey-gold hair flowing behind her. Three minutes later and breathless she knocked on the door of room 312 and Steve opened it.

Order additional e-Book copies or a paperback edition of *WWII Soldier Flyer Prisoner Partisan* from amazon.com, barnesandnoble.com or other e-Book distributors. You may also use the Kindle app on your mobile device.

Also by Richard Noyes and co-author Pamela J. Robertson: *Larceny of Love*, a contemporary novel of action, love, danger and emotion. Meet characters you care about, plus inside looks at cutthroat technology, big-time sports and Machiavellian Hollywood deals, 280 pages, Amazon.

"What a great story! I loved the movie angle. Really great plot and variety of themes, thoroughly enjoyable, entertaining, engaging read." –Joyce Clough, Esq., Chicago, Illinois

Also by Noyes and Robertson: *Guts in the Clutch: 77 Legendary Triumphs, Heartbreaks and Wild Finishes in 12 Sports*, Illustrated, 329 pages, Amazon, with a Foreword by Drew Olson of ESPN and Past President of the Baseball Writers Association of America.

"The best compilation of fascinating sports stories I have read." –David Houle, Emmy and Peabody award winning producer of documentaries on Hank Aaron and the Harlem Globetrotters.

ORDER affordable e-Book copies of all or any one of the books listed above from amazon.com, barnesandnoble.com, googlebooks.com and other e-Book distributors. You may also use the Kindle app on your mobile device. Order paperback copies from amazon.com

Made in the USA
Charleston, SC
26 June 2013